LONG HOLLOW

–

A Charlie LeBeau Mystery

Gregory L. Heitmann

.

Long Hollow

Dedicated to the great people of South Dakota.

Gregory L. Heitmann

Many thanks to my family, gracias!

As always, a big thank you to my editors:

Angela

Dorene

Gwyneth

Gregory L. Heitmann

Author's Note

This is a work of fiction and the usual rules apply. The characters, the conversations, and the incidents portrayed in this novel have been invented by the author. Nothing in this book is to be construed as real. Any resemblance to actual events or persons, whether living or dead, is coincidental. Again, none of the characters are real. This is a fictional story conceived for entertainment purposes only and is not to be construed as a historical tome.

Gregory L. Heitmann

Other novels by Gregory L. Heitmann:

Fort Sisseton – Dakota Territory

Chief Red Iron – The Lakota Uprising

The G MANN 2 – Pay-2-Play

Teener Baseball

Gregory L. Heitmann

Chapter 1
Cold

Red taillights of the car illuminate the roadside sign behind it as it passes. The red hue cast upon the green sign with white lettering creates an eerie brownish tint as the complementary colors merge to produce a muddy sheen denoting the town of "SISSETON." In smaller letters underneath the information "POP. 2575" is revealed, but the highway sign darkens as the light source moves away, trailing behind the generic sedan. The November night is cold. Small flakes of snow drift and dance to the ground, falling onto an existing two inches of week-old snow. It's not unusual to have snow this time of year in Sisseton, South Dakota. The town of Sisseton, located in the northeastern corner of South Dakota, is adjacent to its better known cold-winter partners: North Dakota and Minnesota. Both state borders are less than twenty miles from Sisseton.

The car travels alone on South Dakota Highway 10, heading west out of Sisseton. Up the hill the car climbs the Coteau Des Prairie, "the slope on the prairie," as designated by the first French explorers a few hundred years ago. The slope is the remnants of multiple ice age events that left the area with its present day nickname: the Glacial Lakes Region.

The headlights pierce the shroud of darkness covering the scenic beauty of the Coteau. In the light of the day, the shallow canyons, known locally as draws or hollows, provide a contrast to the prairie grasses. The hollows are filled with a variety of deciduous trees dominated by numerous oak species. In summer the lush green leaves provide a shiny glimmer to the countryside. In the fall, the leaves turn the colors of a painter's autumn palette and feed the eyes of Sunday drivers. In the winter the barren trees whip in the wind, scraggily swaying, worshipping the cold gray skies. In the darkness tonight only the black road with the reflective striping shine before the driver's eyes. A few miles out of town and a couple hundred feet higher in elevation, the snow picks up its pace, whirling and swirling in the beams of the headlights. The driver clicks the lights to low beam in an effort to lessen the dizzying designs traversing the windshield.

Slowing now, the car eases off South Dakota Highway 10. A right turn steers the car north down a gravel road, past a simple small billboard briefly illuminated by the vehicle; the sign denotes "Long Hollow District" at its top edge; the bottom edge displays: "Sisseton-Wahpeton Sioux Tribe."

No traffic has traveled the gravel road on this late night, and the snow blankets the road, making it disappear into the adjacent farm fields. The grass at the edges of the road is the only guide to the driver. Gravel sticks in the treads of the tires thanks to the snow in the grooves, and the wheel wells provide a constant "ticking" of rocks on the metal under carriage. Even at the low speed, the gravel bouncing off the car frame is steady, without a defined rhythm. The driver reaches for the volume knob on the radio and turns up the song, *Seven Nation Army,* by the White Stripes. The song rumbles out of the speakers, camouflaging the stones cast from by the tires and bouncing against the undercarriage of the car in accompaniment to the driving bass line.

Past the Long Hollow Community Center the car continues slowly. The wind whips a little more, exposing the gravel road for a couple more miles as the car slowly and steadily moves along, crunching the snow beneath its tires. The brake lights come on, and the car turns back to the west down a two rut trail. The wheel ruts are deep, and the bottom of the sedan grinds along the hump of soil and snow formed by the time tested tire paths. The engine revs struggling to plow its way down the trail. After a mile the trail dips and is a steady down grade the last five hundred yards. The end of the trail is harshly lit by the headlights of the sedan. The driver clicks on the high beam lights for a moment, exposing the tree-filled drainage at the foot of the Coteau. This is the inflection point where the grade flattens, and the croplands begin at the base of the glacial hills. To the west is the steady incline of the slopes covered with the oaks, maples, ash, and other trees. The lights reveal a dilapidated one room shack. A quick inspection in the bright lights shows nothing else in the area, and the driver kills the engine. A thump emanates from the trunk, and the man looks in his rear view mirror and sees nothing but the black night. He dons his stocking cap and tightens his black leather gloves. Over the stocking cap he stretches a headlamp on an elastic band. "Well, time to get to work, I guess," the man says out loud as he pulls the door handle letting in the cold air.

"Sheesh, shoulda put on a scarf," he whispers to himself, zipping the coat up as high as it will go.

Gingerly the man moves to the rear of the car where a steady thumping can be heard above the rush of the wind. He inserts the key into the trunk lock and turns it, opening the trunk and exposing two teenagers, a girl and a boy, both bound and gagged with duct tape. The man's headlamp blinds the girl's terror-filled eyes as she thrashes in the compartment, fighting her restraints. Opening his coat, the man draws out a stun gun and flicks the button. Blue sparks sizzle between the prongs of the weapon as he clicks the trigger. The whine of the battery charging pierces the air as the wind momentarily sputters. The young girl's muffled screams and thrashing stop instantly as the man touches her with the gun and pulls the trigger, sending one hundred thousand volts with minimal amperage through her body, concurrent with a noise like a crack of a baseball off a bat.

Stowing his weapon, the man reaches for the limp girl and hauls her from the trunk. The teen boy is unconscious, fixed in his restraints. The man looks closely at the boy before moving the girl to the shack. In a moment he returns to the trunk and transfers his other victim.

The snow flurries continue and accumulate on top of the car. Screams pierce the air emanating from the shack but are absorbed in the howling winter wind. Soon there are no cries, only a deafening silence inside the shack as more snow covers the car.

He is a knife connoisseur. Knives are a fetish for this man. Sharp knives. His father had emphasized the importance of the edge. At five years old he watched his father harvest a whitetail deer, a doe, in the woods near his home. The young boy stared wide-eyed at the fallen animal. He held a leg back, assisting his father gut the deer, removing the internal organs. His dad explained the process and demonstrated, wielding the knife like an expert surgeon, because he was. At five years old, the organs and their functions, as described by his father, were not completely absorbed, but it was hypnotic for the boy. The steady patter of his father's voice is synched with the expertly slashing blade. Later, at their home, having hung the deer from the garage rafters, he watched his father peel the hide off the deer. He remembers this time as his cognitive beginning. His first awareness of self, that strange dawning of a feeling of being. It was a lasting impression. A day or two after he had been mesmerized watching his dad skin the deer, he looked on as his father dismantled the *Odocoileus virginianus*, the white-tailed deer. With all the expertise of a professional butcher, the deer was cut, washed, trim pieces ground, and finally packaged in white butcher paper. The final steps involved marking each package and sliding the tightly wrapped bundles into the giant chest freezer in the basement.

As a little boy, he got chills watching his father expertly butcher a deer. Soon he was old enough to hunt and work his own knife through a deer. The chills were converted to thrills. The thrills converted to heat; his heart raced, and he would sweat in the excitement. It didn't matter if temperatures hovered near zero degrees; he would perspire in the excitement.

The knife still dominates his life, almost to a point of worship. He didn't have a massive collection. He only revered his select few favorites. They varied, but half his collection was modeled after the first deer hunting knife his father gave him for his tenth birthday, a folding Buck knife, the Model 110, the Folding Hunter. The knife was sharp and held its edge. If dulled in use, a quick sharpening on steel, and sometimes a stone, would bring the blade to like-new condition. The man smiles as his mind wanders a moment. During the previous night's meal at the bowling alley, he had heard the screech of another diner's knife, scraping the plate as it hacked through a steak. It was the proverbial nails on a chalkboard sound that made his skin crawl. His smile flips to a frown as he shudders at the thought of the knife's edge being abused on the plate. He refocuses his thoughts.

The Buck Model 110 is the knife he uses for this night's operation. These are not deer being butchered; tonight's hunt is human, *Homo sapiens*. He has bagged two and now is his time. "A young doe and a young buck," the man whispers to himself and smiles.

He perspires even in the freezing shack, as he works the knife, piercing the skin of the soft belly of the young boy. He is first. Humans and their soft skin are delicate compared to the tough hide of a deer. However, the same structure is there; the intestines, kidneys, liver, lungs, and heart. These are the easily identifiable organs. The blood. There are always massive quantities of blood. More than you would expect. He is always surprised that *he is surprised* at noticing the blood. Even after all these years, the blood is a pleasant revelation; it gives him the thrill he desires. The blood coagulates quickly. The first thick layer of the liquid freezes on the floor. More blood streams onto the pool of blood on the disintegrating wooden slats beneath his feet, forming lumps and clumps in strange crimson layers as the fluid gels resembling oozing lava.

In his early days he would take a memento from his work. No more. His memory is all the reminder he wants. The thrill of his kills could be recalled by just picking up his knife. He takes his time in his makeshift butcher shop. He carves, fillets, and scalps flesh from bone. Neatly, meticulously he stacks cuts of muscle.

When he is done with the boy, he is tired. He hangs the girl by her wrists from the shack's rafters. He examines her lifeless, naked body. His headlamp is all he needs for a light source. Where he looks the lamp provides light. The girl's pale skin reflects a glare from the headlamp. Her teenage body sports firm, but small, round breasts tipped with erect nipples. He touches each nub with the point of the knife. The body fascinates him. It is not sexual. It is scientific. The evolution of the human body bewilders him. The thin skin, how does it provide enough protection? He slices into her soft belly, careful not to pierce a loop in the intestine. Steam rises from the opening, racing upward toward the ceiling, contrasting with the first drops of blood streaming to the floor.

The adrenaline wanes. He has had enough. He eases the girl's intestines to the floor. The disemboweled figure dangles precariously from the ceiling. The body rotates slowly on its axis. Gruesome shadows from the harsh headlamp dart on the walls.

The pool of blood slowly creeps outward, slowed by the freezing temperature. Blood droplets smear his boots. No matter, his fireplace will burn all his clothes. His dishwasher would cleanse his knife. There will be no evidence that could tie him to this "event," as he calls it.

Two hours pass before the man emerges from the weathered cabin. He is finished. He moves to the trees and disappears following his headlamp, which finally flicks off.

An All Terrain Vehicle engine roars to life beyond the cottage a hundred yards, stashed in the trees a few nights before. Snow continues to fall steadily and the ATV light bursts through the darkness and darts across the snow as the vehicle bounces along the frozen terrain, picking its way through the trees. The headlight jumps and bumps with the jostling of the ATV over the rough tundra like a nervous rabbit in an escape. The driver astride his ATV crosses the coulee. Topping the bank on the other side of the drainage, he momentarily pauses before disappearing behind a hill. Soon the light and the man disappear into the full winter storm leaving behind carnage under a fresh blanket of snow.

Gregory L. Heitmann

Chapter 2
Bale Stack

East Edge of the Coteau

At the base of the Coteau where the oak-filled coulees taper out, giving way to flat openings of cropland, a stack of large round bales rests on the edge of a cornfield. Each round bale weighs almost a ton, two thousand pounds. This bale stack is prairie grass. First mowed by a sickle pulled by a small tractor and then raked into windrows by a bizarre-looking implement made up of spinning wheels tipped with metal prongs, the haying process begins. This is the way the grass is prepared for feeding cattle in winter. The next step is the baler. In the old days a small, tractor-drawn machine would gather the windrows of prairie grass, mash it together, and wrap twine around a block of grass. The square bales were fifty to sixty pounds and could be handled by a man for loading onto the back of a trailer or pickup truck. Those days have passed. Now a larger tractor straddles the windrows as it pulls a machine, "a baler," that makes large round bales. The baler gulps in the grass where larger rubber belts spin the materials into six foot diameter round bales held together by twine. The baler spits out the bales on the new mown prairie where they wait to be gathered by a large tractor with a loader and grappling forks to be stacked on the side of the field making room for the next crop of grass to grow.

The stacking of the bales forms innocuous-looking pyramids throughout the countryside. Six bales long and three bales wide stacked closely together form the base. The flat sides of the round bales are faced to each other in tight formation three wide to provide the grooves for the next layer of bales. The eighteen bale base is topped with the middle layer of ten bales five long and two wide, each bale resting and centered in the saddle formed by the bales below it. The final layer, as high as the tractor's loader can reach, is a single line of bales on top four bales long, each centered in the crook formed by the two bales below.

The architecture of the bale stack is part and parcel to getting the hay home to the farm yard where the cattle will be fed. A large semi-truck with a long, flat bed, "a stack mover," will come, tilt its flat bed, and with the magic of hydraulics, slip the whole 30 ton stack onto its back. The stack mover is simple yet complicated. It's a big truck, like a semi-tractor you would see hauling a trailer down an Interstate highway, but in this case, there is no trailer. A fifteen foot by thirty foot, rolling, spiky platform sits over the multiple axles and wheels of the back of the truck. The operator of the stack mover backs up to a stack, tilts the platform, engages the mechanism, and backs the machine slowly as the bed of the truck slips under the bales, finally lowering flat for the trip home. You'll meet these extremely wide loads coming down the back country roads in farm and ranch country. It's not uncommon to be frightened you'll be forced off the shoulder of the road by a mountain of hay.

But in the meantime, some bale stacks can be left in place a little longer for another use besides feeding cattle. Strategically placed stacks are the perfect deer stands. Inconspicuous to a deer, they blend right into a deer's environment. There is nothing better than a bale stack on the edge of a cornfield between a deer's bedding area and its feeding area. Surely you will have an opportunity to harvest a deer using this method. The bale-stack-deer-blind is a nearly perfect way to hunt deer. It gets you in the air about ten feet higher than your surroundings, giving you a wider field of view to catch those wary whitetails sneaking through trees or low areas.   A hunter can climb up the bale stack, stand on the second row of bales, and rest his rifle on the top layer as he scans the area with his binoculars. It's a windbreak for those blustery days that coincide with nearly every day of South Dakota's weather. Finally, the bale stack is a steady rest for the hunter's rifle. One can lean across the bale stack from any angle and have a firm support to aim and fire a weapon. The bale stack is a damn near-perfect hunting blind for a deer hunter in the Long Hollow District just east of Sisseton.

Hunting magazines like *Field & Stream* or *Outdoor Life* publish stories every fall about pinch points, trails, bedding areas, feeding areas, and where to set yourself up to harvest a trophy deer. Common sense and a hike through your hunting grounds could provide this information for free, and a bale stack at strategic points will aid your harvest.

Chapter 3
Charlie

Bale stack

Opening day of South Dakota East River deer season finds Charlie LeBeau on his favorite bale stack. Sergeant Charlie LeBeau carries a gun everyday for work, but today he carries his rifle to the field for pure joy. His full time job as a Bureau of Indian Affairs policeman is just that, a full time job. Charlie is an enrolled member of the Sisseton-Wahpeton Lakota Sioux Tribe. As if keeping the peace on an Indian Reservation isn't enough, Charlie is enforcing the law amongst his own people, having grown up right here. Today is a reprieve from the daily grind. The tradition of opening day deer season is going on thirty years straight. Actually it is more than thirty years in the field, but thirty years of being allowed to carry a rifle to the bale stack. He went along with his dad before he could legally shoot. His dad had allowed him to fill his grandfather's tag when he was just eight years old.

He stands on the bale stack this morning watching the deer today just as he had all those years ago. The forty year old LeBeau smiles as he uses his binoculars to watch a doe move out of the trees to the edge of the cornfield. The sun has been up for an hour, and no big bucks have appeared this morning. It is time to think about filling one of his several antlerless deer tags and put some meat in the freezer.

Charlie is dressed for the frozen morning. It is about eighteen degrees and agonizingly still. His heavy camouflage coat and coveralls keep him plenty warm. His blaze orange stocking cap and vest, required by law for hunting, make him stand out like a sore thumb atop the snow covered bale stack and surrounding cornfield blanketed with snow. Charlie lowers his binoculars and tucks them between his coat and his thin blaze orange vest. He reaches for his rifle resting on a bale making up the top layer of his blind.

He is a handsome man. His Indian blood combines with his French ancestry, providing dark, attractive features. More boyishly handsome than ruggedly handsome, he's forty but could pass for thirty. The cold air has nipped his cheeks giving his clean-shaven face a rosy glow after sitting on the bales a couple of hours. His striking blue eyes are an oddity that defies his Lakota lineage.

Charlie drapes his six foot tall frame over the edge of the top bale and establishes a firm rest as he aims his Remington Model 700 bolt action at the unsuspecting deer. The rifle is chambered in a traditional .270 Winchester and topped with a Leupold scope with variable magnification from three to nine power. The scope is set on nine power for the shot, just a little over a hundred yards away.

The doe paws at the snow, unearthing a few corn kernels that she readily gobbles up. Charlie watches patiently through his scope. His rifle and scope setup have been successful for the last ten years. If anyone would ever pose such a question, he would dare say that this is the ultimate rifle and scope combination for whitetail hunting.

The doe is not cooperating. She is standing behind a row of cornstalks that block a clear path to her vitals. Charlie waits patiently. He does not want his first shot of the season to be deflected and hit the deer poorly, possibly wounding the deer or damaging the meat. "Come on, girl. A couple more steps," Charlie whispers.

His breath curls upward in the frozen air. Up around the scope the moisture in his breath disappears in wisps as he curses his luck. "Dang it, Pete," Charlie whispers again. "Can't you knock these cornstalks down better with your combine?"

Pete Hakken and his brother Lars farm the ground. Most of the reservation land is a checkerboard combination of private owners adjacent to Indian trust lands. Charlie has known Pete and Lars since they were kids. The cornfield is half trust land and half Hakken Farms Incorporated. Pete and Lars rent the half they don't own. Hakken Farms owns the trees and the next field of alfalfa on the other side of the drainage. The Hakkens don't hunt much anymore, but Charlie has hunted the trust land his whole life and was given permission by Pete to hunt wherever he wanted to on the Hakken farm.

Charlie lifts his head from the scope and stares across the field with his naked eye. The doe is stock still, staring into the trees. Something is moving in the woods behind her. Something has caught the deer's attention. "Uh-oh," Charlie whispers to himself. "What does she see?"

Charlie puts his eye to the scope and scans through the trees. Two more does and four fawns materialize from the tree line and join the original deer in the corn. She turns her attention to the ground in front of her and paws some more snow revealing a few more corn kernels. Charlie can see her working her jaw on her breakfast. "No, no, no, no," Charlie whispers as he feels his chest. His cell phone, set to vibrate, buzzes in his shirt pocket.

He returns his rifle to the bale, looks to the sky, and shrugs. His hands go out, palms skyward, seeking divine intervention. He whines pleadingly. "Damn it." Charlie shakes his head and whispers a little louder. He pulls his glove off, unzips his jacket, and digs for his phone in his shirt pocket over his heart. The phone stops buzzing before he can answer. Charlie scrolls to the missed call register. It was Kipp. The phone buzzes a long note indicating a text message. Charlie taps his phone menu to get to the text. It is short and sweet. The text message is from Captain Kipp, his boss, and only four words: "Code 187. Call ASAP!"

*   *   *

Charlie stands to his full height on the bale stack, no longer concerned with keeping concealed from the deer. The does and fawns are alerted. They stare at the bale stack, having noticed the movement. Heads cocked forward and ears up they gaze in Charlie's direction, frozen. Charlie looks at his phone, then to the deer, and then back to the phone. "Damn it...Damn it," he repeats out loud.

The lead doe has seen and heard enough; she whirls and throws her tail in the air, escaping into the woods. The rest of the deer follow suit, prancing hurriedly through the trees in the opposite direction from Charlie.

Charlie watches the deer disappear as he shakes his head. Without looking at his phone, he presses the "send" button with his thumb. The phone dials his boss, Captain Kipp. Charlie surveys his surroundings, scanning the forty acres of harvested corn immediately in front of him and the trees behind the field.

"What's up, Skip?" Charlie speaks into the phone as he continues to watch the area of the trees where the deer disappeared. "This better be good, because I'm gonna catch heck from my dad when I show up without his deer."

He turns his back to the cornfield and spies his truck parked about a quarter mile away in the distance as he listens.

"What?" Charlie speaks the word crisply. He listens more intently and begins to shake his head side to side. "What?" He repeats again, surprised. "You got to be kidding me." Charlie frowns, "Ok. I'm on my way."

*   *   *

Charlie grips his rifle and slides down from the bale stack. He trudges back over his tracks in the snow, hiking the three hundred yards to his truck, a 1981 rusted Chevrolet. The truck, looking worse for the wear, gives the appearance of an abused farm pickup. It was Pete Hakken that came up with the idea of naming Charlie's truck and thus it was affectionately named "The Bomber," the sure-fire utility vehicle that can bomb up and down the road without a problem.

It is a short drive back to Charlie's trailer. The modern prefabricated home sits on his acre and a half allotment awarded to him by the Tribal Council. Any enrolled member of the Tribe can petition the council for a homestead. Charlie had his eye on this tract since he was a teenager, and now he had it, a beautiful view to the east of the prairie farmland and three sides of his property enveloped by trees. His homestead is just a few miles from Sisseton and any supplies he might need.

As he enters his yard, he pulls up his old four-wheel drive next his new four-wheel drive. It is a stark contrast compared to the Bomber, his brand new BIA police Tahoe decked out with every amenity.

*   *   *

Inside Charlie's trailer sits Claude LeBeau, Charlie's father. The thin, silver-haired man dressed in blue jeans and his favorite blue and white plaid flannel shirt may not have heard the truck pull up, but he heard the truck's door slam. He looks up from his crossword puzzle and keeps his eye on the front door.

Claude hears his son stomping the snow from his boots on the stairs outside. He smiles as his boy enters the trailer. He calls out, "You musta got a good one to be back this early on the opener. Need some help?"

Claude is up from the kitchen table and walks toward the door. Charlie shakes his head as he stomps his feet again on the door mat. He reaches for the closet door as he continues to wipe his feet. He swings the door open, removes his rifle slung over his shoulder, and places the rifle in the closet. "No, Dad. No help needed. I didn't get one."

Charlie quickly unlaces his boots and leaves them on the door mat. He pushes past his father on the way to the bedroom as he removes his hunting clothes. Claude follows his son to the bedroom doorway watching in surprise as Charlie undresses. "You're serious?"

Charlie lays out his uniform on his bed and unbuttons his old flannel shirt, finally pulling off his thermal undershirt. "What? So, you really didn't shoot one?" Claude points at his son, "I'll say this; if you're pulling my leg, you've really committed to the joke...changing clothes and everything. You're kidding, right?"

"No, Dad. I'm not kidding."

Charlie pulls his black uniform pants over his long underwear. "So, you didn't even shoot a doe for me? You gotta fill my tag for me, you know?"

Charlie shakes his head and slips on his uniform shirt and buttons it. "Dad, come on. Can't you see I'm changing clothes? I got called in."

Charlie pulls on his insulated work boots and crouches to lace them snuggly and tie them. He looks up at his father. "Oh. I see," Claude finally nods, smile finally fading from his lined face.

"Heck, Dad," Charlie says, "I don't know why you don't go out and shoot your own deer."

"You always get one for me. That's become the tradition. Besides, I'm a retired old man, and it's cold out there."

Charlie dons his utility belt and holster as he shakes his head, "It was nice out there this morning. No wind. High teens."

"Don't shake your head at me," Claude warns. "You wait. Thirty years from now you'll know how the cold gets in your bones."

"Excuse me," Charlie says as he pushes past his dad, moving to the coat closet. "I gotta get going."

Charlie gets his heavy uniform jacket, a dark brown aviator type jacket with nylon shell and fur lined collar. The embroidered gold badge twinkles as he puts the jacket on. He grabs his fur lined cap with ear flaps.

"What happened, somebody get themselves killed?" Claude questions. "Must be, that'd be the only reason Skip'd call you in on the opener."

Charlie nods slowly and places his fur cap on his head as he frowns at his dad.

"Oh, I'm sorry." Claude forces a smile, "So, you gonna get my deer for me, or what?"

Charlie opens the door and smiles, rolling his eyes. "Yes, Dad. Take it easy. It's only the first day of the season."

"All right then. We'll see you later," Claude nods with a two fingered military salute.

Sergeant LeBeau, in his full police uniform, is out the door, pulling it closed behind him. He pauses and peeks his head back in the doorway. He looks to his dad who waits puzzled by his son's delayed departure. Charlie gazes out to the barren woods to the side of his trailer. Claude shrugs, "What?"

Charlie turns his eyes back to his dad, "Is Nat up yet?"

"Nope," Claude frowns.

"Get his butt out of bed and tell him to get his huntin' stuff ready 'cause he'll be huntin' with me tonight."

"Will do," Claude smiles and provides a thumbs up to his son. "Shut the door already. You're lettin' in all the cold air. See you tonight."

"Bye, Dad, I'll be back tonight. Nat and I will getcha your doe," Charlie calls out as he pulls the door shut. He treads down the steps, quickly moving to his BIA Police truck.

Claude watches through the window as Charlie fires up his truck, reports his duty log in to his dispatcher via the radio, and puts his vehicle in gear. Charlie glances at the house and sees his old man watching him through the window. He waves and Claude returns the gesture as Charlie leaves the yard, kicking snow in the air with his new Sports Utility Vehicle's all-weather tires.

Chapter 4
The Shack

Rural Roberts County

The crime scene is just five miles away from Charlie's trailer, barely enough of a drive to get the cab of his Tahoe warmed up. He is in no hurry and ease down the snow-dusted gravel roads, finally winding his way to the section line dirt trail covered in snow. He lowers the volume on the FM radio. The local station, KBWS 102.9, plays his favorite country music. Randy Travis has just finished singing "Deeper Than the Holler," but now it is time for business.

The last few hundred yards down the dirt trail take some concentration. The other vehicles had punched though the compacted snow drifts, but now the loose snow throws his four wheel drive vehicle to and fro. As Charlie gets to the shack, there are more emergency vehicles present than he can at first count. Yellow crime scene tape is strung from the barbed wire fences to trees encircling the shack. Charlie snickers to himself at the tape and thinks out loud, "As if somebody is going to come way out here in the middle of nowhere and intrude on the site and contaminate evidence."

The shack sits directly at the base of the Coteau up against the tree line and is now overrun by some smaller saplings. It is disappearing, rotting away as abandoned farms and their outbuildings tend to do when the upkeep ceases. Police personnel from all jurisdictions bustle about.

Charlie parks his Tahoe amongst the jumble of other vehicles. He dons his fur lined cap and exits his vehicle as he tightens his heavy, lined black leather gloves. "Hey, Charlie," Deputy Carson calls out as he lifts the yellow tape for Sergeant LeBeau to duck under.

Deputy Wade Carson of the Roberts County Sheriff's Department is just twenty eight years old and new to the force. Deputy Carson is a local, but at the same time, he's not. He's from just down the road, Milbank,

South Dakota, married to Diane, a hairdresser in Sisseton. He is fresh from the law enforcement academy. After five years in a high school classroom, he traded in his college degree in education for a more boots-on-the-ground job. As the rookie, he's stuck with directing traffic today, albeit people traffic. He monitors the comings and goings of everyone from just inside the yellow tape.

"Carson," Charlie nods and extends his hand as the deputy acknowledges the greeting. "What's goin' on?"

Deputy Carson motions his gloved hand over his shoulder toward the shack. "I'd rather be out here than in there." Carson grimaces and shakes his head. "It's a bad one."

Charlie nods and slaps a hand down on Carson's shoulder, trying to provide comfort and a welcome to the gruesome club of dealing in death. "Skip inside?" Charlie inquires.

Carson nods to the shack, and Charlie steps carefully to where the dilapidated front door hangs precariously. He notices the exposed gray siding. Not much of the white paint that coated the house remains. Everything is a dull gray, slowly but surely blending into the same dusky gray of the barren trees. Charlie takes a deep breath and sticks his head inside the shack. His eyes are not adjusted to the darkness. Even with the clouds slowly drifting in from the west, the snow reflects the light remarkably well, making it difficult for eyes to adjust quickly from outdoors to indoors. Charlie might have wished his eyes would not have adjusted if he knew what they would see when he walked through the door.

The one room shack was a tool shed in its former life as part of the buildings making up a farmstead. The house and barn were demolished forty years prior. The shed had managed to escape destruction only because it served as a hunting cabin for the annual deer season, and once or twice during the summers it was the headquarters for a Glacial Lakes fishing getaway. The five acre parcel the shack sits on is owned by the Monahan family. The family hasn't actually used the deer camp in ten years, and its state of disrepair reflects the neglect. The Monahan men in the family had aged to a point that the few that still return to hunt or fish rest comfortably at the Super 8 hotel in Sisseton. The hotel was luxurious relative to the shed.

Charlie's head involuntarily shook side to side in disbelief at the scene unfolding before him. The one room shack is filled to capacity with police and emergency personnel. It takes a moment or two for Charlie to finally discern the two bodies, each hanging from a mechanism made of a discount-quality, assemblage of gambrels, ropes, and a pulley system. The inexpensive packaging with a price tag of $14.99 still attached is already bagged as evidence. Charlie sees through its transparent evidence bag, and its promotional exclamation: "Easily hang your deer for skinning! Includes 30 feet of rope!"

Charlie slowly weaves his way through the personnel to get closer to the bodies hanging from the ceiling. His imagination flashes to the time of the murder. He visualizes the dimly lit shack, illuminated only by a battery powered flashlight or small battery operated lantern. He imagines the unconscious teenagers hanging upside down.

Charlie snaps back to the present, noticing his fellow officers working, talking, and gathering evidence. He pushes closer to inspect the victims' feet. Each body is hung from a gambrel, a metal rod in the shape of an obtuse triangle with protruding hooks at each end, bent in acute angles. The obtuse top angle of the gambrel is hooked to the pulley. The protruding metal hooks are inserted into the gap of the heel formed by the Achilles' tendons. Blood streaks trace random patterns from wounds from the Achilles area across the victims' calves.

Charlie reaches for the ropes extending from the pulley but does not touch anything. He follows the ropes, tracing them with his finger to their anchoring point, a two by four nailed to the wall. His eyes note the familiar knots fixing the ropes and holding their loads.

Charlie's mind flashes back again to what he imagines was the scene as the murders took place. The shadows in the dimly lit shack dance in the pale light. An unknown killer choreographs the death of two teenagers. A knife flashes and slices away the clothes of one teenager then the other. Their naked bodies twist, rotating slowly one direction then turning back the opposite way on the axis of the suspended rope.

Charlie is jolted back to the scene at hand. He surveys the room again and for the first time hears the din of conversation of his fellow investigators. Flashlight beams dart back and forth across the room. He crouches and inspects the frozen pool of blood beneath each body.

Almost in a trance, Charlie again envisions the murder. The dimly lit shack is filled with screams of teens regaining consciousness. They are in agony from the wounds that allowed them to be hung by their feet. Bloody, naked, and groggy, they cry and scream, maybe only suffering momentarily. A gloved hand wields a knife slashing one throat followed quickly by a fluid, continuous movement of the knife to the second victim's throat. Blood gushes to the floor. Gurgles of screams choked by blood rise and fall in only seconds.

Charlie's mind is back on the scene. He shakes his head, snapping back to the pools of blood. The frozen crimson pools border on purplish hues. He notes the equal size of each pool and the rippled effect of each pool on the other. He concludes they were killed at virtually the same instant. Each pool affected by the freezing temperature uniformly when compared to the other.

A few feet from the body, Charlie observes the heap of clothes. He stands, pushing up from his crouched position. He notices the ache in his knees from being bent over. He manages the weakest of a smile, his mind noting he's no spring chicken; forty years old definitely isn't thirty. This little joke to himself is the last mental preparation he needs for his final observation of the crime scene.

Charlie rises to his full height and peers into the boy's gaping abdomen. There is nothing where the internal organs should be. The skin flap cut open over the soft belly hangs limply to the side of the rib cage, dangling by a strip of flesh. Charlie can see the muscle structure surrounding the spine. For an instant his mind flashes to his high school biology text book and the human body musculature image printed in a glossy sheen in the chapter on human anatomy. The boy's shrunken penis has disappeared into the patch of pubic hair as if it had attempted to retreat into the body to escape the horror. Blood streaks cross the boy's chest, neck and face. The young man's expression frozen forever, reminds Charlie of a Roman statue. The eyes are open and seemingly focused far away. The mouth is tightly shut, providing a stoic impression.

Charlie turns his attention to the girl, who is similarly gutted. No belly flap of skin hangs on her torso; the opening is clean and symmetrical, baring her body cavity for all to see. A thin, yellow layer of fat encircles the wound. Her pubic hair is just a strip, black and trimmed. Blood has streamed across her breasts forming intricate, woven patterns. Charlie notices her left nipple. It looks as if it had been nicked with a knife. It has been laid open and blood has coagulated and dripped before freezing, forming a bloody icicle. The girl's face is streaked red resembling a painted warrior. Her shoulder-length hair hangs to the floor giving a constant perception of fear, hair standing on end. But, that has nothing to do with the expression of fear frozen on her face. Her eyes are pinched shut as tight as she could hold them. The wrinkles on her forehead and around her eyes make her look ten times her actual age. She was the second to die. She had closed her eyes to escape the carnage. The muscles somehow unable to relax even in death are now held by the freezing temperatures. It is frightening even for Charlie to observe.

"Hey, when'd you get here?" Skyler Kipp questions as he approaches Charlie.

Charlie raises his eyebrows, snapping out of his stare. He pries his eyes from the girl's face and glances only for an instant at his captain. "Just now."

"Quite the scene, huh?" Kipp sighs. "Come on," he gestures. "He left the organs over here."

The pair moves across the room shuffling through investigators over to a makeshift countertop. Kipp shakes his head, "This counter was probably the one used to butcher countless deer. Now this."

Two sets of internal organs are neatly laid out across the table. A thin sheen of frozen blood holds the organs in place. The heart, still attached to the lungs in the center of a wreath-like formation, is surrounded by the liver, kidneys, intestines, stomach, and spleen.

"Good God," Charlie mumbles barely audibly.

Kipp puts his hand on Charlie's shoulder and gives him a nudge, "Let's go outside."

Gregory L. Heitmann

Chapter 5
Kipp

Captain Kipp pushes Charlie outside, back into the painfully blinding glare of snow reflected sun. Even with the hazy cloud cover typical of an early winter's day, the policemen squint. The brightness on the optic nerves gives one a stabbing pain in the brain as the pupils lag behind in their dilation. The men are silent a few moments as their eyes adjust. They each scan their surroundings, their minds still cluttered with the images from inside the shack.

Bureau of Indian Affairs Police Captain Skyler Kipp was nicknamed "Skip" long before he ever became a captain. With the first letter of his first name combined with his last name, he became Skippy at about four years old. At eight years old the daintiness of Skippy had worn off, and he became Skip. The captain is pushing fifty years old now and eligible for his law enforcement retirement of twenty years of service if he wants it. He has nothing else to do, and he loves his job, so he has no plans of leaving unless he is forced out. Skip is the most unassuming, non-threatening man you might meet. He was born and raised in Sisseton, having barely left the state maybe twice in his life for business in Minneapolis. An enrolled member of the Sisseton-Wahpeton Sioux Tribe, he looks more the part than his coworker, Charlie. Skip keeps his hair long, longer than regulations allow, and he parts it down the middle, a style he stumbled on in high school and has stuck with since. He always has a comb and frequently, unconsciously, combs his hair anywhere anytime, when he has to think about something. This provides much entertainment for his coworkers. His hair is jet black without a touch of grey even though he doesn't dye it. His skin is very dark as well. His wide face and high cheek bones tell anyone in a glance he is native. His most distinctive feature is probably his slight buck teeth that, along with his cheeks, give him a slightly chipmunk-ish image. To top it off he wears glasses that are a throwback to the era of his high school days. Aviator style, wire-rimmed glasses with wide lenses provide the nerdish quality of a substitute high school teacher. There is no nicer man than Skip. Along with his hairstyle and glasses, is his high school girlfriend, married since they were eighteen years old. Captain Kipp is a highly respected man in the community no matter whether you spoke to an Indian or white man.

The men lean on the Captain's BIA police Tahoe. The wind gusts and swirls through the trees. Loose snow hisses as it drifts across the trampled snowy blanket, filling in the divots formed by all the foot traffic. They watch as two South Dakota Highway Patrol officers unload a generator and a trunk labeled "High Intensity Lights" from a four wheel drive unit.

Charlie breaks the silence, "What do you think, Skip? You rule out suicide?"

The Captain can't help but smile at the gallows humor. He shakes his head as he looks at his friend. His smile gives way to a small chuckle that ends with a melancholy sigh. "You already know. It's a repeat of five years ago."

Charlie frowns and nods. "Any IDs on the victims?"

Skip shakes his head, "Nah. Not yet. Highway Patrol is checking the car and missing persons report."

Charlie kicks at the ground, chiseling a hunk of snow from a drift near his boot. He leans down and picks up the hardened snow. He throws the snowball toward a nearby tree, but a gust of wind directs the object waywardly. The fragile snowball disintegrates against a hardened drift. He shakes his head, "I can't believe it. Same ropes, pulleys, knots, gambrels...same everything."

Skip swipes away his glasses and pinches the bridge of his nose with his gloved hand. He squeezes his eyes tightly, closing them in pain. He returns his glasses to their position, "What kind of freak show we dealin' with here?"

Charlie shrugs, "Just the usual psychopath deer hunter."

Skip flips his hands up momentarily, and they fall back to his side, "Great," he folds his arms. "That narrows it down to eighty-five percent of the county's male population. What is with you crazy fools? You stand out there in freezing cold weather waiting for a stupid animal to walk by."

"Who is stupid? We're standin' out in the cold right now." Charlie exhales a large cloud of vapor buffeted by the wind.

Skip smiles, "But we are gettin' paid."

"I'll tell you what," Charlie affirms. "Sitting on top of that bale stack is one of the few things that helps me keep my sanity. The peace and quiet. The time to just think." Charlie cocks his head. "And another thing, I take personal offense at your comment about stupid animals. Deer are smart. Smarter than a lot of the people we have to deal with."

Skip snorts a small laugh. "You got me there."

Charlie shakes his head, "What the heck are we dealing with?"

Skip inhales the crisp air and blows out a long breath in a cloud of vapor into the cold wind. "I gotta name for our guy."

Charlie perks up, "Oh, yeah?"

"I call him the 'Deer Slayer' cuz he only strikes during the deer season."

Charlie's serious expression is frozen for a few moments before he finally manages a grin, "Nice. Take you all morning to think that up?"

Kipp smiles, "To tell you the truth, yes."

The Captain rolls his shoulder and reaches his hand up to massage the back of his neck, "Actually, I have been sitting on that nickname for years. I never thought we'd ever see this guy again, but boom, next thing we know, he's back in business."

Kipp reaches his other hand to his neck as he gently twists his head back and forth, "It makes my head hurt."

Kipp closes his eyes and Charlie interjects. "It's going to stir up a lotta stuff...stuff, if you know what I mean."

Kipp opens his eyes, "If you mean stuff equals the FBI, DCI, newspapers, and TV news crawling up our asses, then, yes, I know what you mean."

Charlie gets serious again, "Did you say that the State Patrol is looking for the identification of the victims?"

"Yeah, why?" Kipp puzzles.

"No reason; I guess I was just imagining making that house call to some poor unsuspecting parents. Did they say they would handle that?"

"Shit," Captain Kipp is deflated. "No way I'm doing it. Those are some White kids. That's off the reservation; I'm pretty sure."

Kipp closes his eyes and grabs the back of his neck again. The men stand in silence a few moments. The wind rattles through the trees in the coulee behind the shack, whistling amongst the branches. Another rolling, wind-driven cloud of snow races along the ground. The captain opens his eyes, drops his hand, and points at Charlie. The mood quickly changes along with the subject as Skip grins at his friend. "See any big bucks this morning?"

"Heck no. Thanks to you."

"Come on. Hop in the truck, and we'll warm up. It's the least I could do. I'll buy you a coffee. I'm sure Louise threw in my Thermos."

The men move from the hood of the Tahoe around to the doors, snow crunching underfoot.

Charlie shakes his head, "Yup, just like before. The Deer Slayer is going to ruin my whole season and ironically, no actual deer will be slain."

The men climb inside the vehicle, and Skip fires up the truck. He unscrews the cap from his Thermos. Steam pours from the bottle along with hot coffee into Styrofoam cups. It's relatively quiet as the men sip on the hot coffee; the silence is periodically interrupted by a voice or squelch from the radio.

Captain Kipp adjusts the heater fan, turning it down a notch as the cab warms. "Look on the bright side; the murders were right here in Long Hollow. Just a few minutes from your house."

Charlie sips his coffee and chokes a bit as he grimaces, "How is that the bright side? A murder, for all practical purposes, perpetrated right here in my backyard! This is your idea of good news these days?"

Skip shakes his head and puts up a hand in his defense, "Hey, you're close to home. You'll probably be able to do some huntin' tonight."

"I guess."

Skip lifts his hand as if offering an invisible handful of advice, "Coulda been over in Big Coulee. Over in Meister's territory. Hey, I heard Meister's tracking a big buck over there. A real monster."

"Yeah," Charlie concurs, "I saw Meister at the gas station the other day. He told me all about it."

The men drink coffee and observe the parade of people going in and out of the shack in front of them. A gurney is pulled from the state coroner's four wheel drive transport vehicle and dragged awkwardly through the snow drifts. It is left near the shack's door. An empty body bag sits atop the gurney fluttering in the wind.

The sky darkens and the clouds droop lower and lower; finally the sun is gone. The clouds begin to touch the ground, unable to contain the weight of the snow they hold. Flurries spit from sky in fits and stops. Perfectly formed flakes bounce along the hood and windshield of Skip's Tahoe as the men watch the removal of the first corpse from the shack. The body is in a black vinyl bag.

Charlie breaks the silence, "Well, they got one of the bodies in a bag. I was curious on how they were going to do that with the arms frozen straight down. What do you think, did it thaw, did they manhandle the arms down, or is it an extra tall body bag?"

Skip grimaces at his friend, "Only you, Charlie, could wonder about such things."

"How much longer you need me?"

Skip looks at his watch, "What's a matter? Not havin' fun?"

"I thought I might get back and get an hour or two on the stand tonight. The weather should have the deer moving around into the corn."

Skip shakes down his wrist, moving his jacket sleeve back over his watch. "Before you go, I thought I'd ask how your nephew's doin'?"

Charlie shrugs, "Pshhh. It's hard to tell. Teenagers are bizarre creatures."

"I'm sorry about your sister. How long did she fight the cancer?"

"Five long years."

Skip exhales deeply, "God rest her soul. Tell Nat I'm thinkin' about him and that I can't wait to see him play some ball."

"Well, you can come see him play in Sisseton with the Redmen," Charlie nods in affirmation. "I'm taking him out of Tiospa Zina and putting him in Sisseton Public, now that he's living with me."

Skip pushes himself up against the driver's side door as he gawks at his friend in surprise, "You're taking him out of his school? Are you kidding me? Why?"

"If it was good enough for you and me..." Charlie points a finger back and forth between Skip and himself.

"Yeah, right." Skip shakes his head in disapproval.

"I wanna keep an eye on him. It's a lot closer. I don't want him chasin' down the road morning and night in weather like this. That's an hour a day lost sittin' in the car."

Skip shrugs and nods reluctantly.

"Plus," Charlie continues, "Sisseton's got a good program. Good competition in the Northeast Conference. None of those rinky-dink schools that fill out a roster with junior high kids. I talked to the coach already."

"Nat's gonna be pissed off," Skip shakes his head and relaxes back into his seat.

Charlie waves away the comment. "We've already talked about it. He's on board. He's ready for a change now that his mom's gone."

Skip reaches for the thermos and warms their cups with some more hot coffee. They watch a second gurney topped with a body bag being shuttled by men wearing parkas embroidered with the word "CORONER" on their backs.

Skip sips at his coffee, "There's the second body already. They're moving things along faster than I thought they would."

"Speaking of moving things along," Charlie glances at his boss, "are we talking about overtime yet?"

Skip grins, "Oh, yeah. Burn the midnight oil. Superintendent already called me and said to get on this case and don't worry about the hours. 'Use all resources' he said. It's safe to assume you'll be out here a couple nights *visualizing* things," Skip enunciates the word "visualizing" with sarcastic spin.

"What's your problem?" Charlie questions. "It's part of my process. I want to get a feel for the scene." Charlie extends his hands, closes his eyes, and mimes groping the darkness. He smiles and opens his eyes.

Skip slowly shakes his head. "Hey, whatever it takes." He closes his eyes and rubs his temples. "I *visualize* you solving our case!" Once again he stresses the word "visualize."

There is a lull again as the men watch the body recovery operation before them. Skip nods again before speaking, "Superintendent also said the cavalry's comin'. The FBI is on its way."

Charlie sips at his coffee and watches the men from the coroner's office, "Of course, the FBI will be here." He scoffs, "Probably be just as effective as last time."

"Don't worry," Skip reassures, "I guarantee they will have a brand new crop of agents who hate being assigned to the frozen tundra of South Dakota."

Charlie stares at the men handling the body bags as they struggle to move the gurneys through the snow, a mere thirty feet away to their transport truck. The men finally give up on the use of the gurney and hand carry the bodies to the vehicle. The Band Perry's song *If I Die Young* plays on Skip's FM radio station. He reaches for the knob and turns the music volume down to a faintly audible level.

"Who found the bodies?" Charlie questions.

"Remember Edgar Walters?" Skip replies with his own question.

Charlie nods and sniffs at his coffee cup.

"His cousin. His cousin was huntin', along with his son. Deer huntin'. They were up from Sioux Falls for opening day." Skip points to the trees, "I guess they pulled in here, were going into the coulee to walk through the trees. They saw the frozen blood that had seeped under the door."

"Are they related to Marvin Hattum?"

Skip nods, "Yeah. Uncles. Nephews. Great Uncles. Something like that. I think almost all the Hattums are dead now. This is their property though."

Charlie shakes his head, "Sheesh, what a way to start opening weekend."

Gregory L. Heitmann

Chapter 6
Tiospa Zina

Tiospa Zina Tribal High School

Tiospa Zina approximately translates to Yellow Clan. The school was built from the ground up in the 1990's as an option for the native children on the Sisseton-Wahpeton Reservation. The average class size from kindergarten to the twelfth grade varies from ten to twenty-two students. It is a small school, even by South Dakota standards.

There is plenty of room in the parking lot as Sergeant Charlie LeBeau pulls onto the high school grounds and parks his BIA Police Tahoe. The Tahoe's engine idles roughly as Charlie pauses before exiting the vehicle. Even after all the discussion, doubts still plague him. He steps on the gas revving the engine. His eye catches the metal sign bearing the name of the high school. At the bottom of the sign it notes with an exclamation in smaller lettering: "Home of the Wambdi!" An image of a soaring eagle punctuates the right edge of the sign.

Charlie says the words out loud in a question, "Home of the Wambdi?" He squints and thinks out loud, "Does that mean 'eagle'?"

He turns the key, killing the engine, and dons a black knit stocking cap. He eyes the Coteau in front of him as he faces east. Snow blankets the hills; it is a white curtain only broken up by the stark stands of trees funneling down the drainages of the hillsides. He pauses again as he grabs the door handle. He shakes his head and frowns at the gray skies and the unyielding breeze swirling snow in and out of the porticos of the school building. Drifts of various heights and shapes form before his eyes. No snow has fallen today, but the snow on the ground is repositioned without remorse by the stiff north wind. Charlie braces himself and exits the vehicle. It is just a few yards to the front door of the school and the administrative offices. The crisp air bites at his cheeks and the snow crunches under his boots. In a moment he swings the bright yellow door open and is inside the empty, echoing hallway of the school. Classes are in session, and he is the only person in the hall. He takes his time wiping the snow from his boots on the rugs in front of the door.

Charlie notes again, as he does every time he visits a school, how small things seem now compared to the way his memories of childhood nostalgically remember them. He sees the sign for the principal's office and makes his way down the hall, boots clomping and squeaking on the polished floor as the snow from his treads melts in the warmth of the school.

Chapter 7
Victor

Amy Two Bulls, the Administrative Assistant, jumps from her desk when she recognizes the man in uniform coming through the office doors. "Charlie!" she calls out.

She maneuvers her stout frame around the barrier separating her desk from office visitors. She hugs the policeman, rising up on her tippy toes to make up for her low profile, as Victor appears from his office and observes the reunion. "How are you?" Amy inquires. Her broad face accommodates a wide smile, her golden brown skin shines.

Charlie swipes his cap from his head and manages an uneasy smile, "Seeing you sure brightens up a dreary day. How have you been?"

"Always good!" Amy beams cheerfully. She finally notices Victor standing in the doorway of his office and realizes the reason for the visit. Her smile disappears.

"Hey, Charlie," Victor motions for his friend to come into his office. "Good to see you; I just wish we were seeing each other under better circumstances."

Victor Crawford is forty years old. He was in Charlie's class in high school, and they've remained pals ever since. He is a large man, pushing six foot four and bumping up near the three hundred pound barrier. His long black hair, interspersed with a few gray strands, is in neat traditional braids framing his face. He sports a leather vest decked out with geometric patterns of colorful, precise beadwork over a dress shirt and tie.

"I know," Charlie nods.

The men sit and Victor aligns the folders on his desk centering them uncomfortably. He looks to the right of Charlie's shoulder on the back wall. His eyes are focused on the large bison skull decorating the office. Charlie turns around and examines the milky white skull adorned with beads in zigzag patterns crossing diagonally over each eye. Eagle feathers are affixed to the tips of the glistening black horns. The feathers dangle and twist, moved by an unseen thermal gradient in the warm office. Victor's eyes remain on the skull. He sighs. "You sure you want to do this? Nat's on board?"

Charlie nods. "We talked about it...a lot. He understands. He really summed it up well. Time for a clean slate. His mom actually recommended it."

"I'm sorry about your sister. She was a good woman, great teacher. We miss her." Victor twists his mouth in pain and makes eye contact.

"Thank you." Nodding his head, Charlie can feel his heart beat in his eyes. He notes the same strange, painful symptom every time his sister is mentioned.

Victor's serious expression flips to an infectious smile like the flick of a switch. "You gonna be able to handle it? Being a single parent of a teenager? There's no escape from a brooding or obnoxious teenager when you go from Uncle Charlie to parent."

"I seriously don't know. I got my dad at home to help, and I'm really glad we got basketball as a distraction."

"Yeah, don't we know?" Victor chuckles. "I don't know 'bout you, but it's the only thing that kept me out of trouble."

Victor holds an imaginary basketball in his hands and shoots it at an invisible basket with a flick of his wrist and exaggerated follow through. Charlie turns in his chair as if he is watching the flight of the ball. "Missed it?" Charlie questions. "I can see you still need to work on your shot."

Victor grabs his large belly, laughing heartily in the style of a store Santa Claus. "I should always leave the shooting up to you."

The men laugh a few moments, finally just smiling at each other. "God, we had some good times playing ball, didn't we?"

Charlie leans forward in his chair, his hands on his knees. He fiddles with his stocking cap, eyes focusing on the hat as he rotates it in his hands, "Yeah."

"I still believe," Victor smiles, "we probably would have brought the Sisseton Redmen a state championship if you hadn't wussed out."

"Wussed out?" Victor's words get a rise from Charlie. "I broke my leg!"

Victor bellows forth laughter again and waves a hand of dismissal at Charlie. "Whatever. You coulda played. You on a broken leg was still better than ninety five percent of the players out there."

Charlie bats his eyes and looks to the ceiling nostalgically, sighing. "Ahhh, what could have been..."

"Man, your nephew…" Victor whistles a low whistle of admiration. "What I would give to see you in your prime play Nat." He laughs, "That would be lights out."

Charlie rolls his eyes, "Good memories."

"You're right," Victor states matter-of-factly. "It'll be good for Nat to play against the better competition of the Northeast Conference." Victor nods knowingly, "Maybe get a few more college scouts at that level. Maybe a scholarship."

"I'm not gonna kid ya, basketball is an almost insignificant part of it," Charlie is not smiling. "The truth is," Charlie pauses, "I want him close. I want to keep an eye on him, and he can keep an eye on me. It's only a few miles from my trailer to Sisseton. And he's got his grandpa right there."

Victor nods understandingly.

"I just can't justify having him on the road that much. It's almost 60 miles round trip."

Victor stands and Charlie follows suit. "I'll have Amy get copies of Nat's records for you. C'mon."

Victor sighs and leads the way out of the office. "Honey, can you get copies of Nat's records for me?"

Amy smiles, "Yes, Dear."

Charlie can't stifle his laugh. "I can't believe you guys work together. I can only imagine that a husband and wife would get sick of each other."

Amy bats her eyelashes, "We have true love."

Victor sighs. "Hey, Charlie, I wanted to ask you something. Maybe you can't say, but what's up with those two kids they found in the shack?"

Charlie puts his hands up and shakes his head, "You're right, I can't say anything."

"Talk about shaking the community up," Amy breathes the words, holding her hand to her heart, tears forming in her eyes.

"It's so sad," Victor places a gentle hand on Amy's shoulder. "Where were they from, Watertown?"

Charlie nods and looks at the floor, "Yeah."

Victor realizes he has pushed the limits. "Come on, let's go get Nat." He pats Charlie's shoulder and moves him to the door, guiding him out of the office and into the hallway.

Gregory L. Heitmann

Chapter 8
Nat

Victor and Charlie move down the vacant hallway, their footsteps echoing. Just a few feet from the administrative office they halt and inspect the trophy case. "We're going to miss that kid," Victor whispers.

He points to the State Class "B" runner-up trophy. It sits next to the Region Championship trophy and a photo of the team. In the center of the picture, Nat sits with a net around his neck, he holds up a finger along with the rest of the team indicating they are number one. Victor gives a nod to the Region Champ's trophy, "How many did he get that game? Thirty?"

"Twenty eight," Charlie replies softly.

"Seemed like more. He must have had fourteen in the last five minutes to cut that ten point lead by Rosholt," Victor shakes his head. "That was one of best games I have ever seen. Nat's buzzer beater to send us to the state tourney. I have never heard a gym so loud."

Victor taps the glass trophy case with a fingernail, "Oh, well."

The men continue down the hallway and take a right turn down a connecting corridor. Victor cocks his head, "By the way, do you remember Zeke Gonzales?"

"Oh, yeah. Tough to forget him."

"I guess he's back in town. That guy was crazy." Victor whistles and pushes his hand out, like pushing a person away.

Charlie's eyes narrow, "He never did graduate, did he?"

Victor shakes his head, "Not that I know of. I just wanted to give you a heads up. Be on the lookout for all the trouble that surrounds that guy...you being a policeman and all. He might hit you up for some money."

Victor smiles and gives Charlie a playful shove. "That guy could play some ball, though. It's too bad he quit the team and school. He coulda played in college."

"He's a sad story." Charlie clucks his tongue. "What was he, two years younger than us?"

The men pass by closed classroom doors. Victor glances through the window of each door, mentally noting the teacher and students.

"Yup," Victor confirms.

"He was in prison for a few years. Stolen property, assault, guns. I looked him up. Like I said, very sad."

"Wait, did you say you 'locked him up'?" Victor questions.

"No, I looked him up on our crime data base."

"Oh," Victor acknowledges. "It made me think for a second old Zeke had come back to seek vengeance on you."

"Not quite," Charlie chuckles.

Victor puts up a hand halting his friend, "Here we are."

Victor looks through the window and turns back to Charlie, "It's not too late to change your mind."

Charlie smiles and shakes his head. Victor shrugs and pulls the door open. All the kids in the classroom turn their attention to the door way. "Pardon me, Mrs. Kincaid," Victor speaks softly, calmly. "I hate to interrupt. Nat, can you come with me please? Bring your books."

Nathaniel "Nat" Chasing Wolf is sixteen years old. He eases himself out of his desk in the middle of the classroom with the grace of a dancer. He is a natural athlete, noticeable in his every move. He stands to his full height of six feet two inches shouldering his book bag. With a nod and a couple fist bumps to his friends, he glides his wiry, one hundred sixty pound frame to the door and into the hall.

"What's up, Mr. Crawford?" Nat questions as he reaches the doorway. Nat sees his uncle at the far side of the hallway as he crosses the threshold of the door. "Oh, yeah. I forgot."

Nat twists his mouth as he remembers today is the day. He gives a nod toward his uncle and his long braid bounces off the middle of his back. Nat is distinguished looking, sporting more of the European LeBeau family traits than his Native father. He has the darker complexion and jet black hair of his late father, but his narrow face, high cheek bones, and hazel eyes indicate a hybrid of heredity that leans to his mother's side. He is clad in his everyday school clothes that may as well be a uniform. He wears Levis and a Nike windbreaker over a white t-shirt and a pair of "retired" basketball shoes.

"It's that time, I guess," Nat flashes a melancholy smile.

Victor's head bobs up and down slowly. His eyes dart for a moment to Charlie then back to Nat. "Yup." Victor's head jerks in the direction of the administrative offices. "Let's get you back to the office and signed out."

Gregory L. Heitmann

Chapter 9
Tradition

Nat sits buckled in the front seat of Charlie's Police Tahoe. He is expressionless. The vehicle pulls onto BIA Route 1, heading north to Sisseton, finger drifts of snow begin to extend across the highway as they leave Agency Village. The two sit in silence for the most part. The police radio calls out periodically, but the northwest wind buffets the vehicle whistling and hissing as it permeates even the new window seals. Charlie hits the power window buttons, moving windows up and down, attempting to reseal them and silence the wind noise to no avail.

The gray winter sky perfectly reflects the mood. The low clouds darken and lighten with the sputtering snow. To the left, as they move down the road, the Coteau is barely visible. To the right, the fertile rolling fields rest under the wind driven snow. There is no traffic on the mid-morning road trip. People are at work or in school, and Charlie leisurely cruises under the speed limit, cautiously navigating the accumulating drifts on the seven mile trip from the Old Agency to Sisseton. Charlie momentarily takes his eyes off the road to glance at his nephew sitting next to him. Charlie notices his nephew seems small, shrunken into the passenger seat. He breaks the silence. "How about this weather? Not what I call ideal deer huntin' weather."

Nat acknowledges the comment with a nod. Charlie continues, "Remember last year? I think I hunted in a t-shirt from the bale stack over a three day period."

Nat snickers, "Don't get me wrong, but that's more my hunting weather. I'm gonna leave it up to you to fill the tags if it stays like this."

"Nah," Charlie laughs, "I'm dragging you out there whether you like it or not. I'm gonna haul your grandpa out there too. We gotta get his butt out of the house. All he wants to do is watch TV."

Charlie slows his speed as the drifting snow has built up along a group of trees beside the highway. "First things first," Charlie lifts a finger off the steering wheel and casts a glance at Nat. "We'll need to get you a new letterman's jacket."

Nat looks down at his winter coat, a Tiospa Zina letterman's jacket, blue with white letters "TZ" sewn over his chest. Nat laughs out loud, "Huh, that's hilarious. I never even thought about that."

Charlie lifts his finger off the steering wheel he is gripping rather tightly as they break drifts on the highway, "There's no way I can have you show up at school in any colors other than red, white, and black."

They smile and enjoy a minute of silence as Charlie's Tahoe bumps along, breaking the drifts in his lane. The smallest of weeds along the highway is enough to catch snow and begin a drift. Charlie looks ahead, paying attention to his driving, as he asks the question, "Are you nervous?"

Nat shrugs. His mouth twists as he thinks, "A little I guess." He shakes his head. "I know almost everybody there already. Baseball. Summer basketball league and pickup games. I know all the guys." Nat looks at his uncle, "It's just weird, you know? Maybe I should have just finished out the year."

"Nah," Charlie disagrees with a shake of his head. "It's a good school. Yours truly graduated from there; Grandpa graduated from there. It can't be all bad."

Nat finishes the thought, "...and my mom. That was her school."

Charlie smiles and nods as he focuses on the road.

"I'm not even that sad about leaving TZ. Half the guys in my class have dropped out. Our basketball team was going to suck." Nat's voice gets higher in anger, "A bunch of the players we were counting on are ineligible because of grades." Nat's disgust is obvious, his voice is low and resolute. "The basketball team was going to suck. I'm ready for a change."

Nat reaches for his head. He runs his hands over his hair. He swings his braid from behind him and stares down at the tip of his woven hair. "You know what? Could we stop at Clyde's? I think I really want change."

"What? You're serious?" Charlie casts a quick glance at his nephew as he slows even more on the snowy road. "No more braid?" Charlie pauses, shocked by this conversation. "You want a haircut?"

His whole body rocks up and down slowly, affirmatively. Nat frowns, "It's time."

"All right then."

Nat continues to stare down at his braid in his hand. He reaches for the visor and pulls it down exposing a mirror. He gazes into the mirror at his hair tightly pulled back. He turns for a moment and looks at his uncle then back to the mirror. "Can I ask you a question, Uncle?'

"Sure."

"Did you ever sun dance?"

"Nope," Charlie is quick and succinct with his answer.

Nat purses his lips. Charlie takes a quick glance at his nephew. "Mind you I've never been traditional. Don't get me wrong, I'm not much for telling people how to live their lives or listening to people tell me how I should live mine. Bottom line, it's just that the old ways weren't for me."

"You never wore long hair? Braids?"

Charlie shakes his head, "I didn't want the hassle. My dad, your Grandpa Claude, he wasn't traditional either. He let me make my own decisions on that stuff."

Silence sinks in just a moment before Charlie continues, "How about you? You sun dance?"

"No."

"You want to?"

Nat purses his lips and scrunches his face, "I don't know. All my friends that ever did it...they all dropped out of school! All those guys, they seemed like they got radical after their experience. They were suddenly 'fightin' against the whole world.'" Nat makes air quotes, and frowns in disgust. "I don't really understand it. The clash of the two cultures. It seems like it's one or the other, you just can't survive in both worlds. They want you to pick one and stick with it."

"I know what you mean. Try being a policeman and dealing with both cultures."

The Tahoe reaches the edge of Sisseton's city boundary, and Charlie slows down to the prescribed miles per hour as indicated by the speed zone signs. The two are in silence and with the lower speed, you can hear the FM station for the first time. The song "Smokey Mountain Rain" by Ronnie Milsap is playing. Nat leans forward and turns up the volume. His head bounces, and he hums along until the chorus, when he sings a customized lyric substituting 'South Dakota Rain' for 'Smokey Mountain Rain.' Nat sings:

"South Dakota rain, keeps on fallin'
I keep on callin', her name.
South Dakota rain, I keep on searchin',

Can't go on hurtin', this way.
She's somewhere in the South Dakota rain."

Charlie looks at Nat and grins at the same time fighting back an emotion that wants to put tears in his eyes.

"What?" Nat questions.

"Nothin'."

Nat smiles a smile of true happiness, "That was the song my mom used to sing. She changed the lyrics to South Dakota, and all the towns it references, we changed them too. Hot Springs. Aberdeen."

"So I hear," Charlie grins knowing this kid is special.

An appropriate silence envelops the vehicle until Nat speaks again, "I really miss her."

"Yeah, we all do," Charlie affirms through watery eyes he hopes Nat doesn't seem to notice. He does notice but does not draw attention to his uncle's emotions.

Silence again prevails. Nat gazes out the side window, which begins to fog from the proximity of his breathing. "You know, I like to think the new tradition for Indians are basketball and deer huntin'."

"I concur." Charlie softly states.

"Granted," Nat shrugs, "Indians have hunted deer since the beginning of time, but I'm talking modern methods...rifles, scopes, binoculars."

Nat laughs at himself. "For basketball, did you ever notice the fan favorite at the state tourney is always a reservation team?"

Charlie laughs with a snort, "Who doesn't like run-and-gun ball?"

"That settles it," Nat declares affirmatively. "I think I will stick with my new modern traditions."

They are at the intersection of BIA Route 1 and South Dakota Highway 10. The vehicle slows for the stop sign. Straight ahead is Sisseton High School, to the right is the rest of the town and the barber shop. "Hang a right," Nat says flatly.

"Clyde's it is then," Charlie affirms, steering to the right.

Nat smiles, feeling comfort in his decision. "I was just thinkin,' Uncle Charlie. You should probably be getting nervous."

"Oh, really? Nervous about what?" Charlie is genuinely puzzled.

"You haven't thought about it? Your Redmen basketball scoring records...they are going down," Nat smirks matter-of-factly.

"Records are made to be broken, but they will have to put an asterisk next to your name or mine."

"Why?" Nat's brow furrows.

Charlie holds up a pleading hand and whines, "I had a three point line for only one year."

Nat shakes his head, "Excuses."

Gregory L. Heitmann

Chapter 10
Sisseton

Sisseton is a dichotomy of culture. It is a blend of Native American and white, mostly European, cultures. To be more accurate, it has more than just the two sides of a coin. The special geography of the Coteau Des Prairies has indelibly marked the agriculture-driven modern society. But long before farming and ranching came to stamp the area as it is known now, the historic and pre-historic traces remain. The northeast corner of South Dakota is filled with treasures of the past and present. Ask nearly any family that has lived in the area for at least a couple generations about the artifacts they have gathered over time, and they will undoubtedly show you a surprising collection. Arrowheads, spear points, and hammer stones seem to literally rise out of the ground as tractors work the fields. But, beyond the manmade riches, there is still the wildlife that abounds as it has since before modern man. This is the wildlife, the first people followed as they roamed the land following the herds and flocks.

To describe Sisseton in one word, you might choose the word "sundry." Like the old mercantile that offered "assorted sundries," Sisseton has a reputation that you probably can't quite put your finger on. But that works for most people. The Indian reservation is a dominant feature and will probably always be, but the Interstate Highway connects to Fargo to the north and Sioux Falls to the south. Travel a few hours east on modern highways, and you arrive in the ultra-modern, progressive, and teaming metropolitan area of Minneapolis-St. Paul, the Twin Cities.

Even with all the modern casinos, the highway connections, and cutting edge technologies of cell phones and internet, Sisseton is still a respite from the bustling, and seemingly out of control world. It is not surprising that the area attracts a steady stream of tourists to hunt, fish, and just get away from things. To a passerby, Sisseton probably doesn't seem like much. But beneath the surface, by just peeling the first thin layer, you can see a wide cross-section of inhabitants, not unlike a lot of Indian reservations and their surrounding communities. There are members of the tribe that have nothing and long for nothing. They may live in what might be considered a shack that is not decent, safe, nor sanitary. They may go for months without electricity. Their heat may only be logs in a wood stove or fireplace. Water might be the only steady necessity they have.

In contrast, ranchers, both Native and white, may live within a mile of those with virtually nothing. Ranchers of substantial wealth, both in reputation and monetary aspects, exist in Sisseton's community.

Sisseton is special. The Coteau and its rolling hills and lakes that are perfectly suited to ranching, hunting, and fishing, form an ideal complement to the flat, rich, soils of the cropland to the east. It is a hub of some renown in an area within a radius of sixty miles. Aberdeen, South Dakota may call itself the "Hub City" thanks to its railroad history, but Sisseton was a hub long before engine-powered wheels entered the Dakota Territory.

The point to be made is that Sisseton will be around for awhile. Some say it is on its way down. Some might claim the town has seen its better days, but be cautious with these predictions. Sisseton has been around for a long time and will continue to be an important part of the Glacial Lakes region and Northeast South Dakota. The simple, agrarian lifestyle of the Dakotas and Minnesota do not radically fluctuate to the whims of metropolitan areas. Today's society tends to glamorize the bustling lifestyle, but who is to say that the laid back, rural living is a lesser existence. No, Sisseton is not better or worse than any other place; it is just different.

Chapter 11
The Holiday Gas Station

Sisseton, South Dakota

On the eastern edge of Sisseton, a couple of miles west of Interstate 29, a fixture of the community stands at this location, the Holiday Station. It was a hub of transportation commerce before the Interstate was completed. The towering sign for the corner gas station still stands, but weathered, less dignified, and fading fast. It is in the shape of an arrowhead or some would say a white zeppelin with a top red fin and bottom blue fin stamped with blue lettering. The word "Holiday" is centered on the sign. The "i" in the word is dotted by a red check mark. It has always been a landmark for the community. You can get almost anything in the convenience store in addition to filling your car. Farmers gather for coffee, munch on fresh donuts, swap stories, and roll dice to see who gets stuck with the bill. The building has evolved over the years, having started as a one room gas station with restrooms in the back.

Charlie pulls his BIA Police Tahoe into the Holiday Station sidling up to the gas pump to refuel. For Charlie, this is one of, if not his most favorite place in Sisseton. As a working policeman it is an important stop in his routine, for this is the communication center of the village. Rumors, gossip, and tales spread like wildfire from this gathering point. More than that, the Holiday Station always brings a wave of nostalgia for Charlie whenever he stops. He vividly remembers his childhood from the vantage point of this gas station. The pleasant memories of riding with his father, to fill the truck for the opening day of pheasant hunting, come rushing back every time he stops to refuel. All sorts of family would come out of the woodwork from far off places to hunt birds and celebrate fall. It was an annual family reunion. Every year, from as early as he could remember, to well into his teen years, cousins, aunts, and uncles would show up in Sisseton. The uncles were the real characters, filling the house with excitement and spirit only duplicated by the Christmas season. It seemed like a tradition that would never end. There were plenty of birds to harvest in the cornfields, edges of pastures, and grassy swales. As a kid you don't understand that everything comes to an end. Time passes, and people get older and busier with their kids and immediate families. Farming practices changed, the pheasant population dropped drastically, and the traditional pheasant opener faded like the colors in the gas station sign overhead.

Under the protection of the canopy, Charlie fills the Tahoe. Snow flakes waft down from the gray sky overhead. It is another sunless, dreary day. As Charlie stares into the convenience store, his mind is taken back to his childhood. He can still hear his dad say, "Charlie, go grab a box of shells for tomorrow, five shot."

That's all it took. Those words were like the starter's pistol at a track meet. Charlie vividly remembers those boxes of twelve gauge, Holiday brand, shotgun shells. Charlie laughs to himself as he thinks about the oddity of a gas station with its own name brand shotgun shells. But as a child there was something amazing about those boxes of shells. They were masterpiece works of art. On the outside of the box one side had a scene depicting pheasants, a brightly colored rooster and a dusky hen, flying over brown prairie grasses waving in the wind. The opposite side of the box was a scene of a pair of mallards, a greenhead and a hen, flying over cattails. Other boxes of shells may have bright colors on the box, but these, these Holiday Gas Station shotgun shell boxes had it inside and out. Not only were there beautiful pictures of your quarry on the outside, but inside the box, the plastic shells themselves were a bright sky blue color! All the other shells out there had dull dark red, green, some were even black. It was mind blowing to a seven year old boy that a simple item like a shotgun shell could be so different. It was and is a lasting impression for Charlie, one that still brings a smile to his face.

Chapter 12
Marvin

At the Holiday Station, as Charlie waits for his large gas tank to fill, a small sports utility vehicle pulls up to the pump across from him. Immediately a man emerges from the store. It is Marvin Hattum, the owner of the gas station. The fifty three year old man hustles as fast as a short, stocky man with a cane and walking boot can maneuver to the SUV. Clad in large bulky blue jeans and only a triple XL Green Bay Packers sweatshirt against the frosty thirty degrees, Marvin passes Charlie with a wave and a, "Hey, Charlie,"

A young man with dark-rimmed glasses exits from the SUV. "Sir," Marvin calls out to him, "you have a loose tie-down on your luggage rack."

Before anyone can react, Marvin is holding the loose rope securing a corner of a suitcase on the roof luggage rack of the SUV. With amazing dexterity, Marvin whips the rope back and forth and the offending rope is cinched with a tidy hitch. Charlie observes the knot tying display with admiration. "Much obliged," the driver thanks Marvin with a wave.

"No problem; you are welcome," Marvin nods. "It was my pleasure. Have a great day!"

Marvin shudders in the cold, flashes a smile toward Charlie, and limps back to the station building. Charlie watches Marvin disappear back into the building. Charlie's mind switches channels like a TV, going from the dreamy nostalgic memories of his youth, to the stark landscape at the base of the Coteau and the murdered teenagers. His mind contemplates the knots used to restrain the teens in the frozen shack. The auto-shutoff on the nozzle of the gas pump clicks loudly, bringing Charlie's thoughts back to the task at hand. He squeezes another half gallon into the tank and buttons things down before heading inside the convenience store.

Charlie passes the counter where Marvin mans the register and rings up a customer. Charlie still thinks about the knots as he goes for the coffee pot. It's business as usual in the coffee shop section, and Charlie calls out, "Morning, everyone."

A collective "hello" murmurs through the 9:30 A.M. coffee club. All the usuals are in place, primarily local farmers and retirees. The all-male contingent sips at coffee and dunks donuts while passing time shooting the breeze. The dice shaker sits ready to stick one unlucky guy with today's bill.

It's Old Man Cowell that addresses Charlie individually, "Shoot anybody lately there, Chief?"

It was the usual banter from Cowell. He looked ninety five years old, although he was only in his late seventies. He was stooped and wrinkled from the years of hard labor scratching out a living on a ranch on the edge of the Coteau. He now resides in the assisted living center in town, having handed off the ranch to his daughter. Cowell referred to all Indians as "Chief." Charlie always got a good laugh when he heard it. The overt discrimination was always there for some people and probably always will be. The racial tensions in Sisseton had been steadily on the rise for the last twenty years. A combination of the ever shrinking rural economy and the self-inflicted problems associated with casino gambling took its toll on both cultures.

"No, Mr. Cowell. Everyone is behaving," Charlie smiles.

"Not everyone," Cowell scoffs. "You got some murdering sumbitch right up on the Coteau."

"Sorry," Charlie shrugs, "I can't comment on the investigation." He points a finger pistol at Old Man Cowell, "You guys have a good day. Stay outta trouble."

Music plays softly overhead. It is Pheasant Country, KBWS 102.9 FM and the Zac Brown Band sings about things they love like fried chicken and cold beer on Friday nights. "Howdy, Marvin," Charlie greets his friend while setting the coffee on the counter and digging for his wallet.

"Morning, Charlie. Just the coffee?" Marvin smiles and pecks a finger at the cash register.

Charlie hands a five dollar bill to Marvin. "Yeah, I put the gas on the government credit card at the pump."

Marvin grimaces, "I sure miss the old days when I used to get to talk to everyone because they had to come inside and pay."

Charlie collects his change from Marvin, dropping the coins in his pocket and folding the bills back into his wallet.

"This business has been in the family for sixty years," Marvin continues. "Before I was even born. Now, I only talk to half the people because of those convenient credit card pumps." Marvin sarcastically emphasizes the word "convenient".

"I hear ya," Charlie commiserates. "The world is more impersonal every day."

Charlie gives a nod and looks down toward Marvin's foot, envisioning the walking boot and cane obstructed by the counter. "I saw you limping out there, foot in a boot, and using a cane. What's up?"

Marvin grasps his large belly with both hands, "Doctor told me being large and in charge is unhealthy. Bottom line, I'm too fat; stress fracture in my foot." Marvin laughs half-heartedly at himself.

Charlie grips his coffee cup and sips. He stifles a chuckle, instead commenting, "Well, that sucks."

Marvin gestures up to the wall behind him at a taxidermy mounted head and shoulder display of a whitetail buck with massive, symmetrical antlers sporting seven points on one side and eight points on the other. Marvin shakes his head and pathetically laments, "No way I can do any huntin' this year with a bad foot."

"Sure you can," Charlie counters. "You can just sit in your truck and drive around like a bunch of those gasoline jockeys burning fuel up and down the roads."

Customers filter in and out of the store, and Marvin waves and nods at each one. He smiles weakly at Charlie, "No thanks. I'd rather not hunt than chase around like those fools and jokers in their fancy trucks."

Charlie steps aside as a customer approaches the counter to pay for a candy bar and a Coke. Marvin's eyes narrow as he gets serious a moment, "How would you like to hunt my honey hole? Seriously, I've got those two quarters adjacent to Peever Slough, and I could hook you up with my neighbor. He's got the adjoining section."

Charlie is taken aback by the generous offer, "That's a great offer, Marvin, but I'm used to just huntin' 'round the house. It's a tradition."

Marvin smiles knowingly, "Let me guess, you got a big one already lined up around your place."

Charlie laughs, "No, I've spotted a couple nice ones. Nothing like Bullwinkle you got up on your wall here." Charlie gives a nod to the deer above them on the back wall.

Marvin leans back on a stool behind the counter and folds his arms on his big belly. He gives a melancholy sigh, "This might be the end of my deer huntin' days. It's like a vicious cycle. Can't exercise cuz of my bad foot, can't lose weight cuz I can't exercise. It's a death spiral."

Another customer interrupts Marvin's take on his foot. The man pays cash in advance of fueling. Marvin taps a few buttons, thanks the customer, and returns to his thoughts. "I have such a hard time with my eating. I love food!" Marvin pats his belly.

Charlie shakes his head, "Changing the subject, have I mentioned my disgust for your sweatshirt?"

Marvin brushes the front of his Green Bay Packers sweatshirt and smiles. "Why are you hating on the Pack? Oh, yeah. It's because we keep demolishing your pathetic Vikings."

Another customer interrupts to pay for gasoline and moves out the door. Charlie poses a question to Marvin, "Who was the guy that you tied down that suitcase for just a while ago?"

Marvin shrugs his shoulders, "I don't know. Just some Thanksgiving Holiday traveler I suppose. I spotted that loose rope. I just hate to see loose ropes like that."

Charlie nods, "Yeah, it's dangerous."

"I mean," Marvin continues, "What if that suitcase flew off and caused somebody to crash? I'd feel terrible if I could have done something, but didn't."

"Where'd you learn to tie knots like that so quickly?" Charlie asks innocently.

Marvin laughs loudly, "You should know. You forget Desert Storm already? You don't remember tying stuff down all the time to haul across Iraq in our trucks?"

Charlie laughs the words, "Oh yeah."

Marvin frowns, "It was a long time ago already. Lord knows we'd all be better off if we just forgot about the whole Middle East. The irony is," Marvin laughs, "look at me, I'm in the gas sellin' business."

Marvin leans in close to Charlie, his eyes dart about the room as if looking for a suspicious character. He whispers, "Any word on the killings? Something I can share with the boys?" Marvin tilts his head toward the men drinking coffee. Charlie sips his beverage and leans in closer to Marvin.

Marvin tilts his head up with pleading, sorrowful eyes and searches Charlie's face. "You know it was my cousin that found the bodies?"

Charlie nods, "That's what I heard. Isn't Long Hollow where you shot this big one?" Charlie glances up at the big deer behind Marvin.

Marvin's head bobs, "Yup. It sure was. Hunted up your direction before I picked up the land down by Peever."

Charlie glances around and leans close to Marvin, "Speaking of Peever, I am heading that direction now, but I'll tell you this: They're going to release the names of the victims...two high school kids from Watertown."

Marvin nods with a serious expression. The two men have their attention redirected by the sound of dice in the shaker and spilling onto the table. Charlie straightens, "I gotta go. I don't want to get sucked into rolling dice and getting stuck for everyone's coffee."

Marvin extends his hand, "Thanks, Charlie. Good to talk to you. What's going on in Peever?"

Charlie shakes Marvin's hand, "Stolen ATV, I guess."

Marvin nods, "Well, let me know the details, and I'll keep an eye out for it."

Charlie smiles as he exits. He raises his coffee toward Marvin, "Sure, Marv, will do."

Gregory L. Heitmann

Chapter 13
Theft

Near Peever, South Dakota

The Cullen Ranch sits just a mile and a half west of Peever. The gravel road leading to the house is frozen today, covered with a dusting of snow. In warmer weather the trip might have been a little more of a challenge to navigate the thawing surface and its muddy, slick coating. Not today, the temperatures have dropped below freezing again, and intermittent snow showers pass through.

Charlie found the Cullen Farm & Ranch Headquarters as directed by the placards tucked into the barbed wire fences and directional signs with arrows at the turns. It is a typical setup for the area: machine shed, barn and corrals, stacks of round bales, house and strategically planted rows of tree shelterbelts to provide a bit of relief from the ever present South Dakota winds. Charlie pulls his Tahoe into the yard and is greeted by an entourage of barking dogs, a gray, shaggy mutt, a heeler, and another hybrid mutt with dominate traits of a yellow Labrador retriever. Will Cullen is at the burn barrel dropping in a bag of trash. He waves at Charlie and points him toward the big shed with its open doors. Charlie steers his vehicle in the direction of the metal building, slowly proceeding to make room for the curious dogs escorting him to the concrete slab in front of the shed.

Charlie doesn't know everyone on the reservation, but he knows most of them. Will Cullen is around his age, a little older. They had been in high school at the same time. Will still looks the same to Charlie. His wavy, red hair peeks out of a stocking cap. His wire-rimmed circular glasses give him a professorial appearance, the same way Charlie remembered the debate club leader. Will had married one of Charlie's classmates, Ellen DeGrey. Ellen is an enrolled member of the tribe. Her father had been on the Tribal Council for many years, serving as chairman at different times. The DeGrey homestead is just a half mile from the Cullen Ranch, and Charlie can see part of the DeGrey trailer from where he sits in his vehicle. Charlie's view of the distant farm place is blocked by mature rows of trees that form a shelterbelt surrounding the trailer where Ellen grew up and her parents still live.

Charlie exits his vehicle and steps into the shed as Will makes his way from the burn barrel, weaving his way mechanically though the dogs that had sniffed Charlie for a moment, only to return to their master. Will reaches down and pats each dog's head and scratches each dog's ear, the dogs reveling in the attention. "Thanks for coming out, Charlie," Will pulls off his glove and extends his hand.

"No problem," Charlie pulls off his black leather glove and shakes the rancher's meaty, calloused hand.

Charlie returns his glove to his hand and turns his attention to his clipboard. "You got the serial number and info?"

Will is clad in his everyday winter uniform for chores, a dark brown, heavy duty Carhartt sweatshirt over his coveralls, and insulated lace up boots. He unzips his sweatshirt and pulls a folded piece of paper from the pocket of a heavy flannel shirt in the traditional red and black plaid lumberjack colors. "I have the invoice right here."

Will hands the folded piece of paper to Charlie. "Gosh darn it. It was a 2006 Yamaha Grizzly."

Will turns from Charlie to look out the shed doors as they rattle, disturbed by a gust of wind and accompanying squall of snow flurries. He turns back to Charlie, scratching his head through his stocking cap. "I'm not even sure when it went missing, but it's gone now." Will throws his hands up in the air. "I just need the report for the insurance. Heck, it may not even be worth filing the claim with the deductible and all."

Charlie copies the serial number, make, and model onto the criminal complaint form on his clipboard. He finishes the required information and hands the invoice back to Will. "Where did you keep it?"

Will folds the paper and stashes it back in his shirt pocket. He points both hands and nods, "Right where you're standin'. We just park 'em here. Keys in 'em. Shed's not locked. Like I said, I couldn't even tell you when it went missing."

"I see," Charlie acknowledges as he makes notes on the form.

"Never had nothin' like this happen before. Shoot, they left the new four-wheeler." Will points to the big red ATV next to Charlie.

Charlie's eyebrows go up as he notices the muddy machine for the first time. "Hmmm," Charlie taps the pen on his lip before making another note.

Will continues, "We musta been gone, cuz we would have heard the dogs barking if a stranger pulled into the yard. You heard 'em when you pulled up."

Charlie nods and scratches his eyebrow with his pen.

"Let me guess," Will resolutely states. "We'll never see that four-wheeler again."

"You never know," Charlie smiles. "I'm on the case!" Charlie's tone shifts; it is more soothing, "It's not likely." Charlie shakes his head.

"Son-of-a-gun," Will mimics Charlie's head shake. "Hard to believe they would leave the new one and take the old one."

Charlie makes the note, "Anything else?"

"Nope."

Charlie tears out a carbon copy of the complaint form and hands it to Will. "I would say that it was a very considerate thief to leave you your new ATV, but I believe that criminals tend not to be the brightest bulbs in the bunch."

Will agrees, "You can say that again. Thanks for coming out, Charlie."

"No problem. Sorry about your four-wheeler. You stay warm."

Charlie turns and begins to walk away.

"Hey, Charlie," Will calls out.

Charlie stops and turns to the smiling man. Will holds up his gloved hands to his head trying to simulate antlers on a deer. "Any big bucks up your way?"

It's a November topic the fraternity of deer hunters can all relate to, and it brings a broad smile to Charlie's face. "Not for me," Charlie shakes his head. "I haven't heard of anyone scorin' a big one yet either."

Will drops his hands, "Same here. Good luck to ya."

Charlie gives a wave and walks the short distance to his vehicle. Dogs emerge from different corners of the yard as he starts the Tahoe. He eases away from the shed, and a few barks echo behind him as he looks in his mirror and sees the dogs guarding the end of the driveway.

Gregory L. Heitmann

Chapter 14
Veronica

Long Hollow

Three days have passed since the murder. The initial torrent of the investigation had washed over Sisseton and receded. The FBI and the State Department of Criminal Investigation had retreated to their labs with the evidence. The news from the Sioux Falls television stations as well as the TV stations from the much closer Fargo, North Dakota, market had summarized the brutality in five sentences and a graphic of two chalk outlined bodies. There was no mention in the media of similar murders five years before. The authorities hadn't mentioned it, and the media outlets hadn't dug up any connections, yet.

Charlie had gone to the bale stack earlier and waited about forty five minutes for a deer to show up. A small buck had made an appearance with a running mate, another buck with no rack to speak of, but Charlie passed on the two little bucks. They were outcasts for the time being as the bigger, dominant bucks defended their does. After dark, Charlie made it back to the house, grabbed a blueberry muffin, and left in his police Tahoe. Charlie drove to the location of the murders just seven minutes away at a leisurely pace. He parked outside the shack, killing the lights and the engine.

*   *   *

Charlie waits in the cold dead night. Inside of his vehicle he pulls the top off the blueberry muffin his dad had made for supper. The pork chops would wait until he gets back. Charlie attempts to get in the mind of the killer on the night of the murders. It is cold, but he refrains from starting the engine. An hour passes as Charlie imagines the killer's thrill. The half moon is high in the sky, and his eyes have adjusted to the darkness. The radio is on a pop music station from Fargo and a song with a driving guitar is playing. It is The Strokes and their song *Last Night*. Charlie turns the volume even lower and closes his eyes, but the tune is stuck in his head now. He visualizes the killer driving down the snowy trail. The car with the teenagers in the trunk struggles to get through the compacted drifts. Charlie shakes his head and opens his eyes. He stares at the shack. He shivers and sips coffee trying to stay warm. He reaches for the key, but his eyes catch movement, something is in the trees. Charlie's first thought is a deer. Maybe it's a buck he could put on his wish list. He reaches for his police-issue night vision scope. There is a person moving though the trees lining the coulee on the other side of the shack. Charlie's heart pounds into action. The cold wind gusts, slinging loose snow crystals across the hood of the Tahoe. Charlie pushes the override button for the interior lights of the vehicle preventing them from illuminating when the door is opened. Charlie looks again through the scope. He confirms it is a person. "Who would be out here?" Charlie whispers to himself in disbelief.

*　　*　　*

He pockets the night vision scope, slips the key from the ignition, and draws his service revolver, a Berretta .40 caliber. Charlie silently eases the door open and slips out of the Tahoe. The wind whistles in his ears through his stocking cap, and he pushes it down tighter on his head. One hand holds his pistol, the other his Maglite, ready to flash on and illuminate his target. Charlie is still dressed in his white camouflage hunting clothes that he wore sitting on the bale stack earlier. He's prepared for the cold. He's still in his hunting camo, only missing his bright orange vest. Charlie moves to the shack and stands flat against the side of the building. Yellow police tape dogged and dislodged by the wind, flaps loosely in the breeze. He tries to control his breathing as his heart pounds. He's not cold anymore; in fact, there is a bead of sweat on his brow. The crunching of footsteps through the snow cuts through the wind and gets louder. The wind cannot drown the thud of footsteps through the hardened snow drifts. Now there is a beam of light slashing across the snow. The approaching person has turned on a flashlight. They have no fear of approaching the building. Charlie is confused. His imagination runs wild. Is the killer returning to the scene of the crime like in a clichéd mystery novel? Re-gripping his weapon and flashlight, he catches a glimpse of his Tahoe. He sets his flashlight down and grips the key fob in his pocket. His thumb finds the unlock button on the remote system.

From his position to the side of the building Charlie hears the shack's door handle emit a shrill squeak. He presses the remote unlocking button and his vehicle lights shine to his side as he maneuvers to the front of the building. The intruder turns and is blinded by the vehicle lights. "Police! Freeze!" Charlie shouts. "Get down on the ground!" He commands with authority.

For the first time since he heard the catchy song *Last Night* by The Strokes earlier in the evening, the tune is put out of his head. The blinded intruder screams and drops to a knee. Charlie's instincts as a cop take over, and he flattens the person into the snow. He jabs his knee in the back of the gasping intruder as he digs for his cuffs. He holsters his pistol. He fumbles slightly fighting his gloves and the struggling suspect, finally getting the cuffs in place.

The timer shuts off the lights of the unlocked Tahoe as Charlie stands and hustles to pick up the flashlight dropped by the suspect. "Who are you?" he shouts. "Get to your knees," he orders as he shines the light on the person.

Charlie rips away the hood from the diminutive intruder and pulls off a facemask revealing a woman's delicate features. He pulls on her arm, setting her on her knees. She gasps for breath. She attempts to stand, but Charlie forces her down, "Stay down!" he orders, drawing his gun.

"My name is Veronica Lewis," the woman gasps, spitting the words. "I'm a reporter! Get these cuffs off me!"

Veronica Lewis is five foot three, one hundred ten pounds. Her pretty face is criss-crossed by her mussed dark hair. Charlie leans down, "All right, up you go," Charlie pulls her to her feet. He pushes the hair out of her face, and he can see her attractive features for the first time. Veronica's eyes pierce Charlie as she glares at him. "My name is Veronica Lewis. Please let me go!" She growls. I'm a reporter with the Sisseton Chronicle!"

Charlie frisks the woman pulling a cell phone from her pocket. "Do you have any ID?"

Veronica's shoulders continue to heave up and down as she slowly regains her breath. "It's in my purse. Back in my car...up on the road!"

Chapter 15
Cuffed

"Come on," Charlie commands.

He grabs her arm. "Ow!" she yells. "Take it easy!" she whines defiantly. "Ow, ow, ow, ow, ow!" Veronica protests on every step.

She stumbles and slips her way through the snow to the rear door of the Tahoe. Charlie brushes the snow from her blue jeans. "You already frisked me," she whines.

"Relax," Charlie shook his head, "I'm just brushing some of this snow off you."

"Oh, thanks," Veronica shrugs.

Charlie opens the door and struggles to load the handcuffed woman into the back seat of the high clearance four-wheel drive. He tosses her in the back as a resolution to the difficulty, and she wriggles to get herself upright with her arms bound behind her. Charlie climbs into the vehicle, locates his key in his pocket, and starts his Tahoe. Veronica straightens to a sitting position in the back seat, stooped forward with her hands behind her back. Charlie observes his suspect in the rearview mirror as the dome light fades and only the dashboard lights illuminate the cab. She scowls at him in the mirror, staring back. Her head goes side to side slowly shaking in disgust and disagreement. The FM radio station plays The Killers' song *Mr. Brightside* and the bass pulsates the speakers with little midrange sounds with the volume so low. Charlie turns the radio off.

Veronica shivers in the backseat and Charlie follows suit. The cold sinking in with the adrenaline rush now fading quickly. "Give it a minute to warm up, and I'll put the fan on higher," Charlie says softly as he locks eyes in the mirror with his captive.

"Listen to me!" Veronica growls loudly. "I'm just doing a story on the murders. I came out here to see the crime scene at night and get a feel for it."

She stares at Charlie in the mirror, not blinking or breaking eye contact. Charlie looks down at the cell phone in his hand. He scrolls through the contacts a moment before pausing to look in the mirror and find Veronica's eyes still fixed on him. "Please! These cuffs are killing me! Please!" she cries out pathetically.

Charlie looks down at the phone again and continues to scroll through the contacts. "Ahhhh!" his backseat passenger calls out in frustration as he looks away.

"I am begging you. Please get these handcuffs off me. I'm just a reporter."

Charlie does not look up, quietly addressing the woman, "I have not read you your rights, and I haven't arrested you yet, but I'd appreciate it if you exercised your right to remain silent."

Veronica rolls her eyes and struggles to find a more comfortable position, "Great I get a comedian cop."

Charlie turns the fan to the highest setting on the heater and scrolls through recent calls, received calls, and missed calls. He finally sets the phone on the console, pulls the handle on his door and exits the vehicle. Opening the rear door, he pushes Veronica forward and unlocks the cuffs. She takes a deep breath and rubs her wrists. "Thank you," she breathes the words in relief.

"Come on. I'll help you down. You can get in the front seat," Charlie extends his hand, and Veronica leans on him, stepping down into the snow. "Let's go. Get in the front."

"What? Why? I'm just gonna go back to my car."

Charlie grabs her arm and starts to drag her around the Tahoe. "Ok, Ok," Veronica concedes. "Sheesh, take it easy."

Veronica climbs into the passenger side front seat and rubs her hands and wrists trying to warm up. Charlie climbs in the driver's side and looks at his passenger with pity. Veronica looks back at Charlie, "What? Don't look at me like that." She shakes her head, "I'm sorry. I know I'm wrong, and I apologize."

Veronica picks up her phone from the console. "Oh, you confirmed my identity from my phone contacts?" She looks from the phone back to Charlie and sarcastically announces, "Nice police work."

Charlie flicks his headlights on as well as his spotlight mounted near his driver's side mirror. He scans the woods. "What are you doing here?"

"Tuh," Veronica clicks her tongue. "I already told you. I'm writing a story on the murders. I wanted to get a feel for it. I'm hoping my story will get picked up by the AP." She pauses, "I'm sorry, the Associated Press. Maybe this will be my big break."

"You're here by yourself?" Charlie questions not looking at her.

"Tuh," Veronica's tongue clicks again. "What? A woman can't work by herself?"

Charlie ignores her question. He turns the spot light off and leans toward his passenger. "This is an active crime scene. You didn't see the police tape?"

"I said I'm sorry," Veronica pleads.

She sighs, and the pair sits in silence, sizing each other up. Veronica shivers again. "Why are you out in here in the dark? Are you guarding the crime scene?" she questions sarcastically. "You do something, and your boss is punishing you?" She laughs.

"It's police business. None of your business why I am here."

Veronica's mouth drops open, "Wait, is this a stakeout? You think the killer is going to return to the scene of the crime? Did he leave something? Tell me, is it just one killer or is it a pair? Maybe, like a, a gang?"

Charlie's brow furrows, "Anyone ever tell you that you talk a lot?"

"Yeah," Veronica responds matter-of-factly. "It's my job to ask questions. I'm a reporter." She shivers again, but relaxing ever so slightly. "Brrrr. Thank God for this heater. I'm freezing."

"Where's your car?" Charlie demands, putting the Tahoe in gear. "I'll take you to your car. Where is it?"

"Wait!" Veronica frowns. "Just hold up a minute. You didn't answer any of my questions. You're on a stake out, hoping the criminal returns."

Charlie puts the vehicle back in park, "I can't comment."

"I'll take that as a 'yes'." Veronica smiles wryly.

The corner of Charlie's mouth twitches, revealing a hint of a smile. "Don't worry, I won't quote you," Veronica grins.

Charlie forces a frown, "You want to go to jail for obstruction? Just keep it up. You went across the police tape...you turned the handle of that sealed door of a crime scene..."

"Fine!" Veronica throws her hands up in frustration. "Take me to my car."

"Where is it?"

Veronica stabs a finger in a westerly direction, "Just over the hill. I parked on an approach near a culvert on this drainage. I just came from upstream following the creek through the trees. All I wanted to do was feel what the killer might have felt that night in these woods."

Charlie puts the Tahoe in drive. He pushes the four-wheel drive low button and turns the vehicle around, getting back on the two rut trail. His tracks from a little over an hour ago have all but disappeared, buried by the drifting snow. "Put your seatbelt on." Charlie orders without looking over.

A half mile east, a mile south, and a mile back to the west on the gravel county road and they arrive at Veronica's car. The Tahoe's headlights illuminate a gap in the trees where the stream passes under the road through a culvert. The barren tree branches sway in the breeze. Snow moves across the gravel road in rhythm with the gusts. The road ahead of them begins to rise steeply up the Coteau. Charlie looks down into the abyss of the bottom of the channel. The lights don't reach to the bed of the stream, but he can tell they are on a grade about thirty feet above the flow line. Charlie puts the Tahoe in park, "Give me your keys."

"Why?" Veronica questions.

"You just sit tight. I'll start your car, and you can stay in here while it warms up."

"Hmmm. A real gentleman."

Charlie provides a pained smile and receives the keys. He's out and back in the vehicle in just a moment with her car running. "Thanks for understanding," Veronica offers diplomatically. "I know you are doing me a favor and letting me slide."

"Don't let me catch you around here again," Charlie warns with a wagging finger.

"You'll be out here again?" Veronica questions with eyebrows raised. "Do you really believe that old cliché: that a criminal returns to the scene? I was just kidding around before."

"I was out at the scene meditating on the crime. Not unlike what you were trying to 'feel' with your little adventure." Charlie makes air quotes with his fingers as he says the word "feel."

"I'm just teasing you," Veronica smiles

"And I'm just warning you," Charlie smiles. "Don't come out here again. I won't be so friendly next time."

"I'm sure my car is warm by now," Veronica declares reaching for the door handle. "Say, do you have a card? I'd like to buy you lunch and thank you. We could talk a little...you know, maybe some background info for my story?"

"I might consider lunch...without the talk of the case," Charlie shrugs.

Veronica nods, "Lunch it is. The rest we can play by ear."

"Ok," Charlie concedes.

He digs in the console of the Tahoe and produces a card. He hands it to Veronica, and she examines it. "Great! Sergeant Charlie LeBeau, I'll give you a call in the morning. Is the casino ok for lunch?"

Veronica opens the door, and waits for an answer. "That's fine," Charlie agrees. "Hey, be careful backing out of the approach. It's a long way down to the bottom, and it'll be slick in your car. I'll wait 'til you get backed out, and I'll follow you out to the highway to make sure you're safe."

"Yeah, I'll be careful. I saw there was an ATV down in the bottom of the ravine. Must have slid off the road. Bye." Veronica slams the door.

"ATV?" Charlie questions out loud.

He unbuckles his seat belt, grabs his flashlight, and exits the vehicle. He follows Veronica to her car. "Did you say ATV at the bottom of the ravine?"

"Yeah," Veronica opens her car door and gets in. "Why?"

Charlie shines his light toward the bottom of the creek, "I'm looking for a four-wheeler that was reported stolen from Peever. Go ahead. I'll catch up to you. I want to check it out. Go slow and be careful."

Veronica shuts her door with a nod, and Charlie taps the roof of her car. He begins to move toward the bottom of the creek, following his flashlight and keeping an eye on Veronica's slow progress down the gravel road. In a moment he is plowing through knee deep, then waist deep snow accumulated in the trees. At the bottom of the stream the frozen water is virtually clear of snow, protected by the surrounding brush and trees. He sees a parallel trail made by Veronica as she used the stream on her trek to the shack. Looking upstream he shines his flashlight into the culvert. "I'll be damned," Charlie says aloud.

Inside the culvert is a four-wheeler. Upon closer inspection he finds the word Grizzly emblazoned on the gas tank.

Gregory L. Heitmann

Chapter 16
Dakota Connection

Dakota Connection and Casino

The Sisseton-Wahpeton Tribe operates three casinos within its reservation boundaries, one casino at its northern boundary near Hankinson, North Dakota, that draws customers from the Fargo area. Another casino, at the southern tip of the Reservation boundary near Watertown, South Dakota, draws customers from the east-central population of South Dakota. The third casino serves as an Interstate gas station, restaurant, and gambling establishment as well as employment opportunity for the bulk of the population of Tribal members concentrated near Sisseton, South Dakota. This Casino, Dakota Connection, sits off Exit 232 on Interstate 29, just a couple miles east of downtown Sisseton.

The fuel pumps stay busy with Interstate travelers, and the food is a good draw for regular local customers. Adjacent to the restaurant is a small addition to the building containing slot machines and a couple of blackjack tables that provide entertainment. A larger annex, built onto the rear of the building for the traditional bingo hall, is accessed via the gambling area.

The day after Charlie's night-time run in with the reporter brings sporadic rays of sunshine through cumulus clouds racing in the howling northwest wind. The sunshine attempts to fool the casual viewer into thinking that the weather is nicer, warmer, but the truth is the temperature hovers in the teens with wind-chills below zero. Winter is early this year. The temperatures reflect the weather of late December or early January rather than November.

Veronica had contacted Charlie the first thing in the morning to set a lunch date at the casino restaurant, and Charlie reluctantly agreed to meet her. Charlie had doubted she would want to keep her promise of thanking him, but by 8:30 A.M., she had phoned and convinced him to take her offer. Charlie figured it would be a chance to listen to another perspective on the case and the community's perception on the investigation.

Charlie arrives at the Dakota Connection early. He stops at the gas pumps to top off his tank before heading into the restaurant. The Tahoe accepts a few gallons, better safe than sorry if one gets stuck out in a drift on some remote call he figures. With the vehicle full of fuel, Charlie parks the SUV and enters the building. He checks his watch again, still fifteen minutes early for his 11:45 A.M. lunch appointment. He looks to the casino and observes a few early arrivals in the lunch crowd. He checks his pocket and finds a five dollar bill for just such an occasion. It's not like he's a prude or a degenerate gambler; Charlie falls into the middle ground majority that can take it or leave it as far as gambling is concerned. It's a mixed blessing in his mind. It provides jobs and revenue for the reservation, but he can't help but notice many of his fellow tribal members sitting in the casino spending cash are some of the people that can least afford to lose. For Charlie, it's a few dollars here or there with the expectation that it is a donation to the tribe. No thought of a jackpot crosses his mind when he plays a nickel slot machine. If he's feeling lucky or when in a hurry, he'll slip his money into a quarter slot machine.

Charlie glances at his watch again and finds an open quarter slot machine that he can play and keep an eye on the door to catch Veronica entering the restaurant. The machine accepts his five dollar bill, and he spins the wheels a quarter at a time with a push of the button. His credits quickly disappear. Finally he hits a combination that brings him from the brink back to nearly even and the bells and lights flash giving him a smile. Five minutes pass, and Veronica enters the building. Charlie sees her. He raises his bet on the machine trying to finish the game quickly. Instead he hits another combination on a two dollar spin that credits him fifty dollars. "Hmmph," Charlie proclaims. "I guess I got lunch this afternoon."

He pushes a button and the machine prints out the credit slip, cashing out of the machine as Veronica catches his eye. Charlie gives a wave and holds up a finger, to indicate that he needs a second. He moves to the foyer of the casino, the lobby area between the convenience store, the restaurant, and the casino area. He holds up his ticket to show Veronica as he approaches the cashier's window to exchange his ticket for cash. "Looks like I can pay for lunch," he calls to Veronica, who moves toward him at the window.

The cashier counts out two twenty dollar bills and a ten in front of Charlie. He takes the money and fans it out for her to see. "Nice," Veronica smiles. "I got a couple stories brewing here. On duty cop in uniform gambles, wins big, and actually buys lunch." She laughs, "I think it's safe to say I have a headline for this week's paper."

"Hey, come on now," Charlie frowns. "I'm on my lunch break. And really? Winning big nowadays is fifty bucks? Man, the economy is bad."

Veronica extends her hand, "I'm glad we are both in better spirits than last night. Let's start over." She pushes her hand out further, "Hi, my name is Veronica Lewis, reporter for the Sisseton Chronicle."

Charlie grins and shakes her hand, "Charlie LeBeau, Sergeant, BIA Police."

"Shall we?" Veronica sweeps her hand toward the café inside.

"After you," Charlie replies.

The hostess seats the couple, handing menus to each guest. "Your waitress will be right with you."

They nod and smile, acknowledging the hostess. Veronica turns to Charlie, folding her arms and placing them on the table. "Thank you again for reconsidering my arrest last night." She smiles pleasantly at Charlie across the table.

Charlie waves away the thanks, "Don't mention it."

"So, you're a big gambler, huh?"

Charlie shrugs, "I wouldn't say that. A dollar or two here or there is all. If it were up to me, I'd probably just limit everything to bingo like the good old days. That was more of a social event."

"I'm probably the same as you in my attitude," Veronica's smile slips to a more serious expression. "It's just not good for the people of the tribe or the state, for that matter. Cons outweigh the pros in my opinion."

Veronica reaches down for her tote bag and pulls out a reporter's spiral bound notepad. She opens to a clean page and turns back to her bag searching for a pen. "Whoa," Charlie puts a hand up in protest.

Veronica locates a pen and straightens in her seat to see Charlie with his outstretched hand on top of her notepad. He taps a finger down on the paper as Veronica watches curiously. "This is all off the record. Remember?" Charlie questions.

"Relax," Veronica insists, shaking her head slowly from side to side as her look of surprise morphs into a smile. "I just wanted to make a note to myself about a potential story on Indian gaming and peoples' attitudes after all these years."

"Fine," Charlie leans back in his chair. "I'm sorry."

"Don't worry about it. This is just a friendly lunch," Veronica does not even look up as she speaks while putting a few notes down on her pad.

The waitress, a young Indian girl, steps up to the table. She barely looks old enough to have a job. "Hi, Charlie," she smiles and turns her attention to Veronica. "Hi, Ms. Lewis. Are you ready to order? We got the good special today, burger with the works?"

"Hi, Janice. No school today?"

"No, ma'am. I set my schedule this semester for Tuesdays and Thursdays off, so I can work."

"That sounds like a good deal for you," Veronica picks up the menu and hands it to Janice without looking at it. "I'll take the special and a water."

Charlie purses his lips. He picks up his menu and doesn't open it. He nods, "A burger sounds good, one special for me. I'll take a Coke, too."

The waitress makes a note on her pad, "I'll get those right out to ya."

She turns on her heel and disappears into the kitchen area. The din of the dining area nearly blocks out the music overhead. An acoustic version of John Cougar Mellencamp's "Small Town" plays from the speakers. Veronica stashes her pen and pad back in the bag by her feet. "Let me get right to it. I'd like to spend some time with you," Veronica states.

Charlie blushes uncomfortably.

"I'm sorry," Veronica laughs nervously. "That came out wrong. I'd like to sit on a stakeout with you if you go again back to the shack. Or maybe just go on a ride along. Just to see what you do."

The waitress brings their drinks, and Charlie sips his Coke. "Oh, you get to the point, don't you?"

Charlie takes the straw from its wrapper, sticks it his Coke, and sips again, "Well, maybe a ride along. Nothing on these murders. That's just off limits. We still got the FBI and DCI leading the investigation. Maybe you can go talk to them."

"In due time," Veronica mirrors Charlie sipping her water. "I know you are going to go out there and sit on the murder site. I'd just like to go. See your process. Get a feel for what happens."

Charlie leans in across the table, prompting Veronica to follow suit, "I've read your stuff," Charlie states flatly. "You were the sports writer for the last couple years. It didn't dawn on me right away last night. Only after you drove away, it hit me." He shrugs, "I apologize for not recognizing you. I remember seeing you at some basketball games. Sports, huh?"

Veronica is defensive, "Yeah, so? This is a small town. High school sports are a big deal. But, I write other stuff too."

"Calm down," Charlie holds up a hand and forces back a smile. "Now you're doing the police beat? Well, you timed that right."

"I know it's so weird," Veronica leans in toward Charlie in more hushed tones. "I just asked my editor for some variety. You know: human interest, community, notable people, etc. And this is what I got. We're just a weekly newspaper; I have time for bigger stories."

"Well, I think you did a great job covering the sports, so I'm sure your other stories will be just as good," Charlie states rapping his knuckle on the table.

Veronica blushes a bit, "You read my articles?"

"Sure, you wrote quite a bit about my nephew."

"Who's your nephew?" Veronica asks.

"Nat Chasing Wolf…"

Charlie's response is cut off by Veronica, "…from Tiospa Zina. Oh, my God. I'm so embarrassed." Her face is red, and she holds her hands up to her cheeks and looks away from Charlie. "I can't believe I didn't make the connection. I'm so sorry about your sister."

"Thank you," Charlie whispers the words.

"Boy," Veronica sighs as she feels her cheeks as the heat from the embarrassment fades. "I'm quite the investigative reporter. I don't even know who I'm talking to." She sips her water. "You're nephew is one heckuva basketball player. He's a joy to cover and write about."

"I couldn't agree more," Charlie lifts his Coke in a toast and sips. Veronica follows Charlie's gesture just as the waitress brings the food.

Gregory L. Heitmann

Chapter 17
Elliot

Charlie and Veronica enjoy their burgers with minimal conversation. As the meal winds down and with only a few scattered curly fries to pick at, the conversation picks up again. "I can't believe you are pulling Nat out of Tiospa Zina," Veronica stares quizzically at Charlie with her arms folded on the table in front of her.

"What about it?" Charlie balks as he wipes at his mouth with a napkin.

"That poor kid. His mother passes away. It seems that school would be the one bit of normalcy he would have left."

Charlie shakes his head in disagreement, "Believe me, we talked about it for a long time. He thought it would be nice for a fresh start, and I wanted him close. I live right on the edge of town. School's close. I'm close. If he needs me, I'm there. Plus, he's got his grandfather, my dad, right in the house to help get through this."

Veronica nods and smiles, "Sounds like you put a lot of thought in this." She picks at a curly fry, drags it through some ketchup, and pops it in her mouth. "I'm sure you'll get through this." She leans back in her chair, "Whew, I'm stuffed."

Charlie sips his Coke and works on his last few fries, "Yup, that hit the spot."

Veronica leans forward in her chair, surprising Charlie a bit, "So," she uses hushed tones, "how about it? Can I come out and sit with you on your stake out?"

Charlie flinches back, chewing his fries. He wipes his mouth to cover his smile. He hadn't planned to spend any more time at the shack, but he was now intrigued by this woman. She was easy on the eyes, she seemed smart, knew a bit of sports. What could it hurt to hang out with her?

Charlie puts on his serious face, "I guess I could ask my boss." He grabs his Coke and drinks again. "It might not hurt for me to be able to talk to someone with a fresh perspective on the whole deal."

Veronica's eyes widen along with her smile. What a deal she thought to herself, a story and a nice looking, decent guy. "You'll ask?"

Charlie nods, picking at his teeth with his tongue, "I'll run it by my captain and give you a call."

"Deal?" Veronica stretches across the table extending her hand to Charlie.

Charlie pauses and cocks his head. He looks to Veronica's eyes, to her hand, and then back to her eyes. Veronica holds her hand steady. He wipes his lips then his hand with his napkin and grasps her hand, noting the long slender fingers and the skin's softness. "Deal," Charlie echoes.

A man walking by their table stops and asks, "Big business transactions going down?"

Veronica looks up, "Oh, hey, Elliot. You having lunch here too?"

"I just called in an order for pick up. Still busy with this week's layout."

Veronica flinches, "I'm sorry, I'll be back right after lunch." She stands and gives Elliot a one-armed hug.

Charlie follows her lead and stands, extending his hand toward Elliot. Veronica waves a hand toward Charlie, "Elliot, this is..."

Elliot holds up his left hand, cutting off Veronica's introduction while extending his right hand to Charlie, "No need; I know Charlie from way back. He was a few years behind me in school before I moved away."

Charlie shakes Elliot's hand. Charlie searches his memory for a recollection of this man. He knew him as the owner of the paper and as a citizen of the community, but Charlie could not recall Elliot's school reference. Elliot pats the handshake with his left hand and holds Charlie's hand a little too long before letting go, but the discomfort is found more in the excessively broad smile of the man, as if he and Charlie were old friends.

Elliot Koffman is forty seven years old. He does not resemble a man approaching fifty, except maybe the patches of gray near his temples in his dark, curly, full head of hair. He is a stocky five feet nine inches tall on a muscular build, a contrast to his delicate and distinct facial features. His face is dominated by a long, thin nose as well as matching narrow, unnaturally red lips.

"Elliot's my boss. He's the editor, publisher, owner...everything for the Sisseton Chronicle." Veronica expounds enthusiastically.

"I like the Sisseton Chronicle. I subscribe," Charlie acknowledges.

"That's great to hear!" Elliot nods. "Circulation is up since I hired Veronica a while back." Elliot edges away, "Listen, I gotta get my lunch before it gets cold. Nice to see you, Charlie." He points a finger at Veronica, "See you back at the office."

Charlie and Veronica sit back down as the waitress delivers the bill. "I got it," Charlie declares.

"I won't argue," Veronica offers. "However, I still owe you a 'thank you' lunch, so we'll have to do this again."

"Yeah, about that," Charlie hesitates, "I wanted to ask you something first."

Veronica feels coolness in his tone, "What is it?"

"You and Elliot an item?" Charlie queries. "I don't want to step on toes here."

Veronica's face scrunches as if she bit into a lemon. She laughs with a loud "Ha!" followed by a noiseless laugh with only her shoulders shaking. It takes almost a minute for her to regain her composure. "Heavens no!" she finally manages to whisper. "Why would you ask that? He's just about old enough to be my dad."

"Geez, so sensitive," Charlie shrinks down in his chair a bit. "I was just wondering. You stand up. Give him a hug. Seems a bit much for just a boss."

Veronica is defensive, but amused, "It's called being polite and introducing somebody."

"I'm sorry I said anything," Charlie laughs the words. "I was just wondering. You don't wear a ring, but one never knows. Especially me. I'm not up on all the gossip and comings and goings of Sisseton."

Veronica points at Charlie's hand. "I don't see a ring on your finger."

Charlie shrugs the comment aside. He picks up the ticket and looks it over; satisfied with the numbers, he leans back casually in his chair. "So, what's your story? You're not from around here."

Veronica purses her lips and shakes her head, glancing to the floor just to the left of Charlie. "I'm from Fargo originally." She swings her eyes back to Charlie. "My parents are dead. My dad fifteen years ago, my mom..." She pauses. "I took care of my mom while she was sick. I delayed going to college to take care of her."

Charlie hesitates, "I'm sorry. Cancer?"

Veronica nods. The emotion still there with the talk of her mother, she takes a drink of water to catch her breath. "I'm sorry. Time heals, but

I'm not sure if I'll ever," she makes finger quotes, "'get over it' as some would say."

Charlie reaches across the table and pats her hand as comfortingly as he can. Veronica manages a weak smile. Charlie nods, "I know what it's like to lose people...my mom."

Veronica locks her eyes with Charlie, "Now your sister."

The couple sits wordlessly a minute. Charlie withdraws his hand. Veronica sighs, "Yeah, my mom left me some money. I don't really have to do much if I don't want to. I promised my mom I would get a college degree." The thought makes her smile. "I enjoyed college. I did some volunteer social work down here one summer for college credit." She shrugs and smiles more brightly, "I liked it here and came back."

"So, what are you? Journalist or social worker?" Charlie's brow furrows.

Veronica laughs, "I was a double major. Journalism and sociology." She shrugs her shoulders. "I imagined writing stories and articles reporting on the downtrodden." She laughs more at her idealistic thoughts of her youth. "Look at me now. Reporter for the seventy fifth largest newspaper in the Dakotas."

"If you like what you're doing, so what?" Charlie offers.

"That is so true," Veronica turns her eyes up for a moment. "It's just hard sometimes. I took a little extra time getting through college, North Dakota State University, go Bison!" she adds with enthusiasm.

Charlie looks around, "I wouldn't say that too loudly."

Veronica laughs, "You're right." She ducks down and looks around to see if she's offended anyone. "But, like I said, it's hard sometimes. A person wants to do a lot, but it's overwhelming."

"So this is your first real job?" Charlie questions.

"Yeah, you could say that," Veronica leans back in her chair, folding her arms. "I've been here just a couple years now. I'm getting my feet wet with the grind. You learn every aspect of the business working for a small town paper. It's enlightening." She points a finger at Charlie, "What about you?"

"I'm the police. I ask the questions," Charlie retorts sternly with a wry smile.

Veronica laughs, joining Charlie's chuckle. He looks around the casino, "Not much to say," Charlie shrugs. "Born and raised here on the reservation. Spent a couple years as an MP, military police, in the Army. Came back home..." Charlie surveys the casino again. "I came back home...try to do some good by being a cop."

Veronica nods, "Very noble."

Charlie looks down at his hands folded on the table top, "Yeah, we're a couple of do-gooder, idealists."

Veronica stares admiringly across the table. She leans forward and places a hand over Charlie's, "There's nothing wrong with that."

Gregory L. Heitmann

Chapter 18
Report

Charlie smiles on his drive back to the office after his lunch with Veronica. He enjoyed his meal and the company, but now it's back to work. Charlie is no sooner back at the BIA Police Office before Captain Kipp is hovering at his desk. "You got a minute?" Skip asks. "Come on back to my office."

Charlie's good day is short lived. Thirty feet from his desk, winding through the office hallways, they go to Captain Kipp's office. The office is in a harsh government building of cinder block construction. Built on the edge of town, the BIA Police Facility, as it is officially referred to by the sign on the corner, was and still is the subject of controversy. The building is a remnant of the 1970's American Indian Movement, AIM, uprising centered in western South Dakota on the Pine Ridge Indian Reservation. Even into the late 1980's the federal government was still stinging from the violent and deadly Indian protests on the reservation. Fortress-like structures for post offices and police stations evolved in their design and construction during this time period. The theory was that these strongholds would offer protection and serve as headquarters during any future revolts in Indian Country. Local tribes took this as an affront to their sovereignty and a forfeiture of peaceful coexistence. The practice eventually stopped, but not before many bunker-like buildings were constructed on the reservations throughout Indian Country in the Midwest.

Kipp's office reflects the impersonal government influence similar to Eastern bloc architecture of the Cold War era. It isn't that the people working in the building haven't tried to brighten the atmosphere, but the windowless fortress is dark and dank. Captain Kipp probably has the most eye-catching office decor of anyone in the station, highlighted by an *Animal House* movie poster, but even more definitive of his sense of humor is the infamous John Belushi poster next to it. The black and white poster of Belushi as "Bluto" Blutarsky in his black sweatshirt bearing the simple white lettering of "COLLEGE" never fails to draw a smile or laugh from most of observers. This poster is customized with a BIA police badge and hat formed from construction paper fitted to Bluto's clothing and glued seamlessly onto the poster.

"Have a seat," Skip orders to his friend.

Each man finds his chair and steals a glance at the Belushi poster gracing the side wall. Charlie gives a nod to the poster, "The superintendent ever say anything about your office décor?"

Skip laughs, "Are you kidding me? The super has never been to my office. If he wants to talk, he's on the phone, and I'm busting my ass to his office as quickly as possible."

The men share a laugh and an awkward silence ensues. The superintendent of an Indian reservation is the official in charge of and responsible for everything related to the federal government when it comes to the reservation. The position of superintendent has a long and somewhat tarnished history in Indian Country, but nonetheless, it is the authority on a reservation. All BIA employees, including the BIA Police, answer to the superintendent. The superintendent answers to muckity-mucks up the chain of command at regional offices and the regions in turn answer to BIA officials in Washington, D.C.

Charlie folds his arms and shrugs, "What did you want? You called me to your office."

"Oh, yeah," Skip holds a finger up as if struck by inspiration. "Now I remember." He smiles mischievously, "How was your lunch today?"

"What do you mean?" Charlie plays innocent.

"I'm just having a friendly conversation. Why can't a captain ask his sergeant a question?" Skip shrugs pretending to be naïve. "You know what I mean," Skip accuses his friend jokingly. "I stopped for gas at the Holiday Station. The place was abuzz with talk of you and some reporter woman."

"Sheesh," Charlie rolls his eyes. "What's with this place? The favorite pastime of the reservation has to be gossip."

Skip scoffs, "Sure, act all hurt and surprised that news travels so fast. There's nothin' to do on the rez except talk. Especially during the winter."

"You're right," Charlie concedes.

"Hey, she's a cutie," Skip conveys the comment as his voice goes higher.

Charlie shifts uncomfortably in his chair, "Just FYI, I'm going to take her on a ride-a-long."

"Nice," Skip nods in approval. "I take my wife for a ride-a-long once in a while. You know, to provide some spark to the fire."

"Please," Charlie covers his ears. "I don't want these kinds of details."

"Hey, whatever. You kids have fun," Skip waves his blessing over Charlie with a sign of the cross. "Seriously though, I really wanted to congratulate you on some excellent police work this morning. Case closed on the missing ATV, eh?"

"Are you mocking me?" Charlie's eyes narrow at the question.

"Hell no," Skip's face reflects the hurtful accusation. "Will Cullen and the Cullen Ranch are good friends of the superintendent. Need I say more?"

"Huh?" Charlie questions.

"I got a call from the Superintendent thanking me for returning the four-wheeler to the Cullen Ranch." Skip throws his hands in the air. "Will Cullen was on his cell phone immediately after you helped him load it out of the ditch, bragging you up to the super. Good job, Charlie. We'll take any victories we can get in this job."

"Not so fast, boss," Charlie holds up a hand in a halting motion. "I'm not sure we should've released the ATV. I have a theory, and it relates to the Deer Slayer."

Skip slumps in his seat, "What is it?" he asks in a monotone.

Charlie sighs, "It's just a theory, but I think our suspect stole that ATV and planted it at the shack."

Skip listens as Charlie leans forward in his chair. "The killer had his car stashed someplace a couple miles away on a road that would stay clear of snow, the county road. He killed those kids, then left the site via the ATV. Then he ditched it at the bottom of the creek."

Skip emits a low whistle, "Makes sense; the guy seems to plan everything to a 'T.'"

"Do you think we should ask for the four-wheeler back as evidence?" Charlie questions.

"Tshh," Skip clicks his tongue and looks over Charlie. "What the heck we gonna do with the ATV? Any and all evidence would be compromised now with a broken chain of custody." He straightens in his chair. "Tell you what, just write up your conclusions in the report. That's good enough for the record."

Charlie shakes his head, "We're dealing with a mad genius here. Snow covering the tracks. There's never a trace of evidence except dead bodies."

Skip smiles mischievously again, "Not this time. He left the four-wheeler. That's evidence, and he doesn't know we know. He had to stick his vehicle out there sometime as well as plant the ATV at the shack. Somebody may have seen something."

"Yeah," Charlie agrees. "We actually have some questions to ask people in the area."

"Huh," Skip grunts. "For the first time in this case, we may have a lead."

Chapter 19
Stakeout

Charlie had picked Veronica up at a quarter to seven that evening. He had called her and warned her to dress warmly, but his instructions fell on deaf ears. The clouds with their ever present snow flurries had cleared, but a cold front pushing down from the Arctic that forced the precipitation eastward had its unpleasant, below zero temperatures. The stars were bright in the frozen air and, along with a partial moon, an eerie blue luminescence glows off the reflecting snow. The policeman and the reporter were in place near the shack by seven p.m. Charlie had killed the lights to the vehicle and steered via his night vision scope the last three quarters of a mile on the gravel road. The last half mile, down the two rut trail Charlie drove by the moonlight, the ruts doing most of the steering. The Tahoe plowed through the drifted tracks, once again crunching across the frozen snow. Temperatures had been no where near a thaw, and the snow crumbled and swirled in stillness of the cold when disturbed by the tires.

With the engine off and the window down an inch or two the vehicle cools quickly. The creaking and ticking of the engine's temperature is an undirected orchestra of sound as the pair sits in relative silence for the first hour. Charlie periodically scans the surroundings with his night vision scope, but it is still and quiet as temperatures continue to plummet.

Veronica shivers, exaggerating for Charlie's benefit. "Can't you at least roll up your window?" she queries in a whisper.

Charlie will not look at her. Instead he peers through his night vision scope. He finally whispers still not looking at his companion. "I told you to dress warm. Instead you dressed like you were going to a casual dinner."

"I know, and I said 'I'm sorry'. What do you want me to do, catch pneumonia?"

"I can't roll up the window," he points to the windshield. "The windows will fog over in a few moments if we don't have this colder air to equalize things with our breath." He sighs and looks at Veronica with a hint of a smile, "I also told you I need to be able to hear if somebody is approaching."

Veronica imperceptibly shakes her head side to side. "I can see you rolling your eyes at me even in the dark," Charlie speaks the words quietly but crisply. "We'll head out shortly. It's probably too cold for any reasonable person to be out tonight."

"Amen to that," Veronica mumbles. "Two unreasonable people sitting out here in a freezing car right now."

They sit in silence for a few minutes more before Veronica whispers again, "What is the deal? Why are you sitting on the shack? I just don't get it."

"We're off the record, right?" Charlie responds, eyebrows raised.

"Absolutely. I'm taking notes, but I swear," She raises her right hand up, pencil between her thumb and fingers in a mitten clad hand. "I swear it. These notes will sit until this crime is solved."

Charlie peers through his scope again, "I like your confidence...the crime is solved." He chuckles quietly.

Veronica manages a smile, "I was going to add to that statement, solved or you tell me it is ok to publish the story."

Charlie drops the scope from his eye and looks squarely at Veronica. "We're off the record..."

Charlie can barely get the words out before Veronica is interrupting him, "Yes, yes, off the record!" she whispers hoarsely in frustration. "All notes are confidential until you say!"

Charlie nods, "Fine." He turns his body to face his passenger more directly. "The previous Deer Slayer crime scenes..."

Veronica is interrupting again, "Whoa, whoa, whoa. Deer Slayer?"

"Yeah," Charlie shrugs. "That's what we call the guy. Captain Kipp came up with the name."

Veronica stares blankly at Charlie. She shakes her head and hunches her shoulders a bit, asking with body language, "What?"

The pair stares at each other in the dark. The whites of their eyes reflecting the bluish hue of the night sky's stars and moon refracted light off the snow, giving their faces an unearthly appearance.

"Like the animal, deer. A four legged creature we hunt?" Charlie tries to clarify. "The murderer hangs, guts, and sometimes skins the victims like you would with a deer. Plus, all the murders have occurred during the deer season."

Charlie can see the puzzled look on Veronica's face. "Oh, boy," Charlie barely breathes the words. "I can tell by the look on your face you are not aware of the murders five years ago."

"Hmmm," Veronica whispers, "what now? Other murders?"

Charlie snickers, "How do you not know this? You're supposed to be a reporter."

Charlie enjoys having the upper hand and sits quietly waiting for Veronica to respond. She doesn't vocally respond. Her mouth moves, but no words emerge. Finally, with much sarcasm she manages to speak, "Wow. So mean and hurtful."

Veronica stares expressionlessly at her stakeout partner, but she can't keep her stoic expression. A smile betrays her as she makes notes in her notepad.

"I'll do some research," Veronica whispers as she jots notes in her notepad.

"Good," Charlie grunts as he looks through his night vision scope again. After scanning the area, he lowers the scope and looks at Veronica still writing away. "There was a lot of stuff never released on the previous murders that was repeated here at this scene, with only the slightest variation. We're pretty sure we got a serial killer here."

Veronica looks up for a moment, "I can't believe this." Her head goes back down, focusing on her notepad as she writes.

Charlie waits almost five minutes while he watches his passenger's pencil dart across the notepad paper, finally flipping the page and continuing. Veronica stops writing and rolls her wrist and shakes her hand to try to get some blood moving. "I have some theories," Charlie quietly says as he raises the night vision scope and looks around.

Veronica turns to Charlie, inspecting his profile as he lowers the scope and scans the area with his naked eyes. "You want to share?" Veronica whispers.

Charlie does not look at her, "You'll be the first to know when I do share."

"Can't you give me something," she pleads.

"You're here aren't you? Shouldn't that be enough?"

Veronica tilts her head to the right, "You've been more than generous..."

"Uh-oh," Charlie whispers.

"What?" Veronica stiffens looking intently at the surroundings. "Is something out there?"

Charlie laughs, "No. I said, 'uh-oh' because I thought I could hear a 'but' coming from you. 'You've been more than generous, but…'"

Veronica relaxes and giggles, "You are correct, sir."

"Because you are so honest I will offer you one more item," Charlie holds up a single gloved finger. "I'm pretty sure the killer comes back to visit the crime scene on multiple occasions. It was a small note in the file of the last murder."

"Really? How did you…?"

Charlie does not let her finish her question. "It was my note. I noticed tracks out of place on subsequent visits on the previous murder. It's been documented before in other cases. Killers get some sort of thrill coming to see their handiwork."

Veronica scribbles away at her pad as fast as she can. "Wow. I must say. I am…shocked. What else? Care to share anything else. Oh, my God. I'm just getting blown away here."

Charlie turns to her and pats her on the knee, "That's probably enough for tonight. Come on. Let's head back. I'm starting to get cold."

"You, come on. I'm completely intrigued now." Veronica pauses for a moment, but then keeps writing notes. "Give me…"

She's interrupted by Charlie's hand on her shoulder and a hoarse whisper, "Shhhhhh! Listen!"

The faint high pitched hum of a small engine approaches. "What is it?" Veronica breathes the words.

"Snowmobile," Charlie pauses. "I think."

Charlie scans the trees in the coulee to his left, in the direction of the sound with his night scope. Charlie lowers his scope, presses the kill switch on the vehicle's interior lights, and pulls the handle to open the door. "You stay here."

Chapter 20
Reappear

Undetected, Charlie exits the vehicle, easing the Tahoe door closed, he slips through the snow to the shack. He presses himself flat against the building, his mind filled with déjà vu from the night previous and his encounter with Veronica. His heart pounds, and he breathes the freezing air into his lungs. Any hint of the cold is gone as adrenaline courses through his body. He listens intently. The still night carries the whine of the snowmobile's engine with clarity. The engine is cut off. The only sound in Charlie's ears is the high pitched whistle of his full attention amped up by his adrenal glands as he strains every sensory nerve in his body to hone in on the approaching person. The crunching of snow under feet finally pierces his hearing threshold.

Charlie never saw the snowmobile as it approached without a light and shielded by the depth of the tree filled coulee. His eyes twitch as he focuses on the crunching snow before him. The slope of the coulee blocks his view as the sound of the footsteps in the darkness becomes shorter and effort-filled as the intruder attacks the gradient of the steep coulee. Charlie re-grips his pistol in his right hand. He holds the weapon over his head ready to lower the sight on his target when it comes into view. His left hand holds a Maglite as he was taught in the academy, head high, elbow forward, in a ready position. He has discarded his gloves and his bare hands holding the metal pistol and flashlight can feel the bite of the cold for the first time. His left fore finger is on the power button for the flashlight, his right fore finger on the trigger of his weapon.

The slow choppy steps of the approaching snowmobile driver are louder and louder. A branch breaks echoing through the coulee. The intruder is not cautious in his approach. From Charlie's position at the corner of the shack, he can turn his head and shield his body while scanning the tree lined slope of the coulee. He sees the intruder. It is just a silhouette. The man approaching is clad in a bulbous helmet and that is all Charlie can make out as the figure slowly rises above the horizon of the sloping coulee. He's twenty-five yards away and closing. Charlie closes his eyes and takes a deep breath. His hopes that his eyes would adjust to the darkness are thwarted by the cold air. His eyes water from the cold and the strain to see.

The crunching of the snow is loud. Charlie peers around the corner, and he sees the man in a snowsuit and helmet, twenty yards, fifteen yards, ten yards and the crunching snow beneath the intruder's feet sounds like explosions in Charlie's ears. At less than ten yards Charlie steps around the corner shouting, "Freeze! Get down on the ground!"

Charlie lunges forward snapping his flashlight on and leveling his weapon at the intruder in a black snowsuit and black helmet. The man freezes but only for a moment. Without raising his arm he flicks on his own light. It is a million candlepower spotlight. The light blinds Charlie instantly, staggering him. Charlie stumbles blindly in the dark, losing his footing and falling to his knees into the snow. The intruder is gone, having turned and bolted to the bottom of the coulee and up the other side. He crashes through branches, making his way back to his snowmobile.

*　　*　　*

Veronica watched the scene unfold in front of her in the dark, metaphorically and literally. Time crept by slowly. She thought she could make out the form of the policeman against the side of the building, but her eyes could not convince her brain that what she was seeing was real. The building screened the path of the intruder, and when the snowmobile engine was killed, her heart skipped a beat. She was too far away to hear the approaching steps of the snowmobile rider crunching through the wind-crusted snow; an eternity passed before Charlie stepped from the side of the building to confront the man. She never saw the visitor, only the momentary silhouette of Charlie before the spotlight illuminated the night, exposing and blinding the policeman. The light immediately dimmed and bounced away through the trees as the intruder made his retreat back to his snowmobile.

*　　*　　*

Veronica reaches across the vehicle from the passenger seat to turn on the ignition and the vehicle lights, but she bounces back, restrained by her still buckled seat belt. She undoes the restraint, turns the Tahoe's key to start the vehicle, and searches for the light switch. Finally, she finds the button that ignites the vehicle's lights, and the high beam lights slice through the night, shining stark light on the unearthly looking trees in the coulee. Veronica straightens back to her seat slowly as she peers over the dash. Charlie cannot be seen. Moving quickly she brushes the volume knob on the FM radio, accidentally cranking up the Fargo pop music station they had listened to on the drive out. "All Over You" by Spill Canvas blares from the speakers and scares her. She finds the knob and turns the volume off. She grabs for the door handle but pauses trying to think.

In the snow, on his knees Charlie's head throbs. The blinding light so overly stimulated his optic nerves that his head spins; he is momentarily nauseous as he staggers in the midst of exploding lights in his head as he gathers his wits and stumbles down the slope of the drainage, crashing into trees attempting to follow the snowmobile driver. He tries to gather his bearings and leans against a tree gasping for breath. The adrenaline rush still pounds through his body. It is dark ahead of him. Behind him he can hear the Tahoe's engine roar to life and lights shine over his head illuminating the tops of the trees. He is at the bottom of the coulee, looking up, when he hears the snowmobile engine growl to life immediately followed by the whine of the full throttle crying as the machine begins to move away from him the same way it had arrived. Charlie reverses his course and plows back through the hardened snow path he just broke through as he came down the slope. His feet slip in the powdery snow as he tries to use choppy steps to climb the incline. His feet spin uselessly underneath him. He holsters his weapon and grasps saplings and to tow himself hand over hand up the incline as fast he can.

At the summit of the slope, finally on ground level with the cabin before him, he sees Veronica moving and holds the light on her. "Get in the truck!" he yells.

They run to the Tahoe and get in. Charlie slams the vehicle into gear, turns the vehicle around, and tears down the two-rut trail. Their arrival had broken the hardened snow drifts, but now between the frozen ruts of mud and the powdery snow, the vehicle is thrown crazily from side to side. "What are you doing?" Veronica yells, frightened.

"Get your seatbelt on!" Charlie orders.

"We can't catch him!" Veronica calls out as she bounces in her seat and off the door, struggling to fasten her seat belt.

Finally, her belt clicks into place. Charlie wrestles with the steering wheel and flies around in his seat as he has not fastened his own seat belt. "We're going to try to get to higher ground. I'm hoping to be able to catch his headlight. He can't be foolish enough to be driving blind. And, I have a guess where he might go."

The chase is brief. "Whoa!" Charlie exclaims as the Tahoe is tossed into the shallow ditch of the trail, victim of the unruly, crusted, compacted snow.

The Tahoe is mired in a three foot drift. Stuck in the wind-hardened snow, Charlie bangs both hands down on the steering wheel in anger. He grasps the wheel and shakes it. Veronica is breathing hard, "I can't believe it. Face to face with the killer." She turns to Charlie who has slumped down in the seat, head up, staring at the roof of the Tahoe. "That was him wasn't it? That was our murderer."

Charlie nods painfully, his gesture matched with a twisted grin. The rush is over, and he can feel his muscles stiffen and cramp. "Sit tight. I got a shovel. It'll be some work, but I'll get out of here."

"Can't you just call somebody to tow us?" Veronica asks.

"I don't want to bother anyone. Plus, I don't want to explain what I was doing and why you are with me," Charlie replies.

He tries to force open the door, but the crusted snow impedes his effort. "Damn it," Charlie curses as he laughs. "Door is jammed by the snow," he laughingly explains to his passenger.

Veronica joins with a snicker at their misfortune. "Just not our night." Veronica's eyes get wide as she reaches and grabs at Charlie's arm. "The tracks! The snowmobile tracks! We'll be able to follow them easily!" she bubbles with excitement.

"You didn't notice?' Charlie questions quietly.

"Notice what?" Veronica shoots back as her brow furrows.

Charlie gives a nod to the sky through the windshield in a northerly direction as the Tahoe sits mostly facing east. Veronica leans forward and looks north through the top of the windshield. She sees half the sky covered in stars, but to the north and to the west a bank of clouds darkens the sky. She falls back into her seat.

Charlie groans pushing on his door finally forcing it open. "There we go," he grunts. A gust of wind catches the door and blows through the cab of the truck. "Yup, here comes the wind..."

Veronica finishes Charlie's statement with a frown, "...There'll be no tracks in an hour or two."

Chapter 21
Holding Court

Sisseton High School Auditorium

No one is surprised at how the basketball practice begins. It is Nat's first practice with his Redmen teammates. Nat makes the long walk from the locker room to the court with his new teammates clad in his new practice uniform, black shorts and reversible jersey, black on one side and red on the other. He sports a new haircut, shaved on the sides with just barely enough hair on top to manipulate with a comb. He has a smile on his face for the first time in quite a while as he returns to the court.

Nat likes the wood floor of the Redmen basketball court. He has had success on the Redmen hardwood. In the district tournaments the last two years when playing for Tiospa Zina, he had scored a minimum of thirty points in each game. It is a new day for him now, a new, blank page in his story. A fellow player tosses him a ball from the rack, "Here you go, Nat."

Nat catches the ball, takes one dribble, and launches from the three point line. Swish. Another player tosses him a ball as he moves and shoots. Swish again. It is a thing of beauty, to watch Nat shoot the ball. He has a text book release and shooting form. It's not a high flying jump shot. He saves his legs with only a slight elevation each time he launches the ball. His shooting style was adopted from his Uncle Charlie who had preached, "The three 'C's of shooting: concentration, consistency, and confidence."

Nat knocks down shot after shot as he circles the three point line. Soon everyone on the team is gathered around. A few "oohs" and "ahs" emanate from the audience.

The basketball coach wanders onto the floor, observes three straight baskets, and smiles as he brings his whistle to his lips. The whistle tweets, "All right men, on the line. Five minute warm up run."

The whistle sounds a long blast, and the players begin running up and down the full court.

Chapter 22
Arctic Cat

The workday and school day morning begin with breakfast before sunrise in Charlie's trailer. The winter sun is lazy in its appearance, and the overhead fluorescent lights illuminate the two diners' meals. Charlie and Nat eat their breakfast, and the conversation is minimal. Nat sits at the kitchen table slowly shoveling cereal blindly into his mouth as he reads the Frosted Flakes cereal box and its feature presentation painting of Tony the Tiger as an athletic role model for adolescent baseball players. Charlie stands over the sink and eats a banana and sips his orange juice as he stares out the window into the darkness. He fights the internal reflection on the window as his mind goes through the laundry list of the day's tasks.

The kitchen is a no-frills cooking and dining area typical of a manufactured home, all the conveniences a bachelor would want and more, with white appliances, including a stove with microwave above and an oven below. The refrigerator and dishwasher encircle the open area. The linoleum floor is shared with the eating area, furnished with a simple round wooden table and four wooden chairs. The table is clear except for Nat's morning fare, cereal and a gallon of milk. It's one of Charlie's few rules that the kitchen table be clear of clutter. No mail, no newspapers, no tools. This table is for eating only. Charlie polices the table with a passion stating, "This is the last bastion of hope to keep control of the trailer clutter. We lose the table; we lose the war."

Charlie's second rule of the kitchen is: no dishes in the sink. All dishes are to be immediately rinsed and placed in the dishwasher. His father and nephew know the rule and follow it; otherwise, they receive an earful from Charlie. Nat had already faced consequences of being handcuffed to a kitchen chair for an hour after violating the sink rule. Everyone knows the origins of Charlie's rules. The military had left a deep discipline with him that remained long after he was discharged. "A man has to have a code, a foundation of principles," Charlie often repeats to his family, much to their chagrin.

Charlie is already suited up for work. It is cold, and he still wears his heavy police jacket and black stocking cap, having already been outside to start his BIA police Tahoe. He turns to face Nat, who sits with his back to Charlie hunched over his bowl of cereal. "How was practice yesterday?" Charlie queries as he finishes the last bite of his banana.

Nat doesn't look up. He shrugs, "Good."

It's quiet in the house. The only sounds are Nat's crunching of his cereal and the background noise of the Tahoe's engine warming outside.

"How about school?" Charlie digs deeper. "Did you find all your classrooms ok? You didn't get lost?"

Nat stares at his cereal box and continues to read, half listening to his uncle. "Nope, I found all my classes."

Charlie steps over and tosses the banana peel into the trash as he finishes off his juice. Nat points to the trash, spoon in hand, still not looking up from his reading material. "You should think about a compost heap. You know, for banana peels and junk."

Charlie looks down at the trash bag and makes a face as he looks toward his nephew, "Yeah, I'll get right on that. How about your hair? Anybody say anything?"

"Nope."

Charlie rinses his glass, opens the dishwasher, and places the glass inside. He straightens his cap, wipes his mouth with a dishtowel, and brushes off his jacket. He moves toward the door. "Ok then," Charlie reaches for the door. "Good talk. I'll see you tonight for supper."

Charlie opens the door, and the roar of the truck fills the room. He pulls on his black leather gloves and looks toward Nat in the kitchen. "You're coming deer huntin' this weekend. Get your stuff ready."

Nat holds up a thumb without looking toward his uncle. Charlie chuckles to himself at the teenager's morning interactions. "Make sure your grandpa is up before you head to school. Tell him he's going hunting too. We need to start getting some meat in the freezer."

There is no reaction from Nat. Maybe the slightest acknowledgement of a nod. "Bye," Charlie calls out as he exits, pulling the door shut.

Nat waves goodbye at the closing door without looking up from his reading material.

Charlie crunches through another dusting of snow, making his way to his truck and mumbling to himself, "Got to work on that kid's interpersonal skills. I know I'm not a morning person but sheesh."

*　　*　　*

Before he can get in the truck, Charlie's phone buzzes inside his shirt pocket. He pulls off his glove, unzips his coat, and digs for his phone as he climbs into the warm truck. The phone indicates "Skip" on its screen. Charlie turns the fan down on the heater as he answers the phone without a "hello".

"Yeah," Charlie grunts into the phone.

He looks up and to the east. In a gap through the trees, he can see the town of Sisseton in the distance. On the rose colored horizon, further east the sun begins to emerge. The clouds have passed through again leaving less than an inch of fluffy snow. Charlie is mesmerized by the sun rising over the flat land spread out below him extending as far as he can see. The warm colors: pinks, oranges, and yellows, crowd out the cool blues, purples, and grays of the morning right before his eyes, as if by magic.

Charlie listens to his boss ramble for a full minute. "I'm on my way in now. You got my message on the stake out from last night?" he ends with a question.

Charlie listens and buckles his seatbelt. His eyes are still riveted to the blossoming eastern sky before him. He puts his truck in gear. "I'll be there in ten minutes. We can talk about it."

Charlie closes his police-issued flip phone and shoves it back in his shirt pocket. Maneuvering out of his yard, he heads to the southeast down his driveway, the morning sun imprinting the shadows of the trees all around him. Reaching the county road, he turns right and heads south. Charlie winds his way on the snow covered gravel roads at a leisurely pace. The snow drifts reach across the roads from the previous night's squall. The slightest breeze now causes a headache for maintenance crews. Plowing snow has become a daily event this early winter.

After a few minutes' drive and a few turns later, Charlie passes the approach for the two-rut trail to the murder scene. The shack is just over the rise, nestled into the trees less than a mile away. Charlie stops and looks across the snow drifts. There is barely a divot in the snow where he spent nearly an hour and a half digging his Tahoe out of the ditch. The snow had drifted back in over his tracks, nearly erasing any activity from the night before.

Charlie looks at the clock on the dashboard. Ten minutes have already passed. He's already late getting to the office. He decides to delay going to the office to inspect the roads he didn't get a chance to see the day before after getting stuck. Fifteen minutes later and four miles from the shack, Charlie is on the edge of the Coteau, heading west and up the slope on the county road that serves three ranches in the area. There has been no traffic yet this morning, and he busts the drifts with his Tahoe as he winds his way on the road parallel to a creek alongside the deep fill-constructed section of the road.

Charlie's phone buzzes, and he digs blindly in his pocket as his eye catches an object on the side of the road just up ahead. "Hello," Charlie answers the phone. "I know I'm late."

Charlie slows as he keeps driving forward and listens to Captain Kipp on the other end. "Lake Traverse? Stolen snowmobile?" Charlie parrots and questions what he hears on the other end of the line.

Charlie pulls even with the object parked diagonally, pulled onto the approach on the north side of the road. It is a snowmobile. He puts his Tahoe in park as he shakes his head. He looks around and sees no one. A drift has formed on the downwind side of the snowmobile. It is about a foot high near the machine, tapering down to the level snow line and intersecting the edge of the road after about fifteen feet.

Charlie smiles, "Let me guess. The missing sled is a black and orange, Firefox Arctic Cat."

Charlie listens as he rolls down the passenger side window to get a better look. "How did I know? I'm looking at it right here."

There's a shout on the other end of the line, and Charlie winces and moves the phone away from his ear. "I'm not kidding you," Charlie laughs. "Come on out, Skip. We'll collect some evidence. Bring a trailer. I'll wait."

Charlie listens still laughing to himself, "Where am I?" Charlie cranes his neck to look behind him. "I'm about a mile past the Evans Ranch just starting up the Coteau on the county road."

Charlie listens, "All right. See you in a bit."

Charlie snaps his phone shut still shaking his head in disbelief.

Chapter 23
Twine

The late Saturday morning finds Charlie and Nat atop a bale stack. They are dressed in their warm hunting clothes, and both sport blaze orange vests. It is a slow day on the deer stand, and the morning hunt is winding down. Charlie scans his surroundings with his binoculars. He shakes his head and speaks softly, "Where the heck are all the deer?"

Nat is sitting on his side of the bale stack, not even bothering to look around. He holds his knees to his chest, staring into the trees in the distance on the other side of the cornfield. "The weather has warmed up and still the deer hardly move," Charlie declares in disgust.

The pair has been on the bale stack for two hours; since a half hour before sun up, they have kept an eye out for their quarry, but no deer moved within a mile of their stand. The temperatures have rebounded into the mid thirties with a south wind that makes it feel relatively balmy compared to the last few days. The brown Carhartt coat and coveralls are a size too small for Nat as he sits, causing the sleeves of his shirt to be exposed while his brown coveralls provide the image of short pants referred to as "floods."

The uncle looks down at his nephew, who is lost in thought, not responding to his comments. Charlie laughs at the boy's ill-fitting clothes. "Dang, Nat," Charlie laughs. "We got to get you some new huntin' clothes. You've grown out of those by a mile."

Nat snaps out his trance-like state and holds out his arms, smiling at his exposed wrists and boots. Charlie gives a nod and smiles, returning his binoculars to his eyes to scan the tree line again. Nat pushes himself up with a groan, straining against his tight clothes. He props himself against a bale, hands behind his back. He stares back into the trees and minutes go by. "Uncle Charlie, can I ask you a question?" Nat finally speaks in a soft, flat voice.

Charlie lowers his binoculars, curious at the boy's tone. "Sure," Charlie responds.

Nat continues to stare unblinkingly into the distance as he summons his question. "What was my dad like?"

Charlie lowers the binoculars to his chest and releases them completely from his grip, as they dangle from the strap around his neck. He contemplates an answer and fumbles to pluck a stem of grass bound in the bale's compacted form. His heavy gloves impede his ability to complete this delicate operation of grasping a dried stem to pick his teeth without damaging the grass in the maneuver. A minute passes, and Charlie successfully accomplishes the task, acquiring his dental tool. He finds the words to answer his nephew. "He was a living contradiction. He was torn. He didn't want to be stuck in traditional Indian ways, yet he wanted to stay on the reservation and help people." Charlie grimaced continuing, "He hated what the Indian way of life had become."

"What do you mean?" Nat questions, eyes still fixed in the distance.

"You've seen it. Welfare. Drunkenness." Charlie shakes his head. "I'd never met a man like him. He ached for a better way of life for his people. His body would literally clench in pain when he talked about the difficulties he witnessed. He'd only slightly relax when he talked about what he envisioned for improving people's lives."

"But, what do you mean when you say 'traditional?'" Nat questions.

"Well," Charlie pauses, "He didn't go by his full last name, Chasing Wolf. He shortened it to just Wolf."

"Really?" Nat looks to his Uncle.

"Yeah. Your mom insisted you have his full last name on the birth certificate when you were to be born. They argued about it. They brought their case to me and asked me to be the judge and rule on it."

Nat laughs, "That is funny."

"I only knew your dad for a short time. I actually introduced him to your mom after we were roommates at the BIA police academy." Charlie pulls up his binoculars and scans the area. He talks again before he even lowers his optics, "It was love at first sight for your mom and dad. They were married in less than six months, then before you know it, boom. You were on the way."

Charlie raises his binoculars and looks at a suspicious clump in the distance, but it's just a bush. "I'm sure your mom told you all this before. Didn't she?"

"Some," Nat shrugs.

Charlie drops his binoculars, and they hang from the strap around his neck. "Your dad was a smart guy. Probably should have been with the FBI, solving the tough crimes. But, like I said, he wanted to come back and help the people. The FBI would have assigned him to...who knows where. Anywhere, but here."

Nat looks to the distance again, "Maybe he'd be alive if he'd been with the FBI. It's weird. My dad was dead before I was even born."

Charlie frowns, "I'm sorry, Nat. Being a police officer is dangerous. We all know the risks when we sign up, but you never think it will be you or somebody you know."

"Like I said," Nat shrugs, "it's so weird. I don't think about it that way...in a bad way. That's just the way it was for me. I'm lucky in many ways. I had you and Grandpa always around. It's like I have two dads."

Charlie feels a bit embarrassed and laughs nervously at his nephew's comment. "I feel lucky I had you around too." Charlie throws his hands up in the air, "Speaking of your grandpa, we got to get at least one deer soon. He is driving me nuts asking about filling his tags."

Nat laughs. He hoists his binoculars to his eyes and scans the area. "Why can't he shoot his own deer?"

Charlie jumps right on his nephew's comment, "I know! That's exactly what I keep asking him. You ask him when we get back."

The hunters use their binoculars to glass their surroundings, hoping a deer has wandered into view. A couple minutes pass to no avail. Nat turns his face to the sun, closes his eyes, and absorbs the warm rays. Charlie interrupts the silence again, "Everything go ok at school this week?"

"Yeah," Nat speaks with his eyes closed. "Hey, I wanted to say I'm sorry about breakfast time. I'm not much of a morning person."

Charlie enjoys a laugh, "You and me both."

"I know our conversation was kind of weird at breakfast the other day." Nat smiles, eyes closed still facing the sun.

"Don't worry about it," Charlie says laughingly. "I guess we got that in common; mornings don't agree with us."

The hunters scan the cornfields and trees with naked eyes. "How about basketball? Everything ok after a week of practice under your belt?" Charlie continues his interrogation.

"Sure," Nat answers succinctly.

"What about the offense? You know it?" Charlie digs deeper.

Nat shrugs, "Same flex offense everyone runs nowadays. It's just a matter of execution."

Gregory L. Heitmann

"You gonna run the point at all?"

"Mmm," Nat shakes his head, "Nah. Two guard. I can run the point if necessary." Nat holds up his hands and flicks his wrist as if shooting a basketball. "I'm more of a shooter than a passer."

Charlie laughs, and Nat can't resist smiling at his obvious statement. The sun disappears behind a stray bank of clouds, darkening the fields and trees providing an ominous look to the Coteau Des Prairie to their west. "Where are all the deer?" Nat asks brusquely.

"Beats me," Charlie replies with a bit of impatience in his voice. "Weather screwing 'em up, I guess. It's been the slowest season in quite a while." Charlie points at the clouds coming in from the west. "I hope you enjoyed your fifteen minutes of sunshine today, because it looks like more snow coming."

Charlie picks up his rifle from a bale on the top row of the stack. "Ya ready to head back?"

Nat grabs his rifle, "Yup, let's get outta here."

Nat sits on his butt and begins to slide down the side of the large round bale where he had been sitting. His foot catches in a loop of loose baling twine, "Whoa!" he shouts. "Nooo!" he cries out as he is spun around and suddenly hanging upside down by his foot. "Help! Uncle Charlie, help!"

Nat's rifle plunges into the thawing snow below and disappears. Charlie is by his nephew's side in an instant. "Are you ok?" he questions immediately.

"Yes, just get me down!"

Confirming Nat is all right, Charlie lets loose a laugh. "Just a sec. I'll have you down in a moment."

Charlie unzips his jacket and pulls his cell phone from his pocket. Turning to the camera function, Charlie points the phone at his nephew, "Just need a couple photos for the record."

"Oh, come on, man," Nat struggles to try to free himself. "Do you have to do that?" He gives up and dangles by his foot patiently waiting for his uncle to help.

Charlie laughs again as he stows his phone. "Just like your mom. Oh, so graceful."

"Just get me down," Nat demands.

Charlie digs his knife from his pants pocket and flicks it open. "Wait, wait, wait, wait!" Nat shouts as Charlie approaches "Let me get a hold of something!"

116

It's too late. Charlie slices the twine, and Nat is freed, bouncing off another bale and face planting into the snow drift beside his buried rifle. Nat rights himself in the snow. He appears in the image of a snowman, prompting Charlie to dig out his phone again for another photo.

"Thanks a lot!" Nat's sarcasm drips off his statement as clumps of snow fall from his hat, face, and jacket as he struggles to stand.

Charlie clicks a photo, "One more picture for the scrapbook. The abominable snowman lives!" Charlie laughs. "Hey, don't forget to dig out your rifle from the drift."

Nat stands and brushes snow off his too small coveralls and jacket the best he can. He digs down into the drift and pulls out his snow encased rifle. "Boy, this huntin' season is starting off great," he mumbles as he stumbles through the thigh-deep snow to join his uncle already heading back to the truck.

Gregory L. Heitmann

Chapter 24
FBI

Charlie's week starts with a Monday morning visit to talk to his captain. He strolls though his office building having entered through the security-coded rear entrance. He looks in at his cubicle for any messages or mail; finding none, he moves toward the reception area and front entrance of the BIA police station. He passes the administrative assistant, Kathy Chasing Hawk. Kathy is twenty-eight years old. She is a tribal member of the Sisseton-Wahpeton Band and in her second year as the receptionist. She is short and plump. Her untamed hair is a relic, looking more like a 1980's fashion revival that contrasts her no-nonsense pants suit attire. "Morning, Kathy," Charlie calls out as he passes her desk.

Kathy's finger goes up in the air, and she points down the hall, "Hi, Charlie. Skip wants to see you."

Charlie turns to face Kathy and takes a couple steps, walking backwards for a moment, while continuing down the hall. He smiles. "Where else do you think I'd be going?" He reorients himself and proceeds ahead.

Charlie knocks on the partially open door and enters Captain Kipp's office. The captain sits at his desk poring over some papers. Without looking up from his papers, the captain responds, "Mornin', Charlie. Close the door and have a seat."

"Mornin', Boss," Charlie gently latches the door closed and swings around to the front of his boss' desk, easing into a stiff wooden chair.

Captain Kipp finishes the long paragraph on the page before him, one finger trained on the words, his other hands moving his glasses to better focus. He looks up with a smile at his sergeant. "First of all, we got another report on a stolen four-wheeler from the Big Coulee District."

"No kidding?" Charlie questions, truly surprised.

"Mattingly ranch called it in. I need you to go out there and take a statement."

"Huh," Charlie's brow furrows.

"I'll be very surprised if this related to our Deer Slayer. More like bored, snowed-in kids is my guess. But check it out...thoroughly," Skip sighs.

Charlie renders a mocking hand salute and leans forward in his chair, preparing to stand.

"Hold on. Not so fast," Skip raises his palm to halt his employee.

"Oh? Something else, Skip?" Charlie settles back in his chair.

Captain Kipp flips an extended thumb over his shoulder, gesturing down the hall, "We got your friend from the capitol waiting for you in interview room two."

Charlie laughs. "FBI finally checking back in? What took them so long?"

Skip shrugs and shakes his head, "Go talk to him."

"With pleasure," Charlie smiles and stands.

"Charlie," Skip elongates the long "e" sound. He raises an admonishing finger at his sergeant grinning in front of him. "Be nice."

With the innocence of a saint, Charlie responds, "Aren't I always?"

Charlie exits Captain Kipp's office and strolls down the hall, whistling a quick tune for a few steps while smiling. In a moment he stands in front of the closed door of the interview room. He wipes the smile off his face, putting on his best serious face. He turns the knob and enters a gray room with a table and two chairs. Mirrored glass lines one side of the room for observers to monitor any interrogations without intrusion, though there are no witnesses to today's conversation.

FBI Agent, Austin Brown, leans against the metal frame of the mirror, staring at himself, hands in his pockets. He wears a nice jacket and tie with black denim jeans all under a gray overcoat that matches the paint scheme of the interview room. "How goes it?" Charlie questions as he raises his hand. The clean-cut, thirty-five year old Tommy Lee Jones look-a-like grasps Charlie's hand for a firm handshake. "Oh, you know. Same old, same old."

The men sit on stiff aluminum chairs at the metal table fastened to the floor. Charlie cocks his head, unable to suppress his smile anymore. He likes the FBI guys. Although it is not politically correct with his boss or peers to show any respect or admiration for the "meddling feds," as they were often referred to, Charlie always enjoyed his interactions with the FBI. They were pros in his mind, somebody to look up to and model yourself after. "Where's your partner?" Charlie quizzes.

Agent Brown frowns, "Dead."

Any hint of a smile is immediately wiped from Charlie's face, escaping with some of his color in his cheeks. A chill runs through his spine, "Are you serious?" Charlie grips the table in front of him as he whispers the words.

"Do I ever joke around?" Agent Brown answers with his own question.

Charlie swallows hard,

"It wasn't in the line of duty," Agent Brown's face contorts, twisting his smile. "Heart attack."

Charlie relaxes. His body leans forward, and he turns his gaze to the side wall where it intersects with the floor. He turns to the FBI agent, "What was he...?"

"Age? Forty-six," Agent Brown states matter-of-factly. "Left a wife and two kids. He had good insurance. They've already moved back east."

"Geez. I'm sorry, man," Charlie puts his hands up in surrender. "How can I help you?"

There's a brief pause before the agent waves the morbid part of the conversation away, "They'll be getting me a new partner soon, but they sent me up here to get whatever you got on the case so far, anything new that is."

Charlie nods, "Yeah, I know, the Deer Slayer case."

"Deer Slayer? That's what you're calling 'im?" Brown questions. "Nice."

"Skip came up with it," Charlie continues to nod.

"Kudos to him. It's catchy," Brown frowns and joins Charlie's nodding.

Charlie takes a deep breath, "Well, we don't have much. As you know, it's the same modus operandi as before. You got anything to help us out?"

"Skip mentioned you may have had an encounter with our boy?" Agent Brown questions.

Charlie nods, "I was at the crime scene a few nights after..."

Agent Brown interrupts, "Oh, yeah. Your process. You visualize? Is that what you do?"

"Yeah," Charlie nods.

"Go on," Agent Brown points a finger toward Charlie, urging him to continue.

"You know, I like to go to the spot. Get a feel. Maybe some inspiration. Sure enough I hear a snowmobile engine approaching. It's cold. It's dark. I exit the truck with my weapon and flashlight to arrest whoever it is. Tampering with evidence at our crime scene, even if it isn't our guy," Charlie shakes his head in disgust as he remembers the encounter. "He's in a snowsuit and helmet. When I put my light on him and tell him to 'freeze,' he blasts me with one of those million-plus-candlepower spotlights. I was blinded and whoever it was got away."

"So, you think it was our guy then, huh?" Agent Brown questions.

"I lean that way," Charlie agrees reluctantly. "Got no proof." Agent Brown cocks his head, folds his arms, and stares at Charlie. Charlie grins.

"Do you hunt?" Charlie asks the agent. Agent Brown shakes his head. "I'll tell you this," Charlie leans back in his chair. He feels a bit like he is being interrogated at this point, yet offers his opinion. "Maybe I have some of those same obsessive compulsive feelings these psycho-killers have." Charlie leans forward resting his elbows on the table. "For me, I can channel my memories of my best hunts easily...my favorite bucks I've killed...I can close my eyes and I'm there. When I'm out there in the field, hunting those same bale stacks, those same trees and fields...I re-live those moments ten-fold."

Agent Brown's eyes have narrowed, and he nods ever so slightly. Charlie continues, "It is a powerful feeling, and I'm pretty sure our guy, our Deer Slayer, has the same feelings. Re-living his kills by re-visiting the scene."

The men stare at each other in silence, neither breaking eye contact. Agent Brown is reassured in his earlier conclusions that Charlie LeBeau is an able bodied policeman. Brown had put on the recruiting spiel a few years ago to Charlie, to no avail. He had quickly realized that Charlie was a local-lifer, and it was a waste of breath to try to coax him onto a national scene with the FBI. Agent Brown unfolds his arms slowly, oddly. He leans forward and gradually sets his hands on the table, almost daintily, clasping them together. "I think you are right, Charlie," he whispers. With a deep breath he pushes away from the table and stands. "You got yourselves a little blip on the big boy's radar up in D.C. We've scoured the national records for similar, or near matching kills."

"Really?" Charlie's eyes bulge. "Were there any?"

"Yup."

"Where?" Charlie's mouth hangs open in surprise.

"New Town," Agent Brown replies with his hushed monotone. "Fort Berthold Indian Reservation in North Dakota.

"Wow," Charlie nods slowly.

"I'll e-mail you the file," Brown continues. "Looks like we got our own isolated psychopath here in the Dakotas. Boys in my shop been callin' him Dakota Killer." Brown gives Charlie a wink. "But, I'm going to give 'em your guys' nickname, Deer Slayer."

Charlie smiles. Agent Brown folds his arms again and leans against the wall. "What are you workin' on now?"

Charlie grimaces, "Nothing much. It's really a stretch, but I'm talking to people that have had their snowmobiles and four-wheelers stolen. I believe these stolen ATVs and snowmobiles are involved in the murderer's getaway plans. I got this theory that he uses an intermediate mode of transportation that he can use to park some where inconspicuous. The snowmobile or the ATV is a shuttle between the crime scene and his vehicle to break up any possible link."

"Hmmph," Agent Brown grunts.

"We don't got much," Charlie shrugs. "What can I tell you?"

"Sheesh. Not much is right," Brown shakes his head. "No wild ass guesses? Nobody out there in the wind that is suspicious?"

"I don't know what to tell you, Agent Brown," Charlie stands. "We didn't have anything five years ago; we got nothing now. For all I know, it'll be another five years before we see anything new...like the Deer Slayer striking again."

"I don't think it will be five years," Agent Brown states bluntly.

Charlie blanches, "Why would you say that?"

"You saw the crime scene. Seems like something happened. Somethin went wrong, like he was interrupted."

Charlie shakes his head, "I don't know. What struck me about it was that, and I agree with you somewhat, but it looked like he quit halfway through. Like he just got bored."

Agent Brown laughs, "Don't tell me. Let me guess. Your theory is that he's tired of slicin' people up, and we'll never see this again."

Charlie frowns, "It crossed my mind."

"Oh, Charlie. You're so naïve."

"I know," Charlie smiles. "I'm a glass half-full type guy."

"Doesn't sound like any police I know." Agent Brown extends his hand, and Charlie shakes it. "You got my contact info. I'll e-mail you the Fort Berthold case. If anything comes up, and I mean anything, you let me know."

"Will do," Charlie responds.

"Well, take me to, Skip," Agent Brown remarks with a melancholy tone. "I'll check out with him and get back on the road to Pierre."

The men exit the room and their steps echo down the hallway, heading for Captain Kipp's office.

Gregory L. Heitmann

Chapter 25
Donner & Blitzen

The Sisseton Redmen boys' basketball program is changing quickly. Nat's presence on the team brings immediate championship experience, but, change is often difficult, today is one of those days on the Redmen basketball gym floor. The team is running the offense in a half court set when Head Coach Dan Kinney blows his whistle. Coach Kinney is tall and lanky, a former college player at the NAIA level. He was consistently the first man off the bench for his Black Hills State University Yellow Jackets, but now he was in his tenth year of high school coaching, the last five in Sisseton.

"Run it again!" Coach Kinney's voice booms in the echoing gym.

The players run the play, black shirts on offense versus red shirts on defense. Shoes squeak on the wooden floor, and the starters on offense in the black shirts are stymied, eventually throwing the ball out of bounds. The coach blows the whistle and straightens from his squatting position on the sideline. He approaches the players gathered in the lane. "Good job, defense," Coach Kinney claps his hands. He points to Nat, "Nat switch your jersey to black. You're going with the starters as the number two." Coach taps Curt Swenson on the shoulder, "Curt, you're going on defense, switch your shirt."

Curt Swenson is an eighteen year old senior. He has been on the varsity basketball team for three years and is finally one of the starting five this year. He is just an inch shorter than Nat. His mop of dark hair betrays his Scandinavian roots as it bounces and flops when he is on the floor. The coach's order to switch his reversible jersey from black to red hits him like a ton of bricks. He is frozen as he stares incredulously at his coach. "Hurry up!" Coach Kinney's voice booms again. "Get that jersey switched. Let's go!"

Nat and Curt trade positions on the floor. Hands on hips, head shaking in disgust at his demotion, Curt matches up against Nat. "Run it!"

the Coach cries out, and the point guard brings the ball from the half court line and the offense begins its motion with a series of screens against the man to man defense.

With a juke step, Nat loses his defender, Curt, and is open for a fifteen foot jump shot. He drains the shot. A couple high fives are provided to Nat as the coach calls out, "Run it again!"

The point guard starts his dribble at half court and bends his knees as his defender pressures him into picking up the ball. The offense stalls for a moment before Nat streaks to the ball, getting a bounce pass from the point guard. The defense relaxes for a moment, including Curt guarding Nat. Nat blows by everyone, leaving Curt near the top of the key, as he scores an easy layup.

"Again!" the coach orders, and the point guard picks the ball up at half court and dribbles.

The ball is passed to the wing to start the offense in motion, and the inside screens are executed. The ball reverses to the other side of the court, and Nat makes a sharp cut across the lane, lining up his defender with the post man providing a solid screen that knocks Curt to his knees. Nat is wide open again as no help defense comes, and he scores another easy lay up.

Curt Swenson seethes as he mutters to himself while following Nat to the free throw line extended position. "That's not gonna happen again, Chief," Curt whispers to Nat as he leans over and holds his shorts, gasping for air. The exertion and his anger have robbed him of his breath.

Nat ignores the comment as the coach orders the offense to reset. Once again the point guard starts at half court, and the offense flies into motion. Nat moves inside as Curt grabs and holds him, trying to plaster him with his body as defense. Nat sets a screen for the center and pivots in the lane, shaking Curt for a moment. Curt recovers, stumbles, and blatantly extends an elbow that catches Nat flush in the eye. Nat drops to floor writhing in pain as the whistle pierces the air in blast after blast. "Swenson! Get off this court!" Coach Kinney bellows. "Now!"

Nat rolls on the floor holding his eye, first on his back, then on his stomach. When he manages to get to a knee, his teammates, including Curt, have closed in around him to see if he is ok. "Get back! Get back!" the coach orders as he comes to check on Nat.

Nat drops his hands from his eye. It is already swollen shut, but he can still pick out his attacker. Nat springs forward, landing a punch deep in Curt's gut. Curt drops to the floor, knocked out of wind.

Coach Kinney blasts the whistle until his players are covering their ears. "Enough!" the coach hollers. "That is enough. Curt! Locker room! Now!"

A teammate helps Curt to his feet, and he makes his way across the court doubled over. "Nat, come with me!" The coach stands over his injured player. Nat is bent over holding his hand to his eye.

The coach leans over, grabbing Nat's arms and slowly eases Nat into a fully standing position. He grimaces as he observes the eye, fully swollen shut, grotesquely puffy with a first hint of discoloration. "Ooh," is all Coach Kinney can manage at first. He puts a hand on Nat's shoulder and directs him off the court. "Come on, we'll get some ice on that eye."

They move toward the training room as the rest of the players stand around, watching in disbelief. "Free throws!" Coach Kinney hollers over his shoulder. "Everyone on the lines! Shoot free throws until I get back!"

Before the coach and player are off the floor, the sounds of rhythmically dribbling basketballs fill the gym. The coach walks slowly and talks in hushed tones. "Don't worry, Nat. You're not in trouble. I saw...everyone saw what Curt did. It wasn't an accidental elbow."

Nat keeps the slow pace of the coach with his hand on his eye. His head throbs as he continues to touch the weirdly bloated skin around his eye. Nat doesn't answer with a word; he gives a nod of understanding to his coach. "I'll give your uncle a call. You might consider seeing a doctor tonight just as a precaution."

*　　*　　*

A little over an hour passes, and Nat is showered and changed, waiting for his uncle outside the gym. Charlie pulls up to the curb. He sees Nat still holding a bag of ice to his eye. He holds up his hands in bewilderment as Nat opens the door and climbs in the Tahoe. Nat removes the soothing ice and displays his wound to his uncle. Charlie turns up the interior lights to get a better look, "Holy Cow! What the heck happened?"

"Didn't Coach Kinney call and tell you?" Nat questions, easing the ice pack onto his eye. "He said he called you."

"I never got a message. I bet he called the station's number. I've been out." Charlie shakes his head as he looks at his nephew, "What happened?"

"I had a little run in with an elbow," Nat mumbles.

"I can see that, but I bet you can't," Charlie laughs at his little joke. "Your eye is completely swollen shut. That is a textbook shiner."

"I'm fine. I've had worse," Nat declares quietly.

"Should we run over to Indian Health?" Charlie offers. "They'll get you in right away. I'm still in uniform and all."

Nah," Nat waves the thought away. "Let's just go home. I don't feel like sitting around the emergency for hours on end to have them tell me to put ice on my eye."

Charlie puts the Tahoe in gear, "Tell me how it happened."

"Coach put me on the starting five today," Nat shakes his head. "Let's just say someone was less than thrilled at getting demoted."

"He took a swing at ya?" Charlie questions.

"He was guarding me...trying to guard me as we ran some half court sets. He was still steaming, and I scored like, three times in a row." Nat shakes his head. "He whispered to me that it wasn't going to happen again...he was right. I set a pick for the post down low, pivoted, and boom he was late getting to me, but he came in with his elbow ready."

"How's the other guy look?" Charlie cringes fearing the answer.

"I may look worse for the wear, but he won't forget who he is messing with." Nat sets the bag of ice in his lap and holds up his fists and flexes his biceps. He smiles, "No reminder needed that he's dealing with thunder and lightning...donner and blitzen as the Germans say." Nat kisses each bicep, even though his arms are protected by his heavy winter jacket.

Charlie laughs, "Take it easy, Schwarzenegger."

Chapter 26
Pickerel Lake

Bing's Resort on the north shore of Pickerel Lake is a happening place, at least for ice fisherman. Bait sales are steady for William "Bing" Fryer, proprietor of the resort. Another customer comes and goes with a scoop of minnows in his bait bucket. The early ice has brought out the ice anglers, and they are being rewarded with a steady bite.

Pickerel Lake is one of the deeper Glacial Lakes of the region. Pickerel is another name for one of the most common game fish of the Dakotas, the northern pike. This fish is an abundant, aggressive fish populating nearly every body of water in eastern South Dakota. It is not necessarily sought after as table fare due to its seemingly infinite amount of bones in its elongated, snake-like body, but it is quite the fighter when hooked and with large populations lurking about in nearly all types of underwater habitat, it is a quality sport fish. Just a half hour or so from the Sisseton Interstate 29 exit, Pickerel Lake has become popular for wealthy city dwellers in the Twin Cities, Sioux Falls, and Fargo areas targeting lakefront vacation properties. Its deeper bottom and fairly decent size attracts fisherman, water skiers, and all recreationalists to the surrounding lake side cabins. Many locals succumbed to the high flying real estate boom and could not turn down ridiculous offers to sell their long time cabins to affluent folks looking for somewhere to spend excess money they don't know what to do with. Smaller cabins were razed and lots combined. Large luxury homes have become the norm for Pickerel Lake, replacing the weekend two-room cabin.

Even with the evolving economy of Pickerel Lake, one thing has remained constant, and that is Bing's. "Charlie LeBeau," Bing calls out loudly as Charlie enters the bait shop. "What brings you off the reservation?"

"Howdy, Bing," Charlie replies as he approaches the counter to shake Bing's hand.

"Ya here to do some fishin'?" Bing laughs.

"You might say that," Charlie shrugs and pulls his black stocking cap from his head. The resort is warm. "Fishin' for clues on a case. You reported to Skip about some ATV's missing?" Charlie watches Bing nod slowly. "They might be related to one of our cases and a rash of stolen snowmobiles and ATVs."

Bing's information is enlightening. "I keep four ATVs for the folks to borrow. Yah, know," Bing's high nasally voice is even higher in his agitation. "They give me five bucks, and I let them haul their shacks out on the ice. Ice's not thick enough for cars and trucks yet. Now I got three out of my four ATVs unaccounted for."

Charlie takes notes and chimes in, "You're not going to catch me out there on that ice 'til after Christmas."

Bing looks around, surveying his shop, so as not to offend anyone, "These boys are crazy for fish. I know'd it's been cold, but that ice is tricky."

Charlie shakes his head, "What do you want to bet that at some point you are going to have some guilt ridden souls confessin' to you that they sunk your four-wheeler to the bottom of the lake."

"Har-har-har," Bing laughs as if he is in pain rather than amused. "I ain't bettin' you nothin'." He sweeps his hand in the direction of the one four-wheeler he has left parked out front. "I was paid and the people accounted for that borrowed 'em. These here missing four-wheelers is gone, unauthorized like."

Another customer gets a bucket of minnows. A generous scoop from Bing for a dollar comes with advice on a question of "Where they bitin'?"

"Wilkes point," Bing replies gesturing over his shoulder with the dripping minnow scoop, splashing Charlie's notepad. "You'll see the crowd of fisherman. Just sidle up to the guy with the most fish layin' on the ice an' drill some holes." Bing gives the customer a wink.

Charlie closes his notebook, "I got your info. We'll keep an eye out for your ATVs. We've had a lot go missing lately, most have been recovered alright. Probably cooped up kids joyridin'."

Charlie shakes Bing's hand and exits the overheated bait shop into the crisp air. The fish smell is left behind, and Charlie draws a deep breath through his nose. The cold air burns a bit through his nasal passages, throat, and lungs. He extricates his cell phone from his shirt pocket with some difficulty as an uncooperative button thwarts his effort. He scrolls through his contacts. "Hey, Skip, it's Charlie." Charlie listens for a moment. "Nah, just over here at Pickerel Lake, talking to Bing." Charlie listens again to his boss. "Just finished up taking his statement on the umpteenth stolen ATV."

Charlie walks slowly to his Tahoe, keys at the ready. He observes sun dogs in the sky as the blowing snow in the clear, sunny skies form what look like additional minor suns on either side of the yellow fireball in the sky. Charlie continues his side of the conversation, "I just thought I'd check in and see if there is anything else that might need to be checked out in this area." Charlie shakes his head as Skip responds, "Nothing? I was praying you wouldn't have another report of a stolen snowmobile or four-wheeler." Charlie laughs and listens some more. "All right. I'll be back in the office in an hour or so."

Charlie slides into the driver's seat and fires up the engine. He pulls out of the parking lot onto Marshall County Road 4, but Charlie is looking for a more leisurely route back to Sisseton off the beaten path. Instead of following the curve of the paved road to the east, he bears to the left and continues his northerly direction on a gravel road. His trek across the back roads stops before it even starts. Charlie's eyes catch tracks on a snow covered approach. He brakes quickly and throws the vehicle in reverse. He backs up until he is even with the approach and puts the vehicle in park as he stares at the tracks through the passenger's side window.

Charlie digs for his phone again; finally pulling it free, he scrolls through his contacts and presses the send button. "Wow, only one ring, and you answer," Charlie speaks into his phone. "Hey, Veronica, this is Charlie, by the way."

Charlie listens and smiles as he looks across the snow covered fields and adjusts his police radio to tone down distracting chatter. "Always anticipating a story? Is that how the great reporters do it? They wait by the phone for a big story to call?" Charlie laughs. "What are you doing tonight?"

Charlie listens more and nods. "Well, do I have a deal for you. Two offers, in fact, for your consideration." Charlie checks his mirrors and the road in front of him as Veronica talks. "I was wondering if you want to get a steak at the bowling alley tonight. They have the best steaks in town, if you didn't know." Charlie laughs and his voice goes higher, "Yes, with me!" he emphasizes loudly into the phone. Charlie notices up ahead of him that a vehicle made a three point turn on the road, the tracks still remaining in the snow. The lightly traveled gravel road still holds the sign of a vehicle crossing out of line into the snow askew of the traffic ruts. "Ok, that sounds good. Six-thirty at the bowling alley. I'll meet you there," Charlie nods as he speaks into the phone. He turns his attention back to the tracks on the approach, pulls the handle to open his door, as he listens. "Oh, the other thing? Yeah. Do you want to go to the game on Friday? My nephew's first game with the Redmen."

Charlie swings the door open as he listens. "Good. Sounds like a plan." Charlie unbuckles his seat belt and slides from the vehicle. "There's something else I want to talk about...off the record." Charlie listens, "Where am I? I'm just over here at Pickerel Lake getting a report on another stolen four-wheeler. That's what I want to talk to you about."

Charlie shuts the door on his truck as he listens and begins to move to the passenger side of the vehicle. "Ok, I'll see you tonight. Bye."

Charlie reaches the approach and the tracks are still clearly marked in the snow, yet to be wind battered and covered by the effects of drifting snow. It is clear to Charlie that a four-wheeler was loaded on this approach. The indentations of a ramp and the distinct prints of ATV tires remain in the snow and down into the loose gravel atop the frozen road. Charlie uses his phone to photograph the tracks. He shoots several pictures of the tire tread. He uses his clipboard and a tape measure for a dimensional reference as he photographs the wheel base and the ramp touchdown point relative to the vehicle. Charlie strolls the fifty yards or so to inspect the three point turn around tracks in the snow. He notes the same matching pattern in the tire tread. "Hmmph," Charlie grunts aloud. He takes a few more photographs and returns to his vehicle. Charlie looks to the south. About a mile away he can see the lakeside cabins lining the shore. Even further away, out on the lake, he observes a few ice fishing shacks.

Charlie takes one more look at the tire tracks in the approach and shrugs. He says out loud, "Could be nothing." He climbs into the Tahoe and heads north on the gravel road, imagining the road in the dark and the operation of stealing a four-wheeler at night from Bing's, driving it a mile down this gravel road and loading it into a waiting pickup truck. The question in the back of his head bothers him. It nags at him. Is this a part of the Deer Slayer's preparations to strike again?

Chapter 27
Bowling Alley

The Sisseton bowling alley, Lakeland Lanes and Lounge, is a hotbed of activity in darker, cold-weather months of the year. Bowlers compete in multiple leagues almost every evening of the week. Mixed leagues, men's leagues, and women's leagues get people out of their houses for friendly and serious competition. But most of all, it gets people's minds off the dreary nights elongated by the earth's tilt away from the sun in the northern hemisphere, and the grind of days moving toward the winter solstice. Winter officially begins on December twenty-first, but the days before and after are short on daylight. Depending on your perspective, you might say the solstice is the shortest day of the year, but for some it is the longest night of the year. Either way, the bowling alley is a popular place in winter.

Inside the bowling alley is the top dining experience in the Roberts County area. Rated above the Indian casinos of the region, the high quality steaks served in the bowling alley's lounge is local legend. It is an unusual dining experience to be serenaded by the unique sounds of bowling pins crashing along with the buzz and excitement of periodic cheers of celebration in competition. It may not be appealing to all, but the locals appreciate and love the atmosphere the bowling alley offers.

Charlie is a little late in his arrival; ten minutes after the agreed upon meeting time, he is escorted to the table by the hostess. "Sorry I'm late. Some bad roads out there in the country. The gravel roads drift shut in a heart beat. Slow going." Charlie takes his seat and finds a glass of water and a menu laid out before him. He sets the menu aside. Veronica looks up from her laptop and smiles. Her elongated reporter's notebook lays open on the table. She closes both items. "Sheesh, don't you ever give it a rest?" Charlie jokes.

"Just trying to preserve my notes. Capture some ideas," Veronica whispers in a defensive, mocking tone.

Charlie grins and holds up an admonishing finger. He wags his finger at her and points it at her and her notebook, "This is still off the record."

"Absolutely," Veronica replies putting her hands up in surrender. "I've closed my computer and shut my notepad; what more do you want?"

"Ok then," Charlie laughs the words. Charlie scoots his chair closer to the table and leans forward about to say something, but a waitress appears and interrupts, "Are you ready to order?" she asks.

"Give us another minute," Charlie holds up a finger, and the waitress's massive head of curly hair bobs as she nods.

She turns away and leaves the couple at the table. Barely audible amidst the sounds of rolling balls and pins crashing, the sound of Johnny Lee's Urban Cowboy Soundtrack song "Looking for Love" can be heard in the dining area. "So, you wanted to talk to me about something?" Veronica leans forward, resting her hands, one atop the other, on the table. "Don't keep me in suspense." Veronica removes her glasses and sets them on the table.

"Glasses?" Charlie questions. "You look so scholarly, so professorial with them; now you take them off?"

Veronica smiles, "Oh, thanks. I just need them to give my eyes a rest once in a while." Veronica holds up her hand, "The lighting in here is not great for reading, and I thought I'd give my eyes a break."

Charlie raises his eyebrows and nods. He sips his water and looks around the restaurant suspiciously before leaning across the table, resting part of his weight on his elbows braced on the table. He closes the distance between himself and Veronica and speaks softly, almost in a whisper. "It's all these stolen snowmobiles and ATVs. I have this theory."

Veronica's eyes widen, "Oh, yeah?"

Charlie continues even softer, "I know we saw the killer on the snowmobile. And before, he used a four-wheeler. We recovered them both...but."

Veronica is puzzled, "But what?"

"But why all the other stolen machines? We've had two dozen reports of ATVs and snowmobiles gone missing in the last month. I bet we only had ten all last winter."

Veronica shakes her head, "What's your point?"

"Well," Charlie looks to each side of the table, at his surrounding diners. He evaluates them before he continues in a whisper. "The Deer Slayer. Is he going to kill again this soon? Or is it just some diversion?"

"Huh," Veronica grunts the word as she ponders the question.

"All these stolen machines," Charlie waves his hand. "They are never new models. It seems like there is a concerted effort to not draw attention. New, ten thousand dollar machine goes missing, boom, people notice that right away and give us a call."

Veronica nods at the shared information as Charlie continues. "Almost all the reports we get, and I've filled them all out, 'cause I'm handling them. The people don't have a clue when the snowmobile or four-wheeler went missing. They can't even tell us the last time they noticed the machine. Days or weeks could have gone by before they notice."

Veronica's brow furrows and her face puckers as she winces. She shakes her head ever so slightly, "I just can't imagine another murder. All this attention right now? That'd be crazy."

Charlie shakes his head, "Crazy is an understatement for our guy. Maniacal. That's the word I've settled on for the Deer Slayer."

The waitress returns and takes their orders, steaks for the both of them and the conversation continues. "So, what's the FBI saying?" Veronica launches a question that knocks Charlie back a bit.

"Hmm. FBI, eh?" Charlie responds, eyebrows raised. "I see you've done some homework."

"Oh, please," Veronica rolls her eyes. "Those guys stick out like sore thumbs. They roll into town with all the subtlety of an eclipse of the sun."

Charlie sips at his water again. "The FBI has nada. The only remotely similar case was up on the Fort Berthold Indian Reservation. They said they would e-mail me the file."

"Oh, I guess we're not all that special. Here I thought we had cornered the market on crazy."

Charlie laughs, "Yeah, that's kinda what FBI Agent Brown said. He said his crew was calling the guy the 'Dakota Killer,' but I told him we had the nickname the Deer Slayer already."

"Here I was thinking we were unique," Veronica smirks. "Unique in all the wrong reasons, but then it turns out we share horribleness with our neighbors to the north."

The steaks arrive, and they dig in. With a couple bites under their belts, a visitor appears tableside. It is Elliot Koffman wearing a bowling shirt and bowling shoes. "Hi, guys," Elliot intones with a childish wave of his hand.

Charlie looks up, grabs his napkin and wipes his mouth, "Elliot. Hi. How are you rollin' 'em?"

Elliot nods excitedly, "Good...for me. I've broken a hundred each of my first two games! It's the Chamber of Commerce league. I'm one of the top bowlers."

As Charlie chuckles, Elliot points a finger at him. "Veronica tells me she's working on quite a scoop, an exclusive interview with your nephew...all-state guard, so I hear."

"Really," Charlie smugly nods. "This is news to me, this interview anyway. And as far as all-state...come on already, he hasn't even played a game."

"I guarantee we'll be selling extra copies when his interview comes out. I called the printers and told them we're going to need twenty-five percent more copies that edition. Speaking of phone calls, the coach even called me twice to make sure I come to the game." Elliot looks to the lanes. "Listen, I'll let you eat. Looks like we're ready to go on our third game. See you guys." Elliot walks away, his steps somewhat choppy on his short legs.

Charlie watches Elliot walk away, and he snickers, "That guy cracks me up." Charlie turns his attention back to his steak, sawing off another perfect piece and shoveling it into his mouth.

Veronica's eyes narrow, "Be nice. We can't all be tall, handsome, and athletic like you." Charlie blushes.

"So," Charlie chews and swallows his bite of steak. "You wanna go with me to the game on Friday? Or are you workin'?"

"I can do both; I'm sure I can make some time. Maybe you can arrange an exclusive interview for me with a certain new, star player."

"Again, come on, he hasn't even played a game yet," Charlie pleads. "This hype is going to bring unreasonable expectations."

Veronica laughs at Charlie's discomfort, "It's not a secret. Word's out that we have a bona fide All-State player on the team. First one since, I don't know...you?"

Charlie blushes again and turns his attention back to his steak.

Chapter 28
Redmen Opener

The high school boy's basketball season starts with a battle of Native American mascots. The Britton Braves travel thirty eight miles east on South Dakota Highway 10 to visit the Sisseton Redmen. Britton rests just a few miles off the west side of the Coteau Des Prairie, mirroring its eastern neighbor. It is just off the Indian reservation, but its high school mascot honors the native inhabitants of the region. The town of Britton is an isolated agricultural village. It is at least an hour's drive in any direction before you would find shopping opportunities the likes of a Wal-mart, thus Britton is pretty independent. The historic main street sports brick buildings and small businesses providing everything the inhabitants need on a relative scale: grocery store, hardware store, furniture store, farm implement dealership. This is the commerce of small towns in South Dakota.

The Britton Braves and their fans are literally brave on this night, traversing the hills and the highway's snow-packed and slippery surface. It is still cold, unusually cold; perfect weather to sit in a crowded gym that warms up as the fans cheer their teams. Heavy winter coats overflow the coat racks near the doors. The capacity crowd fills the bleachers. Word has traveled well that the Redmen are a legitimate force this season. In the two weeks leading up to the opening tip, articles in the *Aberdeen American News* and *Watertown Public Opinion* speculated on the success of the Redmen. The recurring theme in every article is the phrase, "Nathaniel Chasing Wolf, who led Tiospa Zina to the state tournament last year, has transferred to Sisseton and joins a Redmen team poised to make a mark this season."

Charlie read the articles and is nervous as the sits in the bleachers with Veronica and Claude. He worries that no one can live up to this hype.

The Britton versus Sisseton rivalry is not all that it's made out to be at least in this opening game. Sisseton is a larger town, almost double in size, and this is reflected in the student population. Sisseton tends to dominate over the smaller school, but Britton makes a run every couple years as talent cycles through. The Northeast Conference for sports also tends to be unpredictable, and this is the season opener and conference opener for both teams. Nobody is confident one way or the other.

The Sisseton high school pep band plays some upbeat tunes as the teams go through their layup drills and warm-up activities. "Rock Around the Clock" and the "Horse" ring through the gym fueling the mood. The stands are abuzz in anticipation. Doubts about the varsity game's quality began with the earlier junior varsity game, which was a sloppy mess, both teams turning the ball over, fouling, and shooting woefully in a Sisseton victory thirty to twenty-five.

Now the band plays "Fight On," Britton's school song, followed by "Minnesota Rouser," Sisseton's school song, and the clock shows zeroes with the buzzer sounding to start the game. Warm-ups are over, and the starters for each team are introduced. The Sisseton student section mockingly pretends to read newspapers in disinterest as the Britton Braves' players are introduced first, followed by howls of delight as the names for the starting five Sisseton Redmen are announced over the public address system. You could hear a pin drop as the announcer requested everyone stand for the national anthem. The band plays the Star Spangled Banner perfectly, and the roof is nearly blown off the gym at its conclusion.

If there were any doubts about the Redmen and Nat's prowess, they were quickly laid to rest. The opening tip was controlled by Britton, but Nat poked the ball away from a Brave player and took the ball uncontested for a layup to start the game. The Britton Braves are overmatched. It is just as the citizens of Sisseton anticipated or hoped, for that matter, something to cheer about in the dark wintry night. Nat is practically a one man show to start the game as he eases his teammates into the flow. Nat shoots and makes four of five unchallenged three point field goals before the Braves' defense starts to make a concerted effort to force someone else to beat them. The perimeter defense of Britton did not stop the bleeding. Nat drives to the basket and, when the defense collapses on him, easily finds an open teammate for a layup at point blank range.

The crowd roars louder and louder at each basket. With a minute left in the third quarter, Nat runs the point guard position. He starts the motion of the offense, dribbling to the wing and waving his teammate toward the baseline. His defender relaxes, and Nat puts his shoulder down, driving into the lane, weaving through defenders he leaps, hangs in the air, and makes a sweeping reverse layup around outstretched hands. It is too much for the crowd to contain itself, and the gym explodes in cheers. Even loyal Britton fans acknowledge the play with a clap or two.

Britton throws the inbounds pass away, and with the dead ball, Coach Kinney pulls a player from his bench to substitute in for Nat. The announcer makes the call over the public address system, and Nat walks to the bench to a standing ovation, acknowledging the student section, he holds up his finger in a number one gesture as he approaches the bench. Coach Kinney calls time out as the scoreboard shows Sisseton 65, Britton 35. The coach empties his bench and the subs enter the game as the pep band plays the "Minnesota Rouser" to fans clapping along in celebration.

Charlie's hands sting as he claps, along with the crowd in rhythm to the school song. Charlie's hands hurt from clapping so much and so loudly. He is proud that his nephew is able to rise to the occasion under such ridiculous expectations and pressure. Veronica leans over and shouts in his ear trying to get above the crowd noise. "How many points did Nat have? Thirty?"

Charlie shrugs and continues clapping. He leans into Veronica's ear, "Twenty-five, maybe?"

Charlie watches his nephew in the huddle as the substitute players get instructions from their coach. Nat waves a towel as he exhorts and acknowledges the crowd. The buzzer sounds, and the players move to the floor while Nat grabs a water bottle and eases himself onto the bench. Nat looks over his shoulder and makes eye contact with his uncle and smiles. Hoisting up his water bottle toward his uncle in a "toasting with raised glasses" gesture he delivers a slight nod. Charlie returns the gesture and a "thumbs up" between his claps. The cheers ease and fans take their seats. Veronica shakes her head in disbelief, "Your nephew is something else."

The final minute of the third quarter plays out, and the buzzer sounds. Fans rise again and cheer. Charlie looks around as he feels a tap on his shoulder. Captain Kipp leans in and talks into Charlie's ear. Charlie nods, and Kipp turns and moves down the bleachers. Charlie, in turn, leans over and whispers into Veronica's ear, "Something's happened." Charlie points in the direction of the side exit door where Captain Kipp is pushing open the door and leaving the building. "My boss needs me," Charlie frowns.

"What is it?" Veronica questions.

"Can't say," Charlie responds as he dons his jacket and stocking cap.

Veronica's eyes widen, "Is somebody dead? A crash?"

Charlie shakes his head. He leans over and kisses Veronica on the cheek. She blushes and covers her kissed cheek with her hand. She grabs at Charlie's hand, holding him in place for a moment as he stands. "I need that interview with your nephew, you promised," she smiles. Charlie breaks her grasp and moves down the bleachers, easing his way through the crowd. "Call me later!" she yells.

Charlie gives her a wave, acknowledging her as he reaches the floor. He meets her eyes as he pauses at the side exit door, adjusting his stocking cap and gloves before exiting, following Captain Kipp into the freezing night.

Chapter 29
Roped

The Coteau des Prairies Hospital is just a mile or so from the Sisseton High School Gymnasium. Charlie and Skip observe the patient from the far side of the compact emergency room. Sisseton's hospital is a regional facility, hosting thirty to forty overnight patients at its maximum capacity. For the most part, it is a simple service medical center. For critical cases, the hospital tends to be a triage center. Traumas can be delivered to Fargo in just a few minutes via a helicopter if necessary.

A rail-thin teenage boy with a shock of red hair rests on the ER bed. His pale face is mostly obscured by an oxygen mask. His body is covered in blankets as the staff tries to warm him. His eyelids twitch and flutter, half-closed, as his head lolls side to side while multiple nurses hover, ready to provide whatever service may be necessary. Bags of fluid hang above his bed; IVs run to each arm.

Deputy Wade Carson of the Roberts County Sherriff's Office joins the two BIA policemen. "What happened?" Skip asks the obvious question.

Deputy Carson shakes his head, "I was on duty and got the call. Naked man on Main Street." Deputy Carson spins his black stocking cap in his hands as he speaks. "I found him just north of the four-way stop. He was mumbling incoherently, shivering. I got him into my car. I could make out the word 'kidnapped'."

Charlie's eyes narrow, "Who is he? Is this some stupid high school prank gone bad?"

Deputy Carson shrugs, "I think he's from Milbank. That red hair...probably a Caldwell family relation." Charlie and Skip look at Carson strangely. "I'm from Milbank. I know a lot of people there," Carson clarifies, as the BIA policemen nod in understanding. "He mumbled and mumbled. I could make out a few things here and there. He said he 'escaped from the trunk of a car.' His car." Carson points to the doctor, now at the bedside of the boy. "The doctor had to give him a sedative.

When I brought him in, the boy was flailing around like a fish out of water."

"Hmmm," Charlie grunts.

"What do you make of it, Charlie?" Skip questions.

"Hmmm," Charlie grunts again.

Deputy Carson continues, "The sedative calmed him down, and he rambled on quite a while before you guys arrived. Gibberish mostly, but some stuff like 'woke up in the trunk of his car.' Things about being tied up."

Charlie and Skip from across the room can see the bruising on the boy's wrists. Carson continues, "He escaped the ropes and when the car stopped moving for a moment, he bailed out."

Skip nods, "Yeah, these new cars all have a safety latch in the trunk nowadays. Must have been the four-way stop right on First Avenue."

Charlie frowns, "Nobody saw anything?"

Carson shakes his head, "Dispatch got the call. We can track it down for more details, I guess, but dispatch called me; I went to Main Street and found him staggering around disoriented."

"Everybody's at the game tonight," Skip chimes in. "Not many eyes on the street; probably just some passerby driving through called 911 after seeing a naked guy."

Deputy Carson's phone buzzes, and he checks a text message.

Skip slaps Charlie on the back, "By the way, great game by Nat tonight."

"He played all right," Charlie shrugs.

"So modest," Skip grins.

"Do you mind?" Deputy Carson laughs. "I made a couple calls already and got this text. There was a missing boy reported to Milbank authorities. Lonnie Caldwell, he's a high school senior from Milbank. Been missing a couple days. His parents are en route."

"Huh. Good work, Deputy," Skip nods. "Anything else?"

"The boy said he thought he was drugged. He couldn't remember anything. He remembers being in school, that's it. Two days ago, by all accounts."

"Drugged with a Roofie?" Charlie questions.

Skip nods, "Sounds like it. But why?"

Charlie and Skip move to the boy's bedside to get a better look at him. The patient is still. His eyes are closed. And his breaths are slow and deep. Charlie picks up his right hand, careful not to disturb the IV; he turns over the boy's wrist observing the bruises. The tell-tale black and blue lines match the looping knots of the Deer Slayer's previous victims.

"I've seen enough," Charlie whispers softly. He eases the boy's hand to the bed.

Skip and Charlie retreat to the foyer near the hospital's admittance desk to resume their conversation, away from Deputy Carson. "I'd say he's a victim of our guy all right," Charlie purses his lips.

"Yeah," Skip replies softly.

"Same knots as always...tied by a lefty as always," Charlie breathes the words in a slow exhale.

Skip emits a low whistle. "My God. It isn't like the Deer Slayer to deviate from his pattern." He kicks at a scuff on the floor tile.

"No kidding," Charlie sighs.

"Are you sure about all this?" Skip questions.

"Pretty sure. It's a pretty common knot in the military, but other than military and boy scouts, I'd say rare. I saw it in Desert Storm. We used it for tarp tie-downs on our transports."

"So, our Deer Slayer is likely a veteran," Skip nods slowly.

Charlie bites his lip and frowns, "Looks that way."

"Well," Skip announces loudly, "I'll give Agent Brown at the FBI a call."

"You know what?" Charlie points a finger at his boss. "Check our victim for stun gun burns. Find them, and I'd say he's definitely the Deer Slayer's victim."

Gregory L. Heitmann

Chapter 30
South Red Iron Lake

Charlie stands next to a snow drift. He is about twenty five yards from the edge of the frozen lake. About twenty miles west of Sisseton, South Dakota Highway 10 divides Red Iron Lake into a north lake and a south lake. A series of culverts under Highway 10 equalizes the lakes. Charlie is out of his comfort zone as he stands on a patch of snow, an island in the bare, exposed ice. Charlie had shuffled out this far from shore, wary of the early ice, and this was far enough. Another twenty five yards away, a handle bar and a tire protrude from the ice. It is a four-wheeler frozen in place.

Red Iron Lake is named after the historical Chief Red Iron, the founding father of peace for the Sisseton-Wahpeton Bands in the tumultuous 1860's. It is a true honor for an Indian Chief to be memorialized with a place name such as a lake. Such distinction for an Indian is few and far between, even with the long standing Native American influence in the region.

The wind blows across the snow-polished ice; some flakes swirl and hang up behind the exposed machine. It is a dreary, wicked day. The threat of snow looms oppressively in the clouds, encircling the tops of the trees that encompass the shore of the lake between the cabins.

The Red Iron Lakes are contributors to the excellent angling of the Glacial Lakes Region. Small mouth bass or "smallies" populate the lake. They are a sought after game fish known for their legendary fight. The Red Iron Lakes are on the small side relative to their close neighboring lakes like the more established Clear Lake and Roy Lake with their resorts and state park facilities. North Red Iron Lake sports no cabins. Marshes and cattails buffer the lake proper, and to fish this lake it takes a boat or canoe. South Red Iron Lake has an established shore line and a scant few cabins ring a part of the north and northeastern shore.

Just a stone's throw from the north shore is where Charlie finds himself standing. He grumbles to himself as he digs for his cell phone, "Nine o'clock in the morning and I'm out recovering an ice cube."

The ice cracks, popping somewhere in the expanse of the lake, and Charlie's heart skips a beat, and he reacts further, sliding his feet a couple steps closer to shore. The eerie, gurgling sound of ice, shifting and cracking, is something most people never get used to, and Charlie is like most people. One does well to respect the wisdom in waiting for a solid cold spell before associating oneself with early ice or ice at any time for that matter.

"Hey, Skip, you were right," Charlie speaks into his cell phone. "Send a recovery truck with cables and somebody in a wet suit and a chainsaw if you want to get this thing out. It's a popsicle."

Charlie listens on his phone. He stares at the handlebar sticking out of the ice. It looks as if it could be a tree branch if not for the balloon like tire of the four-wheeler adjacent to it. "No word on who called in the tip?" Charlie asks and listens.

"Smack dab in the middle of the lake...well not smack dab, more like close to the north shore of South Red Iron. It's near the equalizing pipes. Probably some poor ice near the moving water. No missing person reports, are there? I don't want to find a body attached to the machine."

Charlie spins on his heel, sliding around the slick ice as he listens, checking the surroundings. He sees the first few snowflakes and answers a question from Skip, "Only about three or four ice fishing houses. They're all about four hundred yards away or more."

Charlie listens some more and smiles before answering. "I'll trade ya," he says into the phone with a smile. "Starting to get some snow, and I need to get back to my bale stack. I can't believe you called me this morning for this. I need to put some deer in the freezer yet!"

Charlie listens and laughs. "Sounds good. Come on out, I'll wait for ya."

Chapter 31
Suspect

Inside the Holiday gas station coffee shop, Charlie and Veronica meet for a break in the work day and a snack. Their relationship is becoming more and more comfortable. Charlie has confided in Veronica, and shared facts about the case he probably shouldn't be sharing. But, she is a sounding board, someone to bounce theories off of, and now she is analyzing the photos of the tire tracks and measurements he took near Pickerel Lake. Maybe narrowing down the truck make and model could point them in the direction of a suspect and break the case wide open.

The pair sits in a booth facing each other, the table between them. Their heads are tilted in the direction of the register. The song "Trouble" by Lindsey Buckingham plays softly overhead. Veronica's mouth twists in a frown, "That guy? He's your suspect? Marvin?" she whispers quietly, her tone filled with doubt.

Only a few people populate the coffee shop this afternoon, but a steady flow of customers move in and out of the building as they pay for fuel. Their booth near the window glows in the sunshine for a moment, quickly followed by an alternating light and dark as the cumulus clouds stream past in the sky, blotting out the sun from moment to moment.

"Shhh," Charlie shushes his companion. "Keep it down," he whispers hoarsely.

"He's...he's..." Veronica stammers.

Charlie finishes her sentence with a question, "Old?"

"Yeah, old and with a broken foot," She winces as she stares at the would-be suspect.

"I know," Charlie reluctantly agrees. "That's where I need your help. I want to see if he's faking."

"Really? What can I do?" Veronica questions. "You want me to go stomp on his foot?"

"I was wondering if you could run to Watertown," Charlie sips his coffee.

"Sure."

"Just go to the Lake Region Orthopedic Clinic and see if you can use their phone. Pretend like your cell phone is dead. Call the Sisseton Hospital, on their line, and tell them to fax the x-rays and diagnosis for Mr. Hattum to this number." Charlie slides his card with the appropriate phone numbers and an e-mail address on the back. "Better yet, see if they can e-mail the info to the e-mail address on that card. It's a dummy email address that sounds like a medical clinic."

Veronica's face scrunches in disagreement. "Shouldn't you have a warrant?"

Charlie shrugs, "Probably."

"So, get one," Veronica demands.

"I know this a roundabout way of doing things, but one, I don't want to alert anyone, and two, if it turns out to be nothing, no records need exist."

"Ok, I'll do my best, but why Watertown?"

Charlie shakes his head, "I'm hoping that the caller ID will bail us out. My guess is that they won't think twice about the records request if their caller ID is showing another medical office."

"So, why don't you do it?"

Charlie nods, "I have some other business to take care of. I'm running down a lead over in Britton."

Marvin notices his admirers and gives a wave to Charlie as he heads in their direction. Charlie's eyes widen, and he kicks Veronica under the table.

"Ouch!" Veronica cries out.

"Shhh. He's coming over," Charlie excitedly whispers. "Act normal!"

Veronica is bent over rubbing her shin awkwardly. She glares at Charlie, "You act normal." She hisses. "Why in the world did you kick me?" Noticing the card still on the table, Veronica quickly palms it and moves her hand toward her pants pocket.

She straightens and smiles at Marvin as he nears the table, and feigning everything is fine, she greets the store's proprietor, "Hi Marvin! Care to join us?"

Chapter 32
Dew Drop In

The cumulus clouds from the early afternoon have banded together to provide an overcast sky that now threatens snow. An hour removed from having coffee with Veronica, Charlie finds himself on the west side of the Coteau des Prairies, just outside of Britton, South Dakota. On the edge of the Britton city limits, the Dew Drop In Bar and Lounge is open for business. A couple cars and a pickup truck grace the parking lot as Charlie pulls the Tahoe off South Dakota Highway 10. He puts the truck in park and eyes the vehicles in the lot before turning the key, killing the engine.

Exiting the vehicle Charlie notes the first few jumbo-sized flakes beginning to fall. He enters the lounge, taking a moment for his eyes to adjust to the dim lighting inside. He stands by the door and hears raucous laughter at the far end of the room. The sparse crowd is made up of two groups of four people, each group occupying opposite ends of the bar. With eyes adjusted to the light, Charlie moves to the loud conversation at the far end of the bar. He can make out the man he came to see. It is Zeke Gonzalez.

Charlie moves toward the man, cautiously taking in his environment. The jukebox plays quietly. The Oak Ridge Boys sing a cowboy's evening prayer in "Y'all Come Back Saloon". Zeke has his back to Charlie. The monster of a man is six foot four and two hundred and fifty pounds of lean muscle. He sports a black leather biker's jacket, faded blue jeans, square-toed biker boots, and a blue bandana on his head. The men he is with give a nod of warning to Zeke, who turns and sees the police officer approaching him. Charlie smiles a bit at the small circular designer eye glasses that appear out of place on his wide face in contrast to the man's wardrobe. Zeke's lip and chin sport a thin, almost dainty, mustache and goatee.

"Remember me, Zeke?" Charlie asks as his feet shuffle to a stop a few feet from the big man.

"Charlie LeBeau? You're a cop?" Zeke squints at the policeman standing before him. He cocks his head in curiosity. "LeBeau, a cop?" He pushes away from the man nearest him and moves toward Charlie, hands extended.

Charlie stands with his hands on his belt buckle not moving, only smiling. The big man engulfs Charlie in his arms and hugs him, lifting him awkwardly off the ground. Charlie is at the big man's mercy, hands still on his buckle, arms pinned to his sides.

Zeke sets Charlie down. "Uf-dah," Charlie grunts as he stumbles a bit and regains his balance. "Yeah, I've been a cop for the last fifteen years."

Zeke beams in disbelief as he shakes his head. "I got a son that's going to the police academy out in Bakersfield."

"Good. Good. What brings you around to these parts?" Charlie queries.

Zeke frowns and gives a jerk of his head toward town, "My mom. She's not doing good."

"Sorry to hear that," Charlie nods.

Zeke's lips purse, "She's in the assisted living center over here in Britton." Zeke scratches the top of his head and then moves his hand to his chin. "It's the damnedest thing." He looks at the bartender then back to Charlie. "I got an anonymous note that said 'come see mom' and five hundred cash in the mail."

"What?" Charlie flinches.

Zeke lets loose a breathy laugh, "I thought it was my mom, pranking me. I don't need the money. I got my own landscaping business back in California; my mom knows I got money."

"I don't get it," Charlie stares at Zeke.

"I don't know what the deal is. My mom denies it all, and she sure as heck doesn't have an extra five hundred bucks layin' around."

"Weird," Charlie digs in his pocket for some money. He throws a five dollar bill on the bar. "I gotta go, but Victor Crawford wanted me to buy you a drink if I saw you. You know what?" Charlie digs another five dollar bill out of his pocket. "It's so rude of me to just come and go, have a drink on me." Charlie throws up a thumb over his shoulder, "It's starting to come down out there, and I got to get back to Sisseton."

"I hear you, bro," Zeke nods. "We don't get snow like this out in California."

Charlie shakes Zeke's hand, "It was nice to see you, Zeke."

"You too, Charlie."

Charlie exits the Dew Drop In. Outside the lounge it is a "snow drop in." The sky is a complete white-out with the extra large snow flakes streaking in different directions. An unusual weather event in the Dakotas known as "no wind" is occurring. Charlie knew it wouldn't last, and it didn't. Just a few miles east of Britton, the Tahoe is buffeted by gusty winds that clear the roads of the new snow and replace it with the drifting snow of the ditches. It is a slow drive back to Sisseton, and he mulls over his new found information and conclusions. Zeke is indeed involved with the Deer Slayer. But, more than likely, he is just a pawn, set up to take the fall if something goes wrong. Charlie is still in disbelief that the killer would go to this depth, but then he remembers all the ATVs he has been dealing with and that whole misdirection. This guy knows what he is doing, but something is up with the Deer Slayer. Charlie can feel it. His policeman's intuition tells him that the killer is stumbling, seemingly flailing in his latest efforts. Charlie looks forward to his conversation with Veronica. She will be waiting at the casino for supper, and he can run his thoughts by her. He smiles as he drives slowly in the snow.

Gregory L. Heitmann

Chapter 33
Notes So Fast

Wednesday evening finds Charlie and Veronica in the bustling crowd of the Dakota Connection Casino Restaurant. The night's burger special is a popular evening treat, and the couple enjoys their burgers as well as discussing details of their day. They both completed their assignments and are anxious to share.

"You go first," Charlie insists.

"Ok," Veronica straightens her laptop on the table in front of her and opens her notebook. "I did as you said. I went to Watertown and made the call." She shakes her head, "No problems on my end." She consults her notebook. "According to my notes it was 2:30 pm when I called." She drums her fingernails on the notebook she holds. "And since I was in Watertown, I stopped and got my nails done." She waggles her fingers.

"Nice," Charlie nods. He smiles. "Like clockwork, I got the records in my office." His smile instantly flips to a frown. "Unfortunately, for both Marvin and us, he really has a broken foot according to the files. So, he's off the suspect list." Charlie leans back in his chair, folds his arms, and looks at the ceiling.

"List? You have a list of suspects?" Veronica questions excitedly.

"That's more of a metaphor. I don't really have a list and not even a suspect now."

Veronica frowns, "What about you? Where'd you go this afternoon?"

"I was over in Britton, basically scratching off the other name on my metaphorical suspect list. There was a guy I went to school with...anyway, he's back in the area. It was a dead end."

The country band Sugarland's song "Want To" plays softly in the dining area.

"Just a coincidence, huh?" Veronica questions. "His being in town?" Veronica writes in her notebook.

Charlie straightens in his chair, squaring himself into perfect posture. He leans forward resting his forearms on the table and interlocking his fingers as he looks at Veronica across from him. "It's a weird deal though. It was like somebody was setting him up to be here. They sent him money, five hundred in cash, and a note that said his mom was sick. This all done anonymously."

"Wow," Veronica's shoulders fall a bit in disbelief. She writes in her notebook again.

"Hey," Charlie raises his voice. "This is always off the record! Stop writing!"

Veronica waves a hand at him. She doesn't look up as she continues to write. "Relax. This is for my book! After you solve the case, I'm going to write a true crime novel about it."

Finally done writing, she looks up at Charlie, who laughs. "I wish I had your confidence in solving the case."

"Rome wasn't built in a day. Piece by piece. You'll get this guy. By the way, based on the info you gave me on the tire tracks, there's ninety percent chance that the truck was a Dodge. You can never be one hundred percent, but all the stats line up with a Dodge half ton." Veronica flips through her notepad again, finding the page. "Yup, Dodge, probably from the last three years."

"Great," Charlie scoffs. "What's that narrow it down to a third of the population of the county?"

"It's something," Veronica provides encouragement. "What are you doing tomorrow?"

Charlie shakes his head, "I'm going to hunt deer in the morning. I have to run over to the BIA regional office in Aberdeen later. I'm picking up some new computer equipment. Why?"

"I was just wondering. Tomorrow's a big day for the paper. We got the final proof of the stories before we go to print..."

Charlie interrupts, "Ooh, that's right. I'm looking forward to your exclusive interview with Nat!"

Veronica blushes, "It includes some nice photos too."

"I can't wait."

Materializing out of the busy restaurant crowd and appearing next to their table, Elliot Koffman is suddenly standing over the couple. "Hi, Elliot. What's up?" Veronica, hand under her chin, asks their guest.

Charlie is also feeling the long day. He rests his elbow on the table, hand holding his chin, similar to his date. When Veronica speaks, it jolts him a bit. He never saw the man approach the table, and he now looks around the restaurant, perusing his surroundings more closely. He picks up his glass of soda in front of him and finishes the last ounce. He looks at the glass before setting it back on the table, pondering the effects of caffeine this late at night.

Elliot looks down, first at Veronica then to Charlie. He smiles an odd smile, "I was just getting some gasoline," he turns his body toward the door and flicks his hand in the general direction of the gas pumps to indicate the location of his vehicle. "I saw the police vehicle and wondered if you were here also." Elliot seems to be bursting with energy, excited.

"Yup, just having a late supper," Veronica responds. "I'll be heading back to the office to join you for the final proof before print."

Elliot is truly bubbly, "It's a big edition with your story. I can't wait." Elliot lifts his hand awkwardly waving. "I guess I'll see you there. Bye." He gives a nod to Charlie and moves toward the exit.

Charlie looks at Veronica. He smiles, shakes his head, and rolls his eyes.

"What?" Veronica intones sharply as she reaches out her hand and places it on Charlie's.

Charlie looks down at his covered hand. "Don't let him see you do that." Charlie gives a nod of his head toward the exit.

"What are you talking about?" Veronica questions lifting Charlie's hand and playfully bumping it down on the table.

"You don't see it?" Charlie laughs the words. "You got yourself a little stalker."

Veronica laughs, "Be quiet!"

"I'm serious," Charlie nods. "Whenever you are with me, boom, there he is. It's amazing. He's definitely got a case on you."

"No! This is just a small town. He's my boss."

"Well, I don't know. I call 'em as I see 'em. I'm going to keep an eye on him...and you." Charlie points two fingers at his eyes with his free hand, then points one finger at Veronica. She playfully slaps his hand.

"Stop it! Are you jealous?"

"Of that guy?" Charlie laughs. "Hardly. What was up with him? He seemed pretty twitchy. Does he take drugs?"

"What is with you? It's twelve hours before press time. This is a journalist's adrenaline high."

Charlie rolls his eyes again. He pushes back from the table. "I'm going to roll. Huntin' tomorrow." Charlie stands and pulls his wallet from his pocket.

"No, no. I'll get it. You keep your money. I still owe you, remember?"

"Ok. Thanks. Do you want me to walk you out?"

"No, go ahead. I've gotta make a couple more notes here before I leave."

Ok. I'll see you tomorrow. You'll be bringing me some extra papers, right?"

Veronica smiles and nods, "Yes. You'll get your papers. Good luck in the morning."

Charlie takes a step toward the exit, but stops. He returns to the table, leans down, and kisses Veronica affectionately on the lips. "Thanks for supper," he whispers in her ear. He straightens and begins to walk away. Veronica is breathless. She watches him move away, mesmerized a moment. Charlie turns back and points a finger at her. "Don't forget those extra copies. I can't wait to read that interview."

Veronica snaps back from her trancelike state; her feelings are noticeably evident on her flushed cheeks. She smiles, nods, and waves to Charlie. Charlie is out the door, and Veronica puts the back of her hand to her cheek. She can feel the heat. She mumbles to herself, "I forgot to wish him good luck tomorrow on his hunt. Or did I?"

The flustered woman shakes her head trying to shuffle her thoughts into order and finish her notes.

Chapter 34
Misprint

Charlie is on his bale stack before sunrise. Several small bucks are out and about in his hour and a half on the stand. However, nothing sporting an interesting set of antlers crosses the cornfields in front of him this morning, and Charlie heads back to the house to get to work.

*   *   *

Charlie checks in with Captain Kipp and is on the road by ten o'clock in the morning. The overcast sky threatens snow as he makes his way west on Highway 10. Through and past Britton he monitors the radios, his police radio, and the local FM stations listening to some country music and weather reports. The wind is blowing from the northwest at a relatively mild ten miles per hour, but still enough to push snow across the road. The drifting snow creates an eerie appearance swirling and curling its way across the charcoal colored highway. The effect is similar to a magician's stunt Charlie saw in a traveling act passing through the casino. He smiles at the sight of a jackrabbit materializing on the highway shoulder and dodging into the ditch, completing the illusion.

Charlie makes the turn on South Dakota Highway 37 and proceeds south. He passes the green mileage sign indicating Groton 23 miles. The highways are in good shape, considering the drifting snow. Charlie decides to travel on the state-maintained routes to Aberdeen, thinking he would time it right for lunch at one of his favorite city spots, Burger King. Who doesn't like charbroiled burgers? Charlie's mind wanders a bit as his stomach reacts to a hunger pang in anticipation of rare fast food. Yes, lunch and then pick up the cargo at the BIA regional office in the federal building. It is a nice easy day, no muss, no fuss.

Charlie contemplates life as a truck driver. "Paid to drive," he says out loud as he scans the fields and trees of prime whitetail country.

Marshall County's border with Brown County is notorious for producing
big bucks. It didn't take long for Charlie to spot one. What he deems as a
"shooter," scampers after a doe across a harvested cornfield to a wide
row of trees. The deer stop and foolishly watch the vehicle pass within a
hundred yards. Charlie laughs. "Of course you see a stupid buck in rut
plain as day when you're not hunting," he says out loud as he slows to get
a good luck at the deer. It is easily twenty inches wide with heavy beams.
Charlie tries to do a quick count of the points and decides it is a four by
five with tall tines. "Definitely a shooter," Charlie nods as he picks up
speed. In twenty minutes he is in Groton and turns west again onto the
four-lane divided roadway, U.S. Highway 12. He sets the cruise on
seventy miles per hour and is dining at Burger King within the half hour.

Charlie times it correctly and is at the BIA regional office right as the
property management supervisor returns from lunch. It takes only twenty
minutes, and Charlie is loaded with gear via the basement parking lot. As
Charlie eases his Tahoe out of the underground parking garage of the
federal building, he feels his phone buzz in his shirt pocket. He pulls over
next to the curb as he digs out his phone. He sees it is Captain Kipp and
answers, "Hey, Skip. What's up?"

Charlie listens carefully, gripping the steering wheel, his knuckles
turning white. His face loses color at first, but his breathing becomes
heavier, and his face reddens in anger.

"What? Are you kidding me?" Charlie shouts into the phone. "In the
Sisseton Chronicle?"

Charlie listens. His open hand pounds down on the steering wheel.
He re-grips the steering wheel. "Who is the story by?"

Charlie shakes his head, "Elliot Koffman and Veronica Lewis. I see."

"Jesus," Charlie's voice is a whisper now. He is in disbelief. "Oh,
geez. Yeah, I'm heading back now."

Charlie listens again. He nods and frowns. "Yeah, yeah. See ya in a
couple hours."

Charlie ends the call. The song "Some Fools Never Learn" by Steve
Wariner plays on the radio, and he stares at the one thirty displayed on
the clock a moment before jabbing the radio tuner button. A local AM
radio news station announcer chuckles softly as he reports, "Surprise,
surprise, more snow on the way." Charlie turns the radio off. He puts the
Tahoe in gear and pulls away from the curb.

He points the vehicle east and mindlessly travels U.S. Highway 12 for
an hour, arriving in Webster. He is shocked to find the miles go by so
quickly. His brain turns over the words Skip shared with him: the Sisseton

Chronicle's lead story links the stolen ATVs to the murders and reveals the investigation's nickname of the killer as "The Deer Slayer." These headlines rattle through his mind. Veronica betrayed him. That is where every thought leads.

Moving from Day County to Marshall County as he travels north on South Dakota Highway 25, out of Webster through Roslyn and Eden, Charlie seethes in anger. Deer move nearly everywhere he looks. "Change in weather," Charlie mumbles to himself as he notes another group of does standing in corn stalks. No snow falls yet, but the clouds look heavy, fighting to hold back their flakes. Any hope Charlie had of getting to the bale stack tonight is out the window. He has only one destination in mind and that is the Chronicle's office to confront Veronica.

Reaching the intersection of Highway 10 and Highway 25 near Lake City, Charlie turns east onto Highway 10, and the snow is finally letting loose. "Three-thirty," Charlie says aloud. "She'll be in her office."

Gregory L. Heitmann

Chapter 35
Headline

It is dark when Charlie LeBeau arrives in Sisseton. His anger still simmers. The headache that popped up a half hour ago throbs, synchronized to his every heartbeat. Charlie drives by the Sisseton Chronicle Publishing Office on Main Street. The BIA police computers he is carrying would have to wait for delivery. He glances out his Tahoe window as he passes slowly down the street. He spies Veronica, alone in the office. The large store front windows of the former flower shop turned newspaper office allow the cool fluorescent lights to spill onto the street and sidewalk. Charlie decides to take another trip around the block to gather his thoughts. "I'm pretty sure she's by herself," Charlie mumbles to himself as he takes a series of four right turns around the block arriving back on Main Street. He parks the Tahoe in the diagonal parking opposite the newspaper office. He adjusts his driver's side outside mirror with the power buttons and watches Veronica, still trying to sort through his anger.

Inside the newspaper office, Veronica sits in front of her computer as she has done for the better part of the day. The computer is on and projects a glow across her worried face. It had been a long day. When the first stacks of papers were delivered to the office, she had to sit down in a chair as she saw the headline. The thrill of seeing her interview with Nat was blown away. She was too scared to call Charlie. She knew he'd find her. Veronica waited to confront Elliot as she wondered what had happened. It was obvious what had happened after she had given it a few minutes of thought. All her notes she had typed on her laptop were synched to the server when she set her machine in her docking station. This was an automatic file backup system in case of a computer crash. It was only now that she realized that all her files were exposed to everyone at the newspaper when they were backed up on the server's hard drive.

Veronica was prepared to make her case to Charlie, not if, but when he showed up.

Veronica's mind is far away as she chews on a fingernail when the door chimes as Charlie enters. She stands quickly with her hands up. Her mouth opens but no words immediately come out. It is Charlie that raises his voice first pointing an accusing finger, "How could you?"

Veronica moves toward Charlie, crossing the room slowly, her arms out in front to cushion the words. "How dare you!" Charlie shouts. His anger crests in a wave. He literally sees red as he stares at Veronica. Everything has a tinge of red as his heart races, and he slams a newspaper on the desk between Veronica and himself.

The newspaper headline is about an inch tall and reports: "POLICE TIE STOLEN SNOWMOBILES TO MURDERS."

"How could you do this to me?" Charlie shouts the question as he stares through Veronica.

A smaller headline with half inch script is an inset story under the main headline reading: *"AUTHORITIES HAVE NO SUSPECTS; TWO LOCALS CLEARED IN WHAT POLICE CALL 'DEER SLAYER' MURDERS."*

Veronica stands opposite the desk between her and Charlie. The newspapers blanket the desktop. "Listen, Charlie, I didn't have anything to do with this."

Charlie extends his accusing finger toward Veronica. Veronica clasps her hands together, begging with hands and eyes for Charlie to understand. Charlie shakes his head and wags his finger, "I trusted you." Charlie's words are slow and calm. "All this was off the record." Charlie turns his back and makes his way to the door.

It is Veronica shouting now, "Charlie, wait! You have to believe me!" Veronica follows Charlie to the door and outside. She yells one more plea as Charlie opens the door to his Tahoe and climbs in. Before he shuts the door Veronica shouts, "Please let me try to explain!"

Her voice echoes in the cold night off the surrounding buildings before being squelched by the Tahoe's engine firing to life. Charlie glances quickly toward Veronica, seeing the pathetic woman standing on the cold street. The vehicle is in gear, and he pulls away.

Chapter 36
Sniper

The weekend arrives, and Saturday morning Charlie and Nat sit atop Charlie's favorite bale stack along the edge of the cornfield to their south and directly adjacent to a woody finger draw to their north. This ephemeral stream, populated with young oaks and maples, eventually drains into Long Hollow. This drainage is a natural corridor for deer, turkey, and other game animals. The pair of hunters scans their surroundings with binoculars under an overcast sky. It is cold and damp. The forecast remains consistent, cold and cloudy with a better than fifty percent chance of snow showers. It's been the same every day since last week. Nat lowers his binoculars and sits with his back against the top bale. His rifle lies atop the bale stack. He shivers a bit and braces against the bale seeking warmth. Charlie continues to glass the area, hoping for a deer. "Sure would like to at least fill your grandpa's doe tag before we head back," Charlie finally offers quietly.

"Where in the heck are all the deer?" Nat questions discouragingly.

Charlie doesn't answer. He shrugs and shakes his head and looks further to the north in the next finger draw, hoping for a glimpse of a deer. Nat looks up at his uncle, "So what's the deal with you and Ms. Lewis? You're not seeing each other anymore?"

Charlie stares though his binoculars and answers, "Nope."

"She keeps calling the house."

Charlie steadily pivots as he scans the area in a three hundred sixty degree rotation, "I know."

"She's nice," Nat mumbles.

"Yeah," Charlie responds.

A herd of ten deer race out of the trees west of the hunters' bale stack and head northwest. "Hey," Charlie grunts. "There's about ten does and fawns coming toward us."

Nat is on his feet and reaching for his rifle. The deer cross the snow covered cornfield on the other side of the adjacent finger draw. Nat and Charlie both shoulder their rifles and swing with a deer. With the trees as a shield and running at full speed, neither hunter is afforded a shot as the deer pass at about one hundred and fifty yards. In a few more seconds the deer are fully into the next draw, disappearing into the woody coverage of the drainage. "What the heck?" Nat ponders aloud as he lowers his rifle, setting it atop the bale stack. "What the heck scared them?"

Charlie holds up a gloved finger, "Listen."

Intermixed in the breeze, just at the threshold of hearing, there is a murmur. It is a small engine. The engine of a snowmobile whines, moving at low speed to the west of their bale stack. The men stare in the direction of the sound. "A snowmobile," Nat whispers. "A snowmobile coming down along the edge of the coulee? Kicked up the deer I bet."

Charlie's eyes narrow as he looks at his nephew. "Nobody but you and I have permission to hunt here."

Charlie sets his rifle down across the top bale of the stack. He pulls his binoculars to his eyes and stares in the direction of the sound. The jumble of trees rising from the coulee blocks his view. The whir of the snowmobile engine cuts out, and Charlie pinpoints the noise, but sees nothing through the branches of the trees. Nat looks through the trees with his naked eyes. He is nervous, unconsciously holding his breath, staring and straining to listen. "I think I see somebody moving over there," Charlie states in a whispered monotone.

Charlie's eyes twitch as he glares through the binoculars' lenses. He sees a man in snow camouflage for a moment moving through the trees. Nat stands with his binoculars aligned with where his uncle looks. "I don't see 'im," Nat states.

Charlie lowers his field glasses for a moment, "I think he dropped down. Down in the bottom of the draw."

Nat lowers his optics and looks toward his uncle, "He's probably stalking a big buck right out from under us."

Charlie nods. "I didn't get a good look," he whispers. "He wasn't wearing his hunter orange. I didn't even catch a glimpse of any rifle for that matter."

A couple minutes pass. Charlie grips his binoculars tightly as he scans the area intently. He is looking up at an elevation slightly higher than the hunters' position on the bale stack. He finally sees something. Two hundred yards from where he last spotted the man, he sees a glint of light. In a split second Charlie makes out the outline of what looks like a ghost. It is a man in all-white camouflage. A white rifle is jammed in the fork of a tree. It was the glint of the scope lens that caught Charlie's eye, and now he is looking down the barrel of a rifle.

"Get down!" Charlie shouts, leaping toward his nephew.

Charlie pushes Nat off the bale stack, and Nat, caught by surprise, falls awkwardly onto the lower layer of bales, bounces off this level and lands in a snowdrift that cushions his fall. Charlie hears Nat's grunting "Oof" twice, once when he ricocheted off the bales, then again plowing into snow.

Immediately there is the zing of a bullet ripping through the air overhead, quickly followed by the report of the rifle. Another zing and crack along with the echoing roar of a follow up rifle shot.

Charlie is already ducking behind the bale stack when he is pummeled with splinters on another shot. The third shot from the sniper's rifle has found the wooden stock of Nat's bolt action Remington. Charlie crawls under the protection of the bales to where he was previously positioned. He blindly reaches his arm up and feels for his rifle on the top of the stack. Locating the sling, he drags the rifle to him. Inching his way to the edge of the bales, he peers around the corner of the stack. Moving his rifle into position, he fires two quick shots in the direction of where he last envisioned the sniper's location.

"Nat!" Charlie calls out. He stuffs two cartridges into his rifle and peers around the corner of the bale stack again, rifle ready. Through the scope he catches movement and pulls the trigger, works the bolt, and pulls the trigger again.

The shots' echoes resonate and die away. "Nat! Are you ok?"

Charlie digs for more bullets in his jacket pocket, but remembers he has an elastic cartridge holder on the stock of his rifle. He reloads and scans the coulee for any movement. There is nothing and he turns his attention to the base of the bale stack. He jumps down from his row of bales and slides down the bottom row of bales to the ground. Shielded from the sniper he kneels next to Nat. Nat is grimacing in pain and rolling with much difficulty, pinned in the snow drift. Nat's eyes are pinched closed and tears stream from their corners. "Nat!" Charlie grips Nat's jacket.

"Uhh," Nat gasps. "My ribs." He fights for his breath, gasping. "I got the wind knocked out of me. Corner of the bale, right to ribs." Nat's eyes blink open, "Uhhhhh," he groans and grunts trying to recover his breathing.

Charlie reaches behind his back and plucks his service weapon from his holster. He hands it to Nat. He lifts Nat up by the front of his jacket causing the boy to gasp and creating a coughing spell. "Are you hit?"

"Uhhhhh," Nat groans and shakes his head.

Charlie pushes his nephew into a gap in the bales to another groan from the boy. "Burrow into the bales and don't move until I come get you!" Charlie's words are a hissing whisper. "You know how to use that pistol?"

Nat nods. Straining he wriggles into the loose hay in a gap in the bottom row of bales. Charlie points a finger at his nephew, "Do not move!" he orders sternly.

The roar of snowmobile engine at full throttle pierces the air. Charlie runs for his old pickup truck, rifle in hand. He dashes toward the truck, picking up the speeding snowmobile shrouded partially by the trees in the coulee. Three hundred yards later, Charlie is at his truck sucking for air. In his truck, rifle out the window, Charlie floors the accelerator and steers the truck down the drifted-in section road trying to get around the trees of the drainage to see if he can spot the snowmobile. The rifle bounces out of control as the truck bangs and surges through snow and ruts. Charlie stashes the weapon, barrel down on the floor, braced in the gap of the split bench seat. The four wheel drive truck bogs down in the snow, and plows forward too slowly for Charlie's liking. He peels off the section road, instead choosing to cut across the wind blown open field of corn cut for silage. He can make up some ground across the frozen black soil and he does, pinning the accelerator to the floor. Angling across the barren areas, Charlie zig-zags keeping his head on a swivel, looking first for the snowmobile and then in front of his truck to avoid snow drifts. There it is. A half mile north of him still partially quartering away, Charlie sees the snowmobile cruising. Puffs of snow form around the drift busting machine. Charlie's path finally intersects the county road, and he guns his old truck and gives it a pat on the dash, "You can do this," Charlie whispers encouragement to his truck. Through the snow packed ditch, the truck loses almost all of its momentum, but Charlie is able to urge the truck onto the gravel surface and spin the tires to get going north towards the sniper escaping on the snowmobile. He guns the engine, and the truck picks up speed on the snowy gravel road. The gap is closing, and Charlie leans forward as he has a full view of the snowmobile in the open, racing across a winter wheat field that shows its own bald patches having been wind blown, exposing some of next year's currently dormant crop. The snowmobile cuts diagonally across the snow covered surfaces.

Something doesn't look right to Charlie. He strains to keep the truck on the washboard section of road while trying to keep an eye on his target. A grove of trees in a low area of the wheat field that drains into the coulee blocks Charlie's view for a moment. Charlie slows hoping to get a glimpse of the snowmobile again. He sees a cloud of snow before he sees the machine top a low swale in the field. He punches the gas and looks down the road trying to calculate the intercepting point where the snowmobile will cross the road.

The snow machine bounces wildly across the drifts in the field. Charlie slams on his brakes and slides to a halt on the gravel road. He looks on in disbelief, mouth agape. He cocks his head trying to make sure he is seeing what he is seeing. The snowmobile is going to cross the road within twenty five yards of his truck, but behind him now. The driverless snowmobile skims over the ditch and hits the shoulder of the road launching into the air. It tumbles and crashes into the oak trees bordering the coulee on the east side of the county road. Charlie shakes his head as he exits his vehicle, but not before grabbing his rifle and shouldering it; his brow is deeply furrowed as he scans the area and slowly approaches the screaming engine of the snowmobile. The battered machine has thrown its track, and the engine roars unabated. Charlie keeps an eye out, turning in every direction and screening himself against trees as he approaches the machine. He finally arrives at the snowmobile and is convinced he is alone. He reaches and presses the kill switch on the Arctic Cat, and the engine dies. Charlie observes the liberal use of duct tape wound around the handle bars of the snowmobile. Somebody had sent this vehicle out as a decoy, like a rabbit on the run to divert his attention, and the ploy had worked. "But why?" Charlie mumbles to himself, puzzled.

In an instant he is in full panic mode; he bolts for his truck, one hand on his rifle the other hand in his shirt pocket grasping for his phone as he digs his feet into the snow and gravel on the road to get to his truck.

He dials Captain Kipp. Out of breath as he reaches his truck, he gasps into his phone, "Hey, Skip. How fast can you get to my house? It's an emergency!"

Gregory L. Heitmann

Chapter 37
Recovery Operation

Charlie is breathless as he reaches his truck. "I need you there," he huffs into the phone. "As soon as possible." Charlie listens for a moment as Captain Kipp replies. Tossing his rifle onto the passenger seat and firing up the truck, Charlie pleads, "Just hurry."

Flipping his phone onto the seat next to his rifle, Charlie spins his truck around and floors it. The anxiety is crushing. Is this a diversion to take him away from his house, maybe to get to his father or Nat? The questions in his mind add fuel to his exertion of running back to the truck. His windshield steams from his breath, and he flicks the fan on high. He wipes at the inside of the glass with his hand, forming dripping streaks across his vision. The sun is attempting to burn through the clouds, and the sky lightens for a moment before giving way to the clouds and a few stray snowflakes. The first two miles down the gravel county road pass, and Charlie has to slow to make the right hand turn to the driveway. He was less than four miles away, but it might as well have taken an eternity to get to his house.

The truck slides in his snowy driveway before coming to a stop. Charlie looks strangely at the other car in his driveway. It is Veronica, and she timidly exits her vehicle as Charlie sprints by her, up the steps of the trailer, and flings open the door. He yells inside, "Dad!" as he stands in the doorway.

"What?" Claude replies a moment later.

It's a moment of relief as he finds his father is unharmed. Charlie slams the door shut and is off the stairs, hustling back to his truck, driver's door open, and engine still running. Veronica is in his path, and he points a finger at her. "Get out of my way! Get out of here! I don't have time to talk to you!"

Veronica is frightened by Charlie's demeanor, and she backs out of his way. Charlie passes her and reaches his truck. "Charlie, please! It was Elliot. He got to my files on my computer. He stole my notes!"

Charlie has one foot in his truck, and he hangs on the door. He points his finger at her again, "I don't have time to hear this." His voice is calm and low. "Somebody just took some shots at me and Nat on the bales this morning. Please...I have to go."

Veronica is moving forward, toward Charlie. She is wide-eyed as she listens. "Are you hurt?" Veronica is at the truck's door, holding her hand on top of Charlie's.

Charlie wrenches the door and his hand free as he gets in the driver's seat. "Just go inside and wait. I got to go get Nat." Charlie slams the door shut, puts the truck in gear, and spins out of the driveway down the snowy section road. The truck plows through the track from this morning until it hits the undisturbed snow. The truck bogs down as it travels the last quarter mile to the bale stack.

Charlie pulls the truck next to the stack of bales. He does not see anything and his heart skips a beat. It is either good or bad...Nat is still hunkered down in the bales, or he's gone. Charlie flings the door open and yells, "Nat!" Stepping from the truck he sees the top of Nat's orange stocking cap rise from in between the bales. A weight is lifted from Charlie, and he can breathe. His shallow breaths are replaced with a deep sigh.

Nat groans as he struggles from the bales and through the snow. Charlie is scrambling up the bales as Nat moves to the passenger side of the truck. Charlie is atop the bales and snatches Nat's splintered rifle. He shakes his head in disbelief as he slides down the bale stack and back to the truck. Climbing into the truck he sets the battered rifle between the seats and next to his. He looks at his nephew, sitting awkwardly avoiding the rifles while straining to protect his ribs. Nat has his left hand on his abdomen, and in his right hand he holds Charlie's pistol. Nat's eyes are fixed on the broken stock of his rifle. Nat blindly hands the weapon back to Charlie, "Did you get him?" He extends his hand and feels the splintered wooden stock of the weapon.

Charlie shakes his head and frowns, "You ok?"

"I been better," Nat manages a weak smile and rolls his eyes, finally meeting his uncle's gaze.

"Let's get back to the house," Charlie quietly and assuredly whispers.

*　　*　　*

Veronica watched as Charlie tore down the two-rut track, the trail invisible except for the defined pattern of the morning's tracks. She turned and proceeded up the steps to the trailer. Inside, Veronica moved to the kitchen, her hands were shaking. Charlie's reaction and behavior frightened her. She found a glass and filled it with water at the sink. From the back room a voice called, "Charlie? Nat? Did you get my deer?"

Veronica screamed and dropped the glass on the floor. The glass bounced off the linoleum but did not break. Water puddled on the floor, and Veronica grabbed a dishrag and dropped down to sop up the spill. Claude stepped from his bedroom to the living room peering into the kitchen curiously. Still in his robe, he asked loudly, "Who's here?" Claude looked and saw no one at first, then Veronica was back on her feet, popping up from behind the counter, causing Claude to jump back and grab at his chest. "Jiminy Christmas! Who are you?" Claude looked at the stranger.

"Oh, my God, you scared me. I didn't know anybody was here," Veronica held her hand over her heart. "Charlie's out there...I dropped this glass...and..."

Claude holds up a finger cutting Veronica's rambling off, "Oh, you're Charlie's friend, the reporter. I'm Claude. I'm Charlie's dad. We met at the game."

A car door slammed outside, and Claude moved toward the window. He rotated the handle for the blind and opened it. He peered out the window. "Skip's here." Claude turned to Veronica, "What the heck is going on?"

Skip moved up the steps and was about to knock as Claude opened the door, "Hey, Skip," Claude called out, welcoming the guest. "Come on in. What are you doing here?"

The grave look on Skip's face told the story, and Veronica moved forward into the living room from the kitchen. "Where's Charlie?" Skip asked frowning.

"He went to get Nat." Veronica walked slowly into the room.

Skip noticed Veronica for the first time and flinched a bit, "Veronica? Why are you here?"

The trio was interrupted by the roar of Charlie's old truck pulling into the driveway. More questions than answers were to follow.

Gregory L. Heitmann

Chapter 38
Dawn

Skip, Claude, and Veronica stand silently watching through the front window. Charlie and Nat are in the truck a moment conversing. The doors open. Nat gingerly, slowly eases his door wide open and steps down from the truck. He is hunched to one side, and his left hand still holds his ribs. He lurches forward leaning to the left as he moves toward the steps of the trailer. Charlie's door is open, but he remains in the driver's seat. He works the bolt action rifle running the cartridges out of Nat's weapon before stepping down from the old pickup. He shuts the door and catches up to Nat, who is climbing one step at a time, holding the railing for added leverage. Finally, Nat and Charlie make it through the front door and into the living room where Skip, Claude, and Veronica anxiously await.

"What in the world is going on?" Skip demands.

Nat, still bent to the left as a damaged ship would list on the water speaks up, "Uncle Charlie pushed me off the bale stack." A wry smile curls Nat's lips.

The danger now passed, Charlie can smile and produce a small laugh. Charlie hands the damaged rifle to Skip. "Somebody was having a bad morning and decided to take a pot shot at us."

Skip carefully traces his finger over the splintered stock accompanied by a look of complete befuddlement. "Holy, cow," he whispers. He emits a low whistle as his hand retracts from the sharp edges.

"Some clown outfitted in white camouflage rolled up on us on a snowmobile," Charlie begins.

Nat injects himself into Charlie's story, "We didn't hear him right away. We saw some does running across the cornfield, and we were trying to figure out what scared them."

"Then we heard it," Charlie nods and takes over the story again. "The snowmobile engine, just for a moment. Then it was cut off."

Veronica steps forward, "Come here, Nat. Let's sit you down."

Veronica leads Nat to the couch, and Charlie continues the story. "I saw some movement; then a couple minutes later, the sun was trying to break through, and I caught a glimmer of light off what was the shooter's scope. Everything was white. His rifle was wrapped in white tape. I just happen to catch the glint off the scope when he was aiming at us."

"Yeah," Nat smiles again. "That's when he pushed me off the bales. I didn't bounce too good. Messed up my ribs, got the wind knocked out of me." Nat wheezes a bit.

Veronica puts a comforting hand on Nat's shoulder to sympathize.

"Tshhh," Charlie's tongue clicks. "Next thing I know, zing! Zing! Bullets are flying over us, and one drills Nat's rifle stock. It was on top of the bale stack." Charlie shakes his head, "I fired a couple rounds in the sniper's direction before I checked on Nat and then heard the snowmobile take off." Charlie points at Nat, "I stashed 'im in the bales and tried to give chase with my truck." Charlie makes a move toward the door. "Come on, Skip. You gotta see this."

"What?" Claude demands. "What the heck happened? You're not just walking outta here. Tell us what happened."

Charlie's head snaps back to the story, "Oh, yeah. There was nobody on the snowmobile. It was rigged to go full throttle away from us. And I was meant to chase it, and I did. It was a diversion. When I realized that, I about hyperventilated trying to get back to the house and Nate. I thought maybe he was coming for you guys." Charlie points a finger back and forth between Claude and Nat.

"You didn't get a look at 'em," Skip states matter-of-factly.

"Dressed all in white. White face mask. Couldn't see. It happened so fast," Charlie shakes his head.

"Come on, Skip. Let's go," Charlie waves his hand toward the door. "It's gotta be the Deer Slayer. Same M.O. Diversion tactics with a plan. He goes into the details," Charlie sneers. "But, he didn't make the shot."

Veronica rushes forward and grabs Charlie's arm, "Wait, Charlie. Please. I need to talk to you. In private. Just two minutes."

Charlie looks down at his sleeve and the woman's hand gripping his coat. For the first time today he actually sees the details of Veronica's face. There is a connection and a realization that he does have feelings for this woman. Charlie's eyes travel the rest of the room, meeting everybody else's eyes as they await an answer to Veronica's plea. Charlie nods and pulls Veronica to his bedroom and shuts the door.

*　　*　　*

In the bedroom Charlie unzips his coat; he is warm from the exertion and now standing around in the heated house. Hands on hips, pushing his coat back he speaks, "You got two minutes, but I'm telling you now; I'm still mad at you." He points a finger at Veronica. She stands near the foot of the bed, and Charlie stands next to the door. His left hand moves from his hip to the door handle, threatening to open the door at any moment. Veronica's eyes focus on his hand on the door knob, and she begins speaking quickly. "You have to believe me. It was Elliot. He wrote those articles. He got access to my backup files on the server. My laptop automatically backs up the files when I connect it. You know, just insurance to protect my notes. I never even gave it a second thought that anyone would be snooping in my stuff." Veronica takes a breath. She can see a slight nod from Charlie as her explanation sinks in. "I've waited around that office for the last four days to yell at him and tell him 'I quit,' but he's a no-show. The gutless creep has just disappeared."

Charlie's brow furrows. Veronica shakes her head in disgust.

"Oh," Veronica scoffs, "Does he think the paper is going to put itself out. I'm sure not doing anything. He's gone. Nobody's heard from him. I went by his house looking for him. Snow on the driveway. It's like he's skipped town. "I can't believe he got my notes off the computer," Veronica heaves a deep sigh of disgust. "What does it matter? Ah, what does it matter," she repeats. "Even if I would have locked my computer files, Elliot is some sort of computer whiz. If he wanted my files he could have gotten them. He used to be Army Intelligence is what he told me. He was in the first Desert Storm. He knows all kinds of computer stuff." She rambles, speaking a-mile-a-minute. "The point is... I'm sorry. I had no idea. I reviewed all the Chronicle's pages Wednesday night before they were going to the printer, and the next morning...all different. Dang it." Veronica grinds her teeth in anger, "I should have been more careful with my notes."

Charlie is frowning. His frown turns into a scowl. "Whoa. Wait a minute. What did you say? Elliot was in the Army?"

"Yeah, why?" Veronica cocks her head.

It's like a blinding light hits Charlie. He looks toward the ceiling. His hands go up, palms skyward, elbows bent, hands rising to shoulder height. "It's him. It's gotta be him."

Charlie moves to Veronica and puts his hands on her shoulders. He looks into her eyes and smiles. He kisses her on the mouth and bolts out the bedroom door. Veronica puts her hand to her mouth as she hears Charlie cry out, "Skip! Hey, Skip"

She touches her lips and whispers to herself, "What just happened?"

Chapter 39
The Scheme

Skip and Charlie load themselves into the Captain's Tahoe, and Charlie directs his boss to the location of the wrecked snowmobile. "Could this be just an accident? " Skip questions. "Could this guy just been shootin' at those does, and you guys got caught in the crossfire?"

Charlie grunts, "Are you kidding me? That guy was trying to pick me or Nat off that bale stack." Charlie shakes his head, "Otherwise, why would he send out a decoy snowmobile afterwards?"

The policemen arrive at the location of the abandoned machine and inspect the Arctic Cat now destined for the scrap yard. "I can't believe this," Skip comments. "We probably shouldn't even bother with this piece of junk." Skip holds up his gloved hand, and snowflakes blanket his palm quickly. The clouds overpower the efforts of the sun, and the snow begins to fall as the winds slowly increase and swing to the northwest. "Why are we standing here? We should be going over to where you first saw him and track from there."

Charlie leans against a tree scarred by the flying snow machine and its rough landing. He doesn't say anything. His eyes are fixed on the snowmobile as his mind grinds through the morning's events. "Did you hear me?" Skip throws the question toward Charlie.

"Hmm?" Charlie grunts not listening.

"I said," Skip repeats loudly and slowly, "do you think we ought to backtrack from where you saw the shooter? Are you even listening? Geez, Charlie, you barely said two words to me since we got in the truck to drive over here, and those words were 'turn here.' What's going on with you?"

"I'm sorry," Charlie apologizes and pushes himself away from the large ash tree. "Forget about the tracks. We've probably already lost any chance of that strategy with this weather." Charlie flips a hand skyward.

"But, I do have an idea. Let me run something by you. You know I had my theory about the Deer Slayer being former military, right?"

Skip nods, "I remember."

"Veronica told me back at the trailer that Elliot is missing. Gone for the last few days. Nobody has seen or heard from him, and he's supposed to be getting next Thursday's paper started."

Yeah," Skip frowns, "paper is a full time job and more."

"Veronica also told me something else," Charlie puts his hands on his hips as he steps forward and kicks at the bent right ski of the snowmobile. "Something far more interesting about Elliot."

"What's that?" Skip brushes the gathering snow from the sleeves of his jacket.

"Elliot was in the army during Desert Storm. She told me that he was in an intel unit, and that's where he got his computer skills."

"Huh," Skip grunts then laughs loudly. "That explains the newspaper stories then." Skip laughs and interrupts himself. "Her boss hacked her computer and got her notes."

"That's about the gist of it," Charlie smiles. "But you're missing the bigger picture. I think our guy was in the military." Charlie pauses and lets the words sink in before continuing, "Elliot was in the military. Does anybody even know this guy?"

"Huh?" Captain Kipp's face scrunches, "You're saying you think the Deer Slayer is Elliot?"

Charlie shrugs, "Yeah, I guess I am."

"You got any proof?"

"No physical evidence...," Charlie points a finger at Skip, "...yet. I got plenty up here," Charlie points to his head, "that leads me to conclude he's our guy."

Skip laughs again. "This seems like a reach. I have no idea where you're going with this."

"Oh," Charlie retorts quickly. "I got a plan."

"Let's go," Skip takes a couple steps in the snow toward his Tahoe. "I'll call Ernie to come out and pick up our snowmobile and have him put it in our yard as evidence."

"Yeah, we can wait in the truck for Ernie. I'll share my scheme with you," Charlie smiles and nods as he starts to plod through the snow-packed ditch back to the road. "You know," Charlie continues. "Scheme sounds shady. I'll share my plan, no...strategy. That's what it is. I got a strategy on getting a better look at my suspect."

"Lay it on me, Sherlock," Skip laughs sarcastically.

Chapter 40
Warrant

Monday morning brings a new work week; and the plan, concocted by Charlie, lurches into action. Veronica informed Charlie that Sunday morning Elliot had called over and over, begging for help on the paper. Elliot had explained that his mother had been ill. He had to make an emergency run to the Twin Cities to see to her care. That is why he was out of contact. He apologized in voicemail after voicemail in regards to her notes. He justified the stories as a necessity of public interest and transparency. Charlie had hoped this would happen, and he had counseled Veronica to bite her tongue and go into work as if all was forgiven. This is phase one of what has been dubbed as Charlie's Strategy.

Veronica rides in Charlie's Tahoe as they make a reconnaissance pass by the newspaper office. Monday morning and Main Street is bustling at nine o'clock a.m. "He's there," Charlie notes as they drive north on Main Street. The radio plays softly; it is Sonny James singing "Young Love," and Charlie turns the volume even lower to a barely audible level as he smiles at his passenger.

Veronica is nervous. She fidgets in her seat. "I saw him." She looks straight ahead and chews on a fingernail.

"Are you up to this?" Charlie questions as his brow furrows.

"I don't know if I can keep my cool," Veronica glances at Charlie a moment before returning her gaze to the view in front of the vehicle. "I'm so mad about this whole deal."

"Well, tell me now. We can abort the whole thing if you want. Once we start he's probably going to catch on pretty quick." Charlie shakes his head, "All I want is to confiscate his computer."

"Do you really think he's the guy?" Veronica questions in disbelief even after a weekend of Charlie convincing her of the circumstantial evidence, or as Veronica called it, pure speculation.

"Depending on how he reacts when the police grab his computer will be the final clue as far as I'm concerned." Veronica fidgets more in her seat. Charlie frowns. "You want to call it off?"

"No!"

Charlie jumps back from Veronica's shout. "Do you want to go over the plan again?"

"I got it," Veronica forces a smile.

"You sure you got it?"

"I got it. I got it!" Veronica raises her voice again.

"Are you positive you can do this?" Charlie prods one too many times.

"For the love of Pete! I'm good to go!" she shouts, scowling at her driver.

The trip by the building leads Charlie and Veronica a few blocks away to her parked car near the nursing home. "I can do this, Charlie. I've already lied to Elliot on the phone. I was glad we exposed the truth in the paper. Nice lie by me, huh?" Veronica rolls her eyes. "I just...it's just that it is one thing to talk to him on the phone versus being next to him in person." Veronica shivers. "It makes my skin crawl to think of the things he's done to people if he is the killer."

"Don't think about that. Just think about getting his computer. Say whatever you need to say to borrow his computer for a moment. Say your internet doesn't work, and you need to check something real quick, as long as you're sitting using his computer, we'll get it." Charlie shrugs, "I'll give you ten minutes; I'll come in with our fake warrant, arrest you, and take 'your' computer." Charlie puts air quotes around the word "your." He laughs a bit, "I'll play it up real big on obstruction of justice charges. Get the cuffs on you. It's gonna work." Charlie nods and smiles like a small child anticipating Santa's arrival.

Veronica can't help but smile at the man's enthusiasm. For the first time today she relaxes. "Ok," she finally sighs while whispering the word.

Charlie leans over and kisses her cheek. "I promise you; it's gonna run like clockwork."

"Yeah," Veronica smirks, "like your old, run down cuckoo clock at your house."

"Ouch," Charlie flinches. "That reminds me of something. Let me just say I'm sorry in advance."

"Sorry?" Veronica cocks her head. "Sorry for what?"

"The handcuffs," Charlie tries to remain stoic, but his lips can't fight the smile. "The cuffs are going to hurt. I want to make sure Elliot sees this as real as possible. And he'll be your knight in shining armor, but mostly he'll want his computer back."

Veronica shrugs and shakes her head, "Do what you gotta do."

"Well, what are you waiting for?" Charlie asks.

Veronica pulls on the door handle and exits. "See you in a bit." She gives a head nod as she shuts the Tahoe door. Charlie gives her a little wave as she moves to her car.

Gregory L. Heitmann

Chapter 41
The Ploy

In a minute or two after pulling away from the nursing home, Veronica is parking her car on Main Street in front of the Sisseton Chronicle's office. She enters the building and locks eyes with her boss. "Ah, you're back," Elliot sips his coffee. Veronica, without so much as an inkling of an expression to read on her face, stands in the doorway staring at the man. "Come on in," Elliot invites.

Veronica wags a finger at the man, "I'm still mad at you. You stole my story."

"You'll get over it," Elliot waves a hand. "You know it was for the public good."

"That's the only reason I'm back. The bottom line is information for the readers." Veronica nods at her statement and steps to her desk.

"You workin' on anything?" Elliot questions.

"Corman's family lost a barn to a fire," Veronica replies scooting up to her desk and setting up her computer.

"Hmmph," Elliot sips his coffee again. He stands over the layout table looking over ads on a paper template. "Any photos?"

"Photo of the aftermath. Audrey Jenkins sent me some. I'll show you once I get my e-mail up."

"Come on," Veronica mumbles under breath. She presses keys on her keyboard dramatically. "Dang it! Elliot, you mind if I use your computer to get on the internet? Some update won't let me log in."

"Go ahead."

Veronica moves from her desk to Elliot's. She moves the mouse, and the computer comes to life. She smiles, knowing that she's moments away from the big show. Elliot laughs. "We had a good week last week," he laughs again shuffling the papers in front of him, arranging rectangular blocks where the ads are to be placed. "We sold out. Our big story in the last edition...amazing, people scooped up all the copies. I added four more pages just for ad sales this week."

"You mean my stories?" Veronica voices her question with a heap of sarcasm. "Between my interview with Nat and the notes from the murder, I'd say that I sold a lot of papers." She heavily emphasizes the word "I."

Elliot smiles broadly and laughs. He throws up his hands in surrender, "You're right."

His smile turns to a frown as Charlie barges through the door with a commotion. With long slow strides he moves toward Veronica at the computer. He raises his arm deliberately and points a finger at the woman. "All right, everyone stay where you are. You, Ms. Lewis, back away from that computer. I have a warrant for your arrest. Obstructing an investigation." Charlie digs a piece of paper from his pocket.

Veronica's eyes widen, "Are you kidding me? You've never heard of the first amendment?"

Charlie moves up to Veronica. She sits motionless in front of the computer. He brandishes the paper in front of her, towering over the woman. Elliot takes a step forward toward Charlie, "Whoa, hold on, Charlie?"

Charlie holds up a finger, "Sorry, Elliot. Just stay where you are. I don't want to have to arrest you too." Charlie turns his attention back to Veronica. "Stand up, Ms. Lewis. Stand up and put your hands behind your back."

"No," Veronica pouts her lips and shakes her head refusing to move. She crosses her arms in defiance.

Charlie stows the paper back into his pocket, nonchalantly tucking it away. In the blink of an eye, he grabs a hold of Veronica's arm, pulls her up, and in a smooth motion bends her over the desk one wrist cuffed. Her other falls to the will of Charlie as she is too surprised to react, and her wrists are joined in the steel bracelets firmly cinched behind her back. "Thank you for not resisting. You don't want another charge against you."

"What the hell?" Elliot takes another step towards Charlie who puts his right hand on his pistol while his left hand holds a firm grip on Veronica's arm.

"Elliot," Charlie calmly calls his name, "I told you not to move."

"Veronica, don't' say a word," Elliot's voice cracks as panic creeps into his thoughts. "Don't worry; I'm calling my lawyer right now!"

Charlie pushes down the screen on Elliot's laptop in front of Veronica. "We'll be taking your computer too, Ms. Lewis. It's in the warrant."

Elliot leaps forward, another step closer to Charlie. Charlie draws his weapon and holds it pointing at the floor. "Elliot, I'm not going to repeat myself. Stay back."

"That's my computer!" Elliot shouts, pointing at the machine. "You can't take that computer! She was borrowing my computer!"

Charlie disconnects the cords connected to the computer and clicks the laptop closed. "You can tell it to the judge. It's in the warrant, and she was sitting at the computer. I would say that's her computer. Move," Charlie pulls on Veronica's arm, holsters his pistol, and scoops up the computer as he moves toward the door.

"You can't do this!" Elliot shouts. "That is my computer, not hers!"

Charlie halts and cocks his head as he looks pathetically at the frothing man. "You think I'm a fool, Elliot? I saw her on this computer."

Elliot bolts to the doorway and blocks Charlie's path to the exit. He extends a shaking finger, pointing it at Charlie, "I'm serious. You can not take that computer. This is a clear violation of the freedom of the press."

Charlie shakes his head. His words are low and slow, "I have another set of cuffs. Step back or you can join Ms. Lewis."

Elliot thinks better of his actions and steps to the nearest desk, "I'm calling my lawyer right now!" He digs his cell phone from his pants pocket. He reaches into his shirt pocket and pulls out a pair of reading glasses as he scrolls through his phone, "Do not say anything, Veronica!" he shouts at the door closing behind Charlie.

Gregory L. Heitmann

Chapter 42
The Accused

In the back of the Tahoe, Veronica's adrenaline still courses through her body. Still cuffed, she sits wide-eyed, but now smiling like a madwoman. "You were something else," she chirps, catching Charlie's eye in the rearview mirror. "I was convinced I was being arrested. You play a very convincing cop."

Charlie smiles, "Thank you. I like your irony. You realize I'm actually a cop?"

"You know what I mean," Veronica snaps. "This is déjà vu all over again! Cuffed in the back of your Tahoe. If my mom could see me now!" Veronica talks a mile-a-minute, "You were definitely right; these handcuffs are killing me...again." She rambles. "You gotta get these off me."

"Relax. We're almost there."

It's a two minute drive from the Sisseton Chronicle's office to the BIA Police station. Charlie removes Veronica from the back of the Tahoe. "Ok, get these things off," Veronica pleads.

"Not yet. We're going inside just in case somebody's watching." Charlie holds her arm and leads her to the back door of the station.

"Oh, come on," Veronica's voice rises. "Enough is enough."

"Hold your horses," Charlie orders as he unlocks the back door. He pushes her inside and produces a key for the cuffs and unlocks the shackles. "Oops, I forgot the computer."

Charlie moves back outside to the Tahoe and grabs the laptop. Back inside, Agent Brown from the FBI and Captain Kipp stand with Veronica anxiously waiting for Charlie. Veronica massages her wrists. "Not too fun wearing the bracelets, eh?" Skip smiles and gives a nod toward Veronica.

"I pray to God never again," she answers. "Charlie warned me and apologized in advance, but I still wasn't mentally prepared, even after the same thing just a couple weeks ago. I have this phobia of being restrained. That scares me as much or more as the actual bite of the metal into my wrists."

The door opens and Charlie holds up the computer for everyone to see. "Here 'tis," Charlie affects an English accent for a moment, receiving only stares. "Nothing? No comment on my presentation?"

"Just give me the laptop, Sir Laurence Olivier," Agent Brown reaches for the computer as Charlie hands it over.

"Come on," Captain Kipp motions them down the hall. "Let's go into interrogation room one."

"Hurry up!" Charlie urges. "Elliot was not kidding around. He's going to get his lawyer here on the double."

The crew moves into the cold, dull room. Agent Brown sits at the table, the computer is already running. The rest of the group looks over the FBI man's shoulder, viewing the expert mouse maneuvering of a skilled computer specialist. Mouse clicks continue and menus open, filling the screen with layer after layer of information.

"Here it is," Agent Brown states. "This is the spyware master program. One more click." Brown clicks the mouse. "Do these look familiar?"

Veronica's eyes bug out. "Those are my notes!"

"He's got a pretty complex system in place. Your whole computer is here. He has spyware on your laptop. It didn't matter that you backed up stuff to the server at your office. He's got everything from your computer's wi-fi."

"Oh, my God," Veronica gasps. "I don't even want to think about my personal information I have on that computer." She covers her face in embarrassment.

"Well, now you know," Agent Brown shrugs.

Charlie puts a hand on Veronica's shoulder. "C'mon, Veronica. I'm going to put you in the other interrogation room. I want it to look good when Elliot gets here. It could be any minute."

Veronica and Charlie exit the room and move across the hall to interrogation room two. "Again, I'm sorry about the handcuffs. I know they hurt," Charlie frowns. "I never want to hurt you."

Veronica rubs her wrists. She smiles, "You warned me." She moves next to Charlie and wraps her arms around him, burying her head in his chest. Charlie is surprised by her move and uncomfortably hugs her back. "I'm sorry about this whole mess."

"What do you mean? We're going to solve this case thanks to this mess," Charlie laughs.

"I want to get us straightened out," Veronica turns her head up to look at Charlie's face. "I like you. I'd like to spend more time with you."

Charlie smiles down at her. "We'll see what we can do." He pulls her tight to his body, and Veronica's head nestles back into his chest. "I got to go. I'll wait for Elliot up front. Have a seat. We'll talk later," he whispers as he withdraws from the embrace.

*   *   *

Charlie planted himself at the front entrance of the police station and waited for Elliot. He shared small talk with Kathy at the reception desk.

*   *   *

Meanwhile, as Charlie stands guard, back in interrogation room one, Agent Brown and Captain Kipp peruse the rest of the computer for anything meaningful. Captain Kipp watches in awe as the FBI agent deftly opens and closes file after file, running searches, and snapping photos of the screen periodically, he is almost like a machine. Brown finally speaks, "There's pretty much nothing of any interest on here. I got his browser history that I can comb through, but there's nothing tell-tale like bomb diagrams, or a confessional blog or journal that would incriminate him."

Skip rolls his neck and straightens. He moves around the table and takes a seat across from Agent Brown. "Charlie said he was very upset, much more upset that his computer was confiscated than he was in losing Veronica. There's gotta be something."

"Sorry to say there's nothing that screams 'arrest me' on this computer," Brown shakes his head. "Let's pack it up. We don't have a warrant, so none of this is even admissible. It's better if we don't find something that some judge would tie to other evidence and claim fruit of the poison tree."

"Yeah, if this plays out as Charlie described, ol' Elliot's gonna flip out and do something crazy." Skip leans back in his chair.

"So, you agree with Charlie?" Agent Brown poses the question, moving his eyes from the screen to meet Captain Kipp's. "You think Elliot is the killer."

Skip purses his lips, "The way Charlie paints the picture, and the fact that we haven't had a clue for five plus years, yeah, I wanna believe."

Agent Brown turns his focus back to the computer. He inserts a jump drive into a USB port and copies files. He waits as the machine churns through the operation. Finally finished he ejects the drive before closing the last few windows and powering off the computer. "I'll tell you this much," Agent Brown folds his hands, elbows on the table, forming a tent over the laptop computer. "Based on the brazen, daylight attack on Charlie a couple days ago, we better be prepared for all hell to break loose...if Elliot is the guy." Brown pushes himself away from the table and stands as he stares into the mirror of the interrogation room. He dabs at his hair a moment. "If that assault hadn't happened, I'd suspect our guy might just disappear, never to be heard from again. But, something like that happens, that shows me that this guy is all in on his story, his psychosis. He's got the end of his tale written, and we're gonna see it."

Skip heaves a sigh, "I hope you're not right." He pushes himself up from his chair. "You're staying here, right? In this room? We don't want you seen?"

Agent Brown nods. Skip puts his hand on the door and smiles, "Time for act two. Marvin was loving it when I told him we needed him for a prop in a criminal case. He couldn't volunteer fast enough."

"Good citizens...that's what holds communities together," Agent Brown nods.

Chapter 43
The Law

Like a whirlwind, Elliot arrives, lawyer in tow. He is out of breath as he hisses his question moving nose to nose with Charlie. "Where is Veronica Lewis?"

Charlie is leaning against the receptionist counter, arms folded. "Hi, Elliot. Looks like you kept your promise. Your lawyer is here, too. Howdy, Jim." Charlie leans to see past Elliot looming over him. Charlie raises a hand and gives a wave toward the lawyer.

Elliot's lawyer is no criminal defense specialist. He is James Kepke, the local lawyer specializing in small town matters, wills, real estate transactions, divorces and the like. "Hey, Charlie," the lawyer gives a small wave and switches his brief case from his right to his left hand as he steps forward to shake hands with Charlie. Elliot cringes at the sight of this action and chops down Kepke's arm. "Ow," the lawyer yelps.

James Kepke is in his early fifties. His hair is thin as opposed to his thick, soft, pear-shaped body. The least threatening businessman is currently the president of the Chamber of Commerce and now is the owner of hurt feelings and a bruised arm. He frowns at Elliot. Charlie observes the drama in front of him with bemusement. He laughs, and Elliot's face gets redder in anger. "Where is my employee?" he shouts the question. "I want Ms. Lewis and my computer out here. Now!" Elliot points a finger at the ground as his volume gets louder.

Charlie straightens from his poor posture and throws his hands up in surrender. "I give up. There's no reason to get upset. My boss agrees with you." Charlie points a finger at Elliot. "She's free to go."

From down the hallway Skip rounds the corner, pushing a handcuffed Marvin Hattum in front of him. Skip's voice bellows through the corridor, "Charlie! Get away from Mr. Koffman!" Skip moves within about fifteen feet of Charlie. "I told you to leave Mr. Koffman alone. Here. Take the prisoner to interrogation." Skip shoves Marvin toward Charlie and eases between Charlie and Elliot. He glares at Charlie.

Charlie smiles and turns away, moving forward and grabbing Marvin's arm, "Come on, Marvin. We got some questions to ask you."

Marvin leans awkwardly, his face is solemn, "I didn't do nothing. What do you guys want?"

Charlie pushes his prisoner forward; Marvin struggles to move. His hands are cuffed in front of him, and he holds a cane as he limps on his booted foot. Skip throws one last barb at Charlie, pointing a crooked finger at the policeman, "Hurry up, Charlie. Get him to interrogation room one. And you wait for me before you start the questions."

Charlie's head drops at the public scolding, and he shuffles down the hall, slowly escorting Marvin away from the reception area. Skip turns his full attention to Elliot. "I'm sorry, Mr. Koffman. Ms. Lewis is waiting in interrogation room two with your computer. I'll go get her and bring her to you."

Elliot nods, "Thank you, Captain."

"I apologize for Sergeant LeBeau," Skip puts his hands up in deference. "It's been very stressful here lately. I hope you understand. It's all over, Mr. Koffman. I hope we can put this misunderstanding behind us." Skip gives a slight nod of his head in the direction of Marvin moving down the hallway.

Elliot acknowledges the gesture with a nod and a smile. "I do understand."

"Sergeant LeBeau will be disciplined appropriately. I can assure you."

Elliot is calm. He looks at his lawyer with a satisfied smile. Skip holds up a finger, "Let me retrieve Ms. Lewis. Excuse me." Skip moves away from the two men. He can hear their voices behind him as he turns down the hall where he sees Charlie and gives him a nod. Charlie returns the nod and includes a wink at his boss. He carries a jacket in his hand. It is Veronica's coat and is the third and final phase of the police station ploy. Charlie appears around the corner, and Elliot and his lawyer go silent as he approaches. "It's not over, Elliot."

Elliot points in the general direction of where he last saw Skip. "I'm pretty sure I heard your boss say it was over."

Charlie shrugs, "Sometimes I don't hear too good." Charlie moves the jacket back and forth between his hands as he stares at Elliot. He breaks eye contact and looks down at the jacket in his hands. "Here's Veronica's jacket." He tosses it toward Elliot. Elliot extends his left hand and catches the coat. "Huh, are you left handed, Elliot?"

"What about it?" Elliot's brow furrows.

"It's just interesting. I will note that in the file."

"File? What file?" An agitated Elliot takes a step toward Charlie. His lawyer grabs his arm to stop him.

Skip appears from around the corner of the hallway with Veronica. She looks disheveled, and she rubs her wrists, exaggerating for effect. "Captain," Elliot points a finger at Charlie, "the Sergeant just mentioned there's a file on me."

"File? Skip's face scrunches as he repeats the word questioningly. "Come on, Charlie. What are you doing out here. I told you to wait with Marvin." Skip's words are low and slow, trying to express the disappointment he has with his Sergeant.

"I'm sorry, Captain. I was just returning Ms. Lewis' coat." Charlie lowers his head in shame. "I'll go wait with Marvin in the interview room." Turning and shuffling away, Charlie's posture slumps, mimicking a scolded puppy.

"Charlie!" Veronica yells through gritted teeth as she takes her coat from Elliot.

Charlie turns and looks back pathetically as Veronica yells again and points her finger at him, "I'm not going to forget this. This is harassment!"

Elliot puts a hand on Veronica's shoulder and turns her toward the exit. "Come on, let's go."

The front doors close behind Veronica, Elliot, and his lawyer. The trio moves down the sidewalk under the gray skies and a few snowflakes trace their way through the sky.

Charlie peeks around the corner and whispers, "They gone?"

Skip smiles, "Yup."

"Do you think they bought it?" Charlie asks.

Skip eases next to Charlie and puts a hand on his shoulder as they move to the interrogation room where Marvin waits. "Oh, yeah! Hook, line, and sinker. And we're gonna land him."

They open the door to the interview room, and Marvin stands up. Charlie moves forward and removes the handcuffs. "That's it?" Marvin questions. "Show's over?"

Skip nods, "Yup, that's it. Thanks for your help."

Marvin shakes his head, "My pleasure, guys. Police work is fun."

Gregory L. Heitmann

Chapter 44
The Dark

It had gotten late, and there was still no word from Veronica. Charlie is at home in his trailer. He had phoned fifty times trying to reach her, but there was no answer. At eleven thirty p.m. he called for the fifty first time.

*   *   *

It might as well be the moon. It is remote and as random as anywhere. The cottage on South Red Iron Lake is one of the few on the shore. It is more of a shack. It is not equipped for the season-round use, but tonight in the freezing air, it is home to Elliot and his companion. A cell phone buzzes and lights up. The caller ID indicates that it is Charlie.

Elliot had retrieved the phone from Veronica's purse much earlier, and he looks at the vibrating phone in his and shakes his head. The two room cabin is dimly lit by a kerosene lantern. It is an antique lamp, handed down many generations, and tonight its light produces harsh, sinister shadows. Elliot stares at the phone. Behind him hangs Veronica's limp body. Hung by her wrists bound with duct tape, her head lolls to the side as she breathes. A trickle of dried blood cakes a rivulet of red from her nose to her mouth around her swollen upper lip. Elliot glares at the phone, his teeth gnash. "Your boyfriend is very persistent." Elliot drops the phone to the floor and smashes it with his foot clad in a heavy, insulated boot. The fifteen feet by fifteen feet room is all open except the small enclosure for the toilet. The luxury of indoor plumbing was part of a remodeling project in the 1960's.

The shack would soon warm with the aid of the wood burning stove. A benefit of the small space was its ability to heat and cool quickly. Elliot fed the fire in the stove and turned quickly when he heard the moan. He could see Veronica's eyes flutter in the dull light of the lantern, and Veronica shivers as her consciousness returns.

Veronica groans, still suffering, trying to comprehend the situation. Elliot approaches her, snatching his stun gun from the counter. "You know," he softly whispers as he speaks more to himself than the bound woman in front of him. "You are special. And I know you will be my last, here anyway. I have to find a partner for you. To do this right."

Elliot is close to Veronica now. His eyes look at hers from just an inch or two away. Veronica's eyebrows raise and her eyes bulge as recognition hits her. Her arms ache from lack of blood flow, having been above her head for quite some time, suspended by a hook and a section of chain from the ceiling. She moves her eyes to the ceiling, and Elliot triggers a test of the stun gun. It crackles a moment, before he releases the trigger. He touches the contact points to her exposed skin on her neck and triggers the mechanism again. Her body jolts and goes limp. "I have just the partner for you." Elliot nods satisfied. He tosses the stun gun aside and breathes a deep breath. Steam spews from his nose and mouth, curling toward the ceiling. "Don't go anywhere. I'll be back soon," he whispers. Grabbing the roll of duct tape from the counter, he peels a piece from the spool and places it over Veronica's mouth. "Stay quiet too, please."

*　　*　　*

Charlie is desperate. He is on the phone with Captain Kipp, and Skip can hear the panic in Charlie's voice. "Something has gone wrong, Skip. She won't answer. I should have never let her walk out of the station with that guy."

"Calm down, Charlie. We're on it. I already had Agent Brown pinpoint her cell phone. It's sitting at coordinates that indicate that it is likely a cabin on South Red Iron."

"We got to get out there!" Charlie demands into the phone.

"Hold on now. We got a guy sitting on Elliot's house. I talked to Kemp and he says he's still there. The car is in the driveway."

"Are you kidding me?" Charlie's voice is rising. "He's not there. He's long gone. You know what this guy does. He plants vehicles. Heck, he may have Veronica's car. Anybody think of putting someone on her?" Charlie sighs into the phone. "Something happened. She would never have gone with him willingly after all this."

A long pause between the men is finally broken by Skip. "Fine. Come to town. I'll get Agent Brown from the hotel. We'll go out there."

"I'll be there in ten minutes." Charlie ends the call without saying goodbye.

Claude is in the living room with a question, "Where you going to be in ten minutes? It's almost midnight for crying out loud."

"There's a situation in town. I gotta go." Charlie unconsciously drops his hand down to his belt and feels his holstered gun. He grabs his coat and pulls on his black stocking cap. "I'll see you later," Charlie's voice is flat as he passes through the front door, departing from the house.

Opening the door, Claude yells, "Be careful!" to his son.

Charlie waves without looking back as he trudges through fresh snow to his Tahoe. Claude closes the door and turns to see a bleary-eyed Nat standing in his bedroom doorway. "What's with all the commotion, Grandpa?"

Claude waves a hand at Nat. "I don't know. Your uncle's got an emergency to tend to. Go back to bed."

Gregory L. Heitmann

Chapter 45
Assault Team

At the BIA police station the three men gather. Charlie joins Agent Brown and Captain Kipp who look at the screen of Brown's laptop. The display shows an aerial map of South Red Iron Lake. The computer screen casts an eerie glow on the men's faces as they lean forward to see the small screen. "So," Charlie straightens, "this is at Red Iron Lake, right near where we picked that four-wheeler out of the ice. He must be using an old cabin out there."

"Tell 'im," Skip gives a nod to Agent Brown.

Brown holds up two fingers, "Two things, Charlie. I looked at the property records and one of the cabins is held by EK Corporation. That's the same company that owns the Sisseton Chronicle, so it's not a leap to conclude that the EK of EK Corporation is Elliot Koffman."

"Yeah, let's go then," Charlie nods. "What's the other thing?"

"I've been tracking Veronica's phone since she left," Brown pauses. "I lost the signal a half hour ago. The battery could be dead."

"What are we sitting around here for?" Charlie questions. "The three of us, let's roll!"

In five minutes the men are changed into the black-out uniforms of an assault team. Backpacks are loaded into the vehicles with enough weapons to sustain a small Latin American country's revolt.

"I'll follow you guys," Agent Brown states as they carry more equipment through the parking lot. "I got more stuff in my car that we might need if push comes to shove."

It is snowing again. Despite extreme cold, the moisture is still managing to be squeezed out of the air in giant clumps of fluffy, cottony snow.

Skip and Charlie toss their assault bags in the back seat of Skip's Tahoe. "Try to keep up," Skip yells to the FBI man as each climbs in the driver's seat.

The vehicles peel out of the BIA police station parking lot pointed west on SD Highway 10. The midnight traffic is nil, and the two vehicle convoy speeds down the asphalt. Wafting clouds of the delicate snowflakes scatter across the frozen pavement, disturbed by the vehicles. The headlights illuminate what appears to be a ground fog or clouds of dry ice you would see as a movie effect wispily dancing along the road's surface.

Charlie's phone buzzes, and he pulls the phone from his shirt pocket. He looks at the caller and presses the "ignore call" button. He dons his night vision goggles over his stocking cap and adjusts them. "Who was that?" Skip asks.

"It's my dad. He was still up when I tore out of the house. He doesn't know what's going on, and he was upset. I just told him it was an emergency."

Skip shakes his head, "Well, he must have an idea of what's happening. I'm sure he noticed you trying to call Veronica all night."

The phone buzzes again, and Charlie hits "ignore."

"Just answer it!" Skip orders.

"We're almost there!" Charlie counters.

The lights reflect off the road signs, indicating the road to Buffalo Lake and then past the turnoff to Sica Hollow. In another couple minutes they are at the turnoff from Highway 10 to the trails to the cabins at Red Iron. The vehicles kill their headlights as they sit in the driveway. Skip is out of the Tahoe and moving back to the FBI sedan. Agent Brown is already out of his car and pulling his bag from the back seat. "I'll hop in with you. Snow looks like it might be too deep." In the Tahoe the final polish is given to the plan. "These look like fresh tracks in the snow. I'd say there's only been one car in or out of here in the last hour or two."

Skip looks to Agent Brown in the back seat, "How far is it to the cabin?"

"The one we're looking for is still a mile and a half down this driveway."

Skip nods and puts his night vision goggles on. "We'll go with no lights. Everyone ready?"

The FBI agent attaches his goggles to his head, and Skip turns the dashboard lights to off. The Tahoe is put in gear and eases forward through the snow, traveling on top of the other tracks. "Let's see where these tracks lead us," Charlie indicates with a wave of his hand. He waves his hand in front of his goggles and notes the contrast of the green glow.

He reaches for an adjustment knob on his glasses and adjusts it to provide a little more crispness to his view.

Skip maneuvers slowly along the driveway. They pass two cabins and the tracks continue. Charlie's phone buzzes again. Charlie is nearly blinded by the glowing screen of the caller ID showing "Claude". He punches the "ignore" button and tosses the phone on the dashboard.

From the back seat Agent Brown yells out, "Kill it here!"

Skip slams on the brakes and the Tahoe slips forward, anti-lock brakes chattering a bit, halting the vehicle. "I see 'em."

Brown's voice is husky, "The tracks bend into the driveway ahead. I'm picking up something, from a window it looks like, through my goggles. There's a dim light coming from inside that cabin."

"Roger that. I see it," Charlie echoes the agent's statement.

Skip kills the engine. "Brown, you're on the lakeside. Me and Charlie will go right to the door."

Under the cover of darkness, the men step from the Tahoe. Silently, with only the crunch of cold snow under foot, they advance to the house, weapons drawn. Charlie with a shotgun and Skip with his assault rifle hold their position just outside the front door and waiting a full minute for Agent Brown to maneuver to the other side of the cabin. Charlie puts his ear to the door. He looks toward Skip and shakes his head. Moving a step back from the door he holds up three fingers of his gloved hand. He drops one finger, than another. When his countdown reaches zero he kicks the flimsy door in. Charlie sees Veronica jolt at the commotion of their entrance. She shivers and trembles, eyes wide in fear. The kerosene lantern's wick holds the slightest flame, producing just enough light to defend against complete darkness.

Charlie is at Veronica's side in a flash. Skip is to the lakeside door opening it and calling for Agent Brown, before moving to the lantern and turning the wick as high as it can go, splashing light inside the cabin. Charlie has his knife out in an instant. "It's me, Charlie," he softly whispers trying to provide comfort to the woman. He slices through the duct tape that binds Veronica's hands to the chains and makeshift hoist attached to an exposed ceiling rafter. Veronica groans and falls toward the floor as she is cut loose. Charlie catches her and eases her down. Grabbing every sheet and blanket he can find, he throws them atop Veronica who shakes, sobbing intermittently with gasps of breath. Charlie scoops up the woman, blankets and all and whispers, "It's ok." He pulls the tape from her mouth as gently as he can.

"Where is he?" Skip poses the question to no one in particular.

"I got to get her to the car. She's freezing," Charlie calls out.

"I thought it was going to be you, Charlie," Veronica mumbles the words barely audible to Charlie.

"Yes, I'm here." Charlie responds, pulling her closer.

"No," Veronica gasps for breath. "He's not here. He said he was going to get a partner for me."

The men have moved their night vision goggles to the tops of their heads. Agent Brown looks at Skip. "His M.O. has typically been pairs."

"Who in the hell would he be getting for Veronica?" Skip questions out loud.

Charlie tosses his rifle toward Skip, who catches the weapon. "Who cares? I got to get her to the truck!" Charlie lifts the bundled woman and sidles through the door. He runs. He runs in the general direction of where they left the vehicle. The darkness and snow hide the Tahoe. He runs the three hundred yards as best as he can, Veronica bouncing in his arms. The location of the truck is revealed with a glint of light through the windshield. Inside the empty vehicle, Charlie's phone buzzes on the dash. The caller ID lights up, indicating Claude calling. Charlie is finally at the truck. He places Veronica gently in the passenger seat, scrambles to the driver's side, hops in the truck, starts the engine, and turns the heater on full blast. He notices he is out of breath, gasping for oxygen. He turns on the headlights revealing Agent Brown and Skip rushing to the truck.

Charlie is out of the truck again moving to the passenger side to unwrap Veronica and let the warmth of the vehicle's heater get to her. Skip calls out, "Get in the truck Charlie. We'll get her to the hospital."

Chapter 46
Claude

Claude sits in his chair watching a late night talk show. He winces as the music act, Seether, begins to play "Rise Above This." Claude shakes his head, "What is this noise?" he mumbles as he reaches for the remote. As annoyed as Claude was about Charlie not answering his calls, he is more annoyed by a vehicle's squeaking brakes. A car with no headlights pulls into the driveway. Claude stands up and moves to the window. The only light in the room is provided by the flickering change of the images on the TV as the band rocks. Claude parts the curtain ever so slightly. He looks out into the darkness cut in two by the Rural Electrification Association light atop the utility pole forty yards from the house. The harsh fluorescent light seems to magnify the snowflakes that fall in a slant, pushed by a northwest wind. Claude can see a car he does not recognize in the drive. Reaching for the cordless telephone, he speed dials Charlie. Again, there is still no answer.

Tossing the phone on the couch, Claude moves to the front closet and extracts Charlie's deer rifle. He works the bolt action, chambering a round. He eases back to his position near the front window parting the curtain ever so slightly to peer outside. He leans against the wall and window frame, enveloped by the curtain.

Outside, the interior light comes on for a moment as the door opens and closes quickly. A man in black, holding a pistol, springs from the car. Elliot Koffman moves away from the vehicle with the smooth experience of many a covert mission. Elliot is unaware that he is watched. He treads lightly to the steps of the dark trailer, nearly invisible in the shadows through the aid of his black clothing. He checks the action of the pistol, assuring a round is in the chamber of the automatic pistol. Flat against the wall of the outside of the trailer, Elliot gently twists the door knob. It is unlocked, and he pushes the door open.

*   *   *

From inside the LeBeau trailer, Claude watches the man move up the stairs and check his pistol. The flat angle of his view shields the intruder from Claude's vision, but Claude can hear the rustle of the door knob. He knows the door is not locked. They never lock the door out in the country. Why would one ever think you needed security out in the sticks? It never crossed his mind. Something else blasts through Claude's mind in this instant, Nat. Nat is asleep in his bedroom. It is too late now to alert the boy. Claude shoulders the rifle and aims it at the door. He feels good. Hidden by the billowing curtain, the semi-dark trailer gives him an advantage and the element of surprise.

The door opens quietly, slowly, and then returns to a closed position in the same manner. Claude can see the black outline of a person standing near the door. "Who are you?" he whispers out of the darkness.

Elliot raises the pistol and fires toward the sound of the voice. The crack of the pistol round is drowned by the roar of Claude's rifle. The zing of the pistol's bullet sizzles by Claude's ear, Elliot is struck square in the chest, knocked off his feet. Blown backward into the TV, the large console unit crashes forward. The music and the illumination from the TV halt abruptly as the room goes dark.

Chapter 47
Shots Fired

Charlie holds Veronica as tightly as he dares. He sits in the front seat with her on his lap. Her covers are down to a single blanket as the heater roars, fans on high, blasting heat from all vents. Skip eases the vehicle along, trying to keep Veronica from being jostled by the rough road. There is no conversation; it would be difficult to speak over the heater fan. Charlie strokes Veronica's hair trying his best to comfort the trembling woman. The fear or the cold, it is difficult to try to gauge which one wracks her body with convulsions.

"We'll drop Brown off at his car, then we'll hustle to Sisseton," Skip finally shouts over the heater as the FBI agent's car comes into view. "I hope she doesn't have some frostbite. Hands over her head for a long time, questionable circulation to the extremities."

Charlie shoots a dagger-like glance at Skip. Skip flinches knowing he said too much. He slows as they approach the car and Highway 10. Forgotten in the moment, but still on, the police radio crackles loudly, "Report of shots fired. 911 call. LeBeau residence."

Charlie's heart skips a beat as he hears the words. Skip grits his teeth and slams his foot down on the accelerator. The Tahoe crabs its way sideways down the driveway picking up speed slowly in the snow. They bounce onto South Dakota Highway 10, leaving Agent Brown's car behind in a flurry of snow. Pointed east, Skip flips on his strobe warning lights and pushes the pedal to the floor. "I knew it! I knew it! I knew it!" Charlie yells.

Charlie's cell phone buzzes loudly, the vibrations magnified by the windshield and dash. "My phone!" Charlie shouts reaching around Veronica on his lap. "It's Claude!" Charlie yells again as he sees the caller ID.

Skip turns the heater to low so Charlie can hear. "Dad? Hello?" Charlie speaks loudly into the phone. "Are you all right?"

Charlie relaxes into his seat as he hears his father's voice, "Charlie, I just shot somebody."

"I just heard on the police radio that there were shots fired at our house," Charlie tersely speaks into the phone. "What happened? Are you ok?" His voice changes from fear and anger to pleading.

"I'm ok, Charlie. Nat's ok, too," Charlie repeats the news for everyone in the Tahoe.

"My God!" Charlie shouts into the phone, "We're on our way. Is he dead?"

There is a long pause on the phone, and Charlie repeats the question, "Is the guy dead? Dad, are you still there?"

"I'm here, Charlie...," Claude breathes loudly rasping a bit into the phone, "but the guy's gone."

Charlie shouts orders to his father into the phone, "Ok, don't touch the body or anything. Just get out of there!"

Charlie listens again to his father. "No, Charlie. I'm trying to tell you, the guy I shot. He left. I don't know where he went. I shot him. The TV went over and crashed down. It was dark and by the time I got lights on, the guy was out the door, gone."

"What?" Charlie's voice resonates in the truck as he yells into the phone. "I don't understand."

Claude shares the story again as Charlie listens and repeats each sentence to the other passengers as Skip flies down the highway. "You shot him with my deer rifle. He flew against the wall. He bounced off the wall into the TV. The TV was knocked over and smashed. You thought he was dead. You turned away for a moment to get the lights on. He was gone."

"What the hell's going on?" Skip hisses.

Charlie meets Skip's eyes and shrugs. "Dad, get Nat and get out of there. Take my truck and go straight to the hospital. Don't stop for anything or anyone. We'll be there in less than ten."

"Hospital? I don't need to be in a hospital!" Claude shouts over the phone.

"No, Dad. Meet us there. We're bringing somebody."

Claude's voice is shaky, "Are you all right, son?"

"It's Veronica. Something's happened. Just meet us there."

Chapter 48
Medical

The LeBeau family is reunited at Coteau Des Prairies Hospital. Everyone is still a little shell shocked. Veronica is admitted and held for observation. She is sedated and treated for bruising to her face and minor wounds on her wrist. It appears that the largest physical injury she has suffered is a knick on her wrist from Charlie's knife when he cut her free from the duct tape, much to Charlie's chagrin. The doctor briefs Charlie with the news of Veronica's status emphasizing the physical condition. Her mental condition may be the issue that lingers. Agent Brown and Skip traveled to Charlie's trailer to inspect the crime scene and gather evidence. They had returned to the hospital to let Charlie know that his place was cleared, and he could take Claude and Nat Home. It is three thirty in the morning when Charlie gets the news, "All clear, Charlie," Skip calls across the waiting room where Charlie, Nat, and Claude rest uncomfortably on the modern furniture.

Charlie pushes himself up stiffly, "What did you find?"

"We got the slug from Elliot's pistol. It was head high in the wall. And get this, we got the pistol itself," Skip smiles. "Maybe we'll get some information from it."

"He left his weapon?" Charlie questions.

"The TV fell on it. I'm guessing he was in a hurry to get out of there, took a quick look for it, and bolted rather than risk getting another round from Claude." Skip gives a nod to Claude.

Skip continues, "We went back and got Agent Brown's car. He's got some evidence gathering equipment, i.e., a vacuum. He wanted to see if he could get some fibers. So, you'll get yourself some free house cleaning, at least around the entry way." Skip scratches his head. "What else," he thinks for a moment. "We got all the photographs of everything inside, and your driveway. You're good to go home."

"So, we can go home?" Charlie asks again for confirmation.

"Sure. It's late. Get your guys home, and I'll see you tomorrow." Skip clasps a hand down on Charlie's shoulder, "How's Veronica? Did they say anything else?"

Charlie shakes his head, "Cold and dehydrated. They're going to keep her tranquilized for awhile."

Skip points to the door, "Get out of here then. I'll see you in the office tomorrow afternoon. We'll talk then."

Nat stands and lends a hand to his Grandpa, pulling him out of his chair to his feet.

"See you, guys," Skip gives a wave as Charlie leads his family out the door.

Chapter 49
Debrief

Charlie dressed ready for duty, appears in Captain Kipp's office at one p.m. sharp to find Captain Kipp and Agent Brown talking. "Hey, Charlie. Come on in and have a seat."

"Morning, Skip...I mean afternoon," Charlie manages a smile. "Agent Brown. You back to Pierre today?" Charlie sits down, leaning forward in his chair; he spins his black stocking cap in his hands.

"Nah," Agent Brown shakes his head, "Still snowing and the road report is bad. I'll hang with you guys one more night."

"Wait 'til the wind comes up, you'll be here a week," Charlie laughs weakly.

The men sit silently for a moment, not sure how to start the conversation. A gap in the small talk is blitzed by Charlie, "What the hell happened? How did any of this happen? How did Elliot get away?" Charlie is getting agitated.

"Take it easy, Charlie. Everybody's still working this case."

"I'm sorry, Skip," Charlie stands and paces next to the door. He leans against the door frame. "I didn't sleep last night. My brain was goin' a million miles an hour, turning over all this stuff in my head."

"I was just telling Skip," Agent Brown interjects, "it just came over the wire that they recovered Veronica's car in Minneapolis. It was double parked at the bus station."

"Sheesh," Charlie's hands flip up in the air. "He's in the wind."

"I wouldn't be so sure," Agent Brown points a finger at Charlie. "Get this. They found a Kevlar body armor vest with a hole in it. Stashed in the trunk. Little bit of blood. We're gonna have DNA on our guy."

Charlie throws his hands up in the air, "What am I going to tell my family in the mean time? We're going to sit here and live in fear?"

Agent Brown twists his mouth, narrows his eyes, and shakes his head. "He's not coming back, Charlie."

"How do you know? What would make you so sure?" Charlie folds his arms a moment, but then gesticulates as he continues. "We know nothing about this Elliot guy. What did the FBI records show? Elliot Koffman was...is missing in action in Desert Storm?"

Skip and Agent Brown exchange troubled looks. Charlie shakes his head back and forth as he goes on, "Whoever this 'Elliot Koffman' is," Charlie makes air quotes around "Elliot Koffman" before continuing. "Did the Deer Slayer steal Elliot's ID and assume his life?"

Agent Brown holds up his hands to calm Charlie, "We're working on a bunch of leads. The important thing is that we got a light on this guy. You solved it. He's not gonna kill anymore. He's gonna spend the rest of his life hiding, but we'll get 'im."

"Psssh," Charlie grunts. "We are probably more confused than ever. Do we even have fingerprints? You said you had DNA from the vest?"

Skip looks to Agent Brown, "The DNA is going to take a couple days. I've already been to the newspaper office and personally lifted prints. Don't worry, we'll have prints and DNA, and if he's in our database, we'll have an ID by the end of the week."

Charlie sighs, "That's not soon enough. You can't go around taking shots at a policeman's family!"

Skip and Brown nod in agreement. Charlie folds his arms and leans against the doorframe again. He shakes his head and looks back and forth at the men in front of him. He frowns and grinds his teeth. "I'm gonna kill him."

"Come on, Charlie," Skip holds up a hand. "Take the rest of the day and go visit Veronica. You're not expected to be at work." The captain shakes his head, "You know you can't be working this case anymore with your family involved. Heck, take the week off. Take Nat out on the bale stack and see if you can get a deer."

Charlie rolls his eyes and sighs. He knows the discussion is over. He knows Skip is right. He's off the case. "Fine. I'm outta here for the rest of the week. Give me a call if you need something."

"Ok, good," Skip forces a smile.

Charlie reaches down, extends his hand toward the FBI man, and Agent Brown shakes it. "Agent Brown. Skip." Charlie throws up a mock salute as he heads out the door, moving deliberately, stalking down the hallway.

Chapter 50
Visitor's Hour

Charlie wastes no time. He leaves the police station and drives directly to the Sisseton Main Street Flower shop. He picks up thirty dollars worth of flowers in a vase and heads to the hospital. On cue the snow lets up and the sun breaks through as Charlie eases quietly into Veronica's room. The sunshine fills the room, bathing the sleeping woman in an angelic glow. Charlie sets the vase on a stand near the window. The clunk of the vase on the table wakes Veronica, and she turns her head, recognizing Charlie with a smile. "Hi. I brought some flowers," Charlie whispers.

"Hello," Veronica responds sleepily, eyelids straining to stay open. "Sorry. I'm so groggy. They keep giving me sedatives."

"That's ok. I just wanted to check and see how you're doing."

Veronica smiles, "Thank you. For the flowers. And for saving me."

"Shhh," Charlie holds up a hand, "just rest."

"I'm ok. I twisted my shoulder a bit. They said I was just cold and dehydrated." Veronica holds up her arm with an IV stuck in it. They're giving me fluids and holding me for observation at least through tomorrow."

"Good. I'll let you rest and check back with you tomorrow." Charlie moves to the bed and grabs her hand, interlocking his fingers with hers.

"What happened with...?" Veronica starts to ask a question, but Charlie cuts her off.

"We'll talk about what happened later. Everybody's fine." Charlie uses his free hand to run through Veronica's hair. "I'll check with you tomorrow. Hopefully, I'll be giving you a ride home from here." He smiles at her. "I'm on my way home too. Skip sent me home for the rest of the week. I'll be trying to finally get my deer."

Veronica laughs and begins to cough. Charlie pulls himself from Veronica and pushes her water to within easy reach. She sips from a straw and recovers. "I better go. Get some rest, and I'll see you tomorrow."

Veronica closes her eyes. "Thanks again, Charlie. Bye."

Charlie bends down and kisses her forehead, "Bye."

Chapter 51
Together

The sunny blue sky is short lived. By the time Charlie picks up milk and other groceries from the Super Valu, the clouds have reconvened. The wind is steady from the east, but Charlie is relaxed. His radio plays an oldie but a goodie, Sonny James yodels about "Young Love," and it seems like the first bit of normalcy for Charlie in forty eight hours.

Charlie is up the steps and into his house where he spots Nat packing his duffle bag, basketball shoes tied together by the shoestrings; he's ready to go. "What are you doing?" Charlie's eyes narrow as he looks at Nat.

"I'm going to practice."

"No. You weren't in school today. No practice." Charlie stomps his feet on the entry rug to rid the snow from his boots. "Come here and get these groceries."

Nat moves forward, relieving Charlie of the paper sacks. "Get your huntin' stuff. We're going out." Charlie looks around the trailer. "Quiet in here. Where's your grandpa?"

Nat shrugs as he marches the groceries through the living room and sets the bags on the counter. "TV's broken."

"Good. Nothing to do except go huntin'. You too, Dad!" Charlie shouts. Get your stuff on. You're comin' with. We're going to get your deer if we have to sit there all night! A family that hunts together, stays together!"

Claude pokes his head out of his bedroom, "Fine with me, but remember, we only got your rifle."

"We'll get by just fine," Charlie smiles. "You obviously know how to use it."

*   *   *

Charlie, Nat, and Claude stand on the bale stack overlooking the trees in the coulee and the snow covered cornfield. Charlie scans the area with his binoculars. Claude and Nat have backed themselves into the bales, fighting the biting, damp east wind.

Nat breaks the silence, "What do you think? A sixty inch flat screen fit in the living room?"

Claude purses his lips, "I think so, but we could get by with a fifty."

"Shhh!" Charlie tries to shush the conversation. "Can we forget about the TV? Look for a deer, would ya?"

The sun starts to drop to the horizon. "I'm freezing," Nat shivers, hands tucked deep in his pockets. "Where are all the deer this year?"

Silence falls for a few minutes as the sun disappears behind the trees on its way to sunset. Charlie spots a doe moving from the trees no more than seventy-five yards away. The unsuspecting animal steps clear into the cornfield, pawing at the ground trying to reveal some corn in the snow. Charlie reaches for his rifle. He settles across the bale, putting the cross hairs on the deer's chest. "We definitely need high def," Claude speaks up.

The doe's head is up looking, hearing the human voice. She stares at the bales for a brief moment, ears point at the bale stack. Before Charlie can pull the trigger, the whitetail doe makes a giant leap, waving its namesake as it drops into the coulee out of sight. "Dad!" Charlie laughs the words. "What are you doing? Couldn't you see I was going to shoot a doe for you?"

Nat chimes in, "You're right. It's about time Uncle Charlie moved into the 21st Century. Definitely high definition."

Charlie is incredulous. He sets his rifle back on top of the stack. He holds up his hands in a shrug. "Seriously, you didn't see the deer? You didn't see me pick up my rifle and aim at it?"

Nat pulls his phone from his pocket. "You know what? I bet we could get a good deal at Karl's in Watertown."

Claude nods, "Get on your phone and see what Best Buy up in Fargo can do."

Charlie smiles, enjoying his family. "We'll get one tomorrow," he mumbles, laughing softly and shaking his head.

Gregory L. Heitmann

The first chapter of the next book in the
Charlie LeBeau Mystery Series:

Buffalo Lake

Gregory L. Heitmann

Chapter 1
Lake Cabin

Marshall County, South Dakota – Sisseton-Wahpeton Indian Reservation

Waves lap at the shoreline of Buffalo Lake in the darkness. In the shadowy night, the soothing, rhythmic wash of the waves permeates the home next to the shore. The summer heat is mitigated by the cool lake breezes, and the windows and doors are open in the small cabin. Screens are in place to guard the windows and to keep the mosquitoes at bay; the cool air circulates well in the tiny dwelling. The cabin is a simple 850 square foot two bedroom cottage. Two small bedrooms, a living room, kitchen, and bathroom form the basic floor plan.

A lone figure dressed in black, moves outside through the darkness. The trespasser is illuminated only by the new moon and stars under the cloudless night sky. The late night visitor eases through the spring-held screen door in silence. The darkness of the cabin shrouds the figure as it moves to the back bedroom of the cabin where snores emanate.

The figure in black flicks the bedroom light on, and a sleeping gray-haired man awakens with a surprise, squinting at the intruder. The old man's eyes do not focus on the person in front of him. He finally reaches for his glasses on the bedside stand. He knocks over a black and white photo of his once younger self, dressed in his black priest outfit and collar. The old, yellowed photo shows the young priest holding a small boy in front of a St. John's Catholic Church sign. Flanked on each side of the priest are three nuns and another priest.

The framed photo falls to the floor and shatters as the same man in the picture, the now seventy-five year old retired priest, Father Michael Franzen, gets his glasses in place. His head nods slowly. Still under the covers of his bed, he leans on an elbow, "Hmmph. It's you. My very own devil."

The figure in black, dressed like a modern-day ninja, points a gun at the man, silently motioning him to get out of the bed. The old man refuses with a shake of his head and defiant smile. The intruder pulls the trigger on the pistol. A deafening roar cracks the quiet of the tiny bedroom. The bullet whizzes by the priest's ear, the headboard of the bed splinters, and the bullet lodges into the wall.

Father Franzen grunts, "Uhhhnn," as he grasps at his chest. He throws the bed sheet aside and moves unsteadily to his feet. The priest is shirtless, dressed only in boxers; his large round belly and chest are covered in silver hair. His thin legs seem incapable of supporting his rotund body. He holds his chest and gasps for air as he leans on the small dresser, the single piece of furniture in the bedroom besides the bed. "Help me," he pleads.

The intruder spies a gold cross buried in the gray chest hair of the priest. It hangs from a chain, around the old man's neck. A black-gloved hand reaches out and tears the cross and chain from his neck. Father Franzen's body heaves. He pants, "I'm having a heart attack. If you are not going to help, just…just shoot me now."

The breathy words come as a whining plea. The aggressor silently shakes its head, having no pity for the man. The intruder in black motions the old man to walk. The stooped over priest manages to stagger toward the screen door of the cabin. Out the door the old man stumbles, bent almost in half, clutching at his chest. The visitor in black follows behind, the screen door on its spring restraint, closes with a crack, like a small arms report.

Light spills from the cabin providing harsh shadows on the shoreline. The assault continues on the old priest with a jab of the pistol into his ribs as they move toward the lake. From his stooped position, the priest eyes a canoe beached on the narrow strip of sandy shore. The pair moves, crossing the short distance from the cabin to the stub of a dock protruding into the lake. The attacker prods the priest forward with pokes in the back from the barrel of the pistol. Stepping onto the dock, the old man stumbles, falling onto his belly. Rolling onto his back, the priest pleads with tears in his eyes, "For the love of Christ. I beg you…"

The attacker moves close to the incapacitated man, hovering over the wheezing priest. The figure extends the pistol, slowly, painstakingly aiming the weapon a few inches from the man's head. Prostrate on the dock, the man clutches at his chest with one hand, with the other he crosses himself and mumbles, "The Lord is my shepherd…"

He gasps for any hint of breath. He cannot finish the verse. With all his strength remaining, the priest speaks, "Father, please forgive them, they know not what they do."

The attacker's head shakes. Holding the weapon in one hand and with the other the cross and chain, the figure in black tosses the jewelry in the lake. An almost imperceptible splash is heard as the items hit the water. In a grunting, guttural voice, the assaulter finally speaks, "You're wrong, Father. I know exactly what I do. Burn in hell, Franzen."

The assailant fires the weapon. The muzzle flash pierces the night, reflecting like a flash of lightning off the lake. The echo of the pistol's report roars one direction then the other in an eerie reverberation in the still, night air. The bullet splinters a wooden plank of the dock an inch from the priest's head. The old man's eyes widen and he gasps, choking a moment as he squeezes and clutches his chest. Then there is nothing but silence.

The assailant stands over the victim, admiring the completed task. A leg twitches as the attacker bends down, listening for a breath. Nothing. Mustering strength, the figure in black rolls the corpse off the dock into the water. With a gurgling splash the priest's body hits the water forcing waves to wash along the shore from the disturbance on the still lake. The beached canoe grinds in the sand, rocked by the waves.

The attacker looks around in the dark, surveying the surroundings, while moving to the canoe. In a fluid motion the intruder pushes the canoe away from shore, gracefully leaping into the vessel, picking up the paddle, and silently stroking the water, skimming away from what appears to be a white-bellied whale beached on the shore.

*   *   *

Buffalo Lake is really a group of lakes that combine to form two bodies of water in wet years, or in dry years, several individual lakes. Located eleven miles west of Sisseton, South Dakota, Buffalo Lake forms its own District and community on the Sisseton-Wahpeton Indian Reservation. The reservation covers the heart of the Coteau Des Prairies, "the slope on the prairie." The Coteau was carved and shaped by the glaciers ten thousand years ago. These lands feature the Glacial Lakes region in the higher elevations, areas gouged by the glaciers, but not scarred smooth by the ancient seas that flattened most of the Great Plains. The uneven wear of the ice sheets scraped out a pock-marked landscape, each dip holding water. The hills of the Glacial Lakes region are dotted with hundreds, if not thousands of bodies of water and Buffalo Lake is just one of many.

The Coteau juts up steeply in the flat land on its east and west sides, rising 350 feet in a mile or so, and holding that elevation for thirty or forty miles. The elevation is enough to affect the climate. The additional snow and rain in hill country, thanks to the altitude, tend to keep the lakes, ponds, and sloughs brimming. Along the South Dakota Highway 10 corridor, the Coteau begins in earnest about three miles west of Sisseton and continues for approximately twenty five miles through rolling terrain before dropping into the remnants the long dry lake bed of a prehistoric sea. The modern Great Plains in this area are made up of the level, fertile grounds of the James River Valley and the town of Britton, South Dakota.

The Sisseton-Wahpeton Indian Reservation is predominantly defined by the Coteau in its eastern and western boundaries. The reservation's north and south limits also relate to the Coteau. Starting at its southern tip, just north of what is now Watertown, South Dakota, it is said that an Indian Chief held his arms in a "V" as he faced to the north. The chief proclaimed his Tribal Bands' lands with this gesture, the north boundary just jutting into what is now the southern border of North Dakota. The lands of these Lakota people, the Santee Bands of the Sisseton and the Wahpeton, were later reduced to approximately 165 square miles in the rough outline of a thin, triangle-shaped nation in the 1860's.

The modern day reservation is home to a sportsman's paradise of hunting, fishing, and boating, as well as the dominant agricultural economy of the Dakotas. Many of the Glacial Lakes sport a thriving community of vacation cabins. The bigger, deeper lakes, like Roy, Clear, and Pickerel have a mix of seasonal cabin dwellers and permanent residents. Buffalo Lake a shallower lake has limited accessible shore line and is an off-the-beaten-path sort of getaway. Tonight, the body of a holy man bobs in the undulating waters of Buffalo Lake.

Long Hollow

Greg Heitmann has worked for the Federal Government for 20 years, which pays the bills while pursuing a career in writing. His life experiences have been an inspiration for much of his writing. Look for something new from Greg soon!

Made in the USA
Middletown, DE
05 September 2019